"BREATHE, CHIUN," REMO SAID

The dragonflies seemed to form a solid wall in front of him. He would never see it when he reached the edge, and now his flesh was screaming. He was being skinned alive. He felt one foot come down on nothing and he drew back.

"Breathe, Chiun!"

He felt nothing, not even a breath, from the small figure in his arms.

"We're going in," Remo said. He launched himself and Chiun out into space, and dropped. Sixty feet of emptiness separated the edge of the land and the Mediterranean waters, with a thin beach at the bottom.

Remo inhaled, knowing his lungs weren't right. The dragonflies fell away suddenly and for a moment the world was clean and bright. Then Remo saw how much blood there was on Chiun, on himself. Every exposed inch of flesh was flayed, and here he was putting them in saltwater.

"This," he said to himself, "is gonna hurt."

Other titles in this series:

CREATED BY MURPHY & SAPIR

THE DESTROYER

UNPOPULAR SCIENCE

REPRISE OF THE MACHINES
BOOK 1

A GOLD EAGLE BOOK FROM

WORLDWIDE®

TORONTO • NEW YORK • LONDON
AMSTERDAM • PARIS • SYDNEY • HAMBURG
STOCKHOLM • ATHENS • TOKYO • MILAN
MADRID • WARSAW • BUDAPEST • AUCKLAND

First edition July 2004

ISBN 0-373-63251-7

Special thanks and acknowledgment to Tim Somheil
for his contribution to this work.

UNPOPULAR SCIENCE

Printed in U.S.A.

And for the Glorious House of Sinanju,
sinanjucentral@hotmail.com

One day you're a young man and the next day you're old. One day your eyes are sharp enough to make out Cloudcroft, better than fifty miles to the northwest, and the next day it's just another blur on the horizon. One day you're strong enough to walk to Cloudcroft for a sack of beer, and the next day you're tuckered out just from shuffling down to the latrine pit.

One day you've got your sanity. Next day, well...

Bo Janks expected his eyes to go bad and he knew his legs would get tired, but somehow he never expected his mind to give up on him. Not that he relied on it all that much, anyway. Not that he had to think through any new problems. Bo Janks was living the exact same life today as he'd lived thirty years, forty years back. What was there for him to think about?

But he did need his old brain to show him what was real and what wasn't, and for the first time ever it wasn't pulling its weight in that regard.

It started on April 15, Bo recalled, the day that Mel came out to fill the water tanks and wouldn't you know it, the rain came that same night. Bo was at home, drinking his one nightly beer and watching the rain from the porch, when his mind betrayed him.

"What is that?" he asked. Bo talked to himself all the time. That didn't make him crazy, did it?

"I know what that is, don't I?" Bo remarked a minute later, and by this time he was so intrigued he got up, knees creaking, and walked out into the rain with his thumb over the top of the beer bottle to keep it from getting diluted. He followed the thing, only to become disoriented when he came near enough to recognize what it was. What he recognized couldn't be real, so he had to be hallucinating. Bo fell over, knocked his head and he spilled his beer.

WHEN HE CAME TO his senses again it was morning. Bo Janks found himself looking up at an Air Force man.

"You okay, there, old-timer?"

Bo got to his feet with the help of the Air Force man, who had more than a few uniform decorations. "You gave me a scare when I saw you stretched out like that," the officer said.

Bo looked around to find he was in the scrub only a hundred paces from his place. His head hurt like hell and he saw the rock he had banged it on. There was a little blood on it.

"I should get you to a doctor."

"I'm all right," Bo said, but he didn't feel all right. He felt as though his life was over. Once your mind goes bad, that was all she wrote.

"Maybe you ought to go easy on the Budweiser," the officer suggested.

Bo picked up the bottle, showed the officer the dregs. "You'll find five unopened bottles in the cooler at my place and not another empty bottle around. I ain't a man who drinks to excess."

The Air Force man nodded. "Okay. What were you taking, a premature dirt nap, then, old-timer?"

Bo saw no reason to kid himself or this stranger. Bo was a straight shooter, always. "I was seein' things. Chasing my past in the desert."

"Chasing your past?"

"Something walked right out of my past and by my place and then into the desert. I saw it plain as day."

"Somebody you knew once?" the Air Force man asked.

"Not a somebody. A something."

The Air Force man looked at his black sedan, parked up by Bo's place, and he looked around the sandy desert, and then his eyes sort of just wandered on back to Bo. "You saw a thing that walked?"

"It warn't real."

"What did you mean when you said you know what it was, old-timer?"

"I know it because I've seen it before."

"Well, then? What was it, anyway?"

Bo Janks looked out into the desert himself, mind going back to what he'd seen the previous night, and then going back to when he'd seen it before. Out loud, to the stranger from the Air Force and to God and to the world, but mostly to himself, he said it as if he was making a confession, "It was Ironhand."

IRONHAND. JESUS, MARY and Joseph, but he hadn't even thought that name in forty years.

Where had his daddy's old books gone to anyway? Probably sold off with the rest of his daddy's belongings. When Bo's daddy died, Bo's sister couldn't erase his memory fast enough. She sold or trashed everything in the house, then sold the house, and she sent half the money that was left over to Bo. The check in the mail was how Bo found out his daddy died.

Daddy used to have some books that Bo read when he was twelve years old. Those books were old already. The ones with covers, and there weren't many, showed grimy old drawings of what Bo saw in the desert on that night.

"What's that mean, Ironhand?" the stranger from the Air Force asked.

Bo got suspicious then. "I don't mean to be disrespectful, but who are you anyway, and why'd you come to my place?"

The Air Force man smiled. "We lost a missile. I came by to see if maybe you spotted it."

They lost a missile that went maybe a thousand miles per hour and what Bo saw was a thing that walked no faster than a man.

"A missile?" He laughed.

BO DRANK TWO BEERS that night, just as if it were Christmas or the Fourth of July. Drowning his sorrows.

He started chuckling again when he thought of the Air Force man. "A missile!"

After the Air Force man left, Bo looked around, hoping against hope to find some evidence that what he saw in the night had left a mark of itself, but there was nothing. 'Course not. It wasn't real. Ironhand didn't exist.

Once there was an Ironhand. Bo's daddy saw it at the World's Fair in St. Louis. He told Bo about it time and time again. That World's Fair was more than a hundred years ago, and Ironhand must be long gone now.

"Don't look for excuses for your old brain, Bo. It's just worn down. Face it, Bo, you're losing it."

It was a hard pill to swallow. If his mind went, he couldn't live alone anymore. He would have to go to town, check himself into the home for old geezers, and that was unthinkable. He had lived in the desert for thirty years, independent and happy enough, and he couldn't change his life now. When a man was eighty-nine years old, he was too old to change. So what options did that leave him?

Next day, more strangers from the Air Force came by, and they weren't as friendly. They wanted Bo to talk about what he'd seen, and they accused him of being a drunkard. Bo asked them to leave politely, then got on the phone to the sheriff, and that convinced the Air Force men to leave Bo's land.

But the visit got Bo thinking. Not that he could trust his thinking, but it seemed odd, all this attention from the U.S. Air Force. There had been stray missiles from White Sands before, and Bo had talked to the Air Force men before. They never sent men on the first day, with all the decorations. They never came back for a second visit. They never sent the goon squad.

What did it mean?

He spent all the following day in the desert, searching the ground for any sign left by the thing that his mind had made him see.

"Darn fool!" He was home at dusk, a whole day wasted, his neck sore from bending so much.

Then the next day he got up and he looked some more.

On the third day, he found something strange. It was a flake of heavy, corroded iron, small as a fingernail, lying atop the sands where nothing made of iron ought

to be. Bo held it in his shaking hands. He looked at the
ground again and noticed how the sand sunk down in
a way that wasn't right.

That night, Bo drank three beers and woke up sick.
He heard pounding and it took a long time to figure out
there was somebody outside his place. It was more Air
Force. They were nicer this time, but they kept talking
and talking and all Bo wanted to do was to lie down and
sleep or maybe just lie down and die.

But when they left at noon he got his shovel and he
went to the place where the iron chip had been sitting
on top of the sands, and he started to dig.

The rain started coming down. The day got dark,
and by the time of the real dusk, Bo was exhausted,
his old arms on fire and his head pounding. He was too
old for this.

But he had to know. Bo kept digging, the powdery
sand piling up on either side. He kept thinking the sand
was too loose, as if something had been digging here
recently, when it should be hard as sandstone.

His shovel hit something metal under the sand, and
Bo scrambled out of his newly dug hole in a panic. He
stared down there, terribly afraid. Whatever metal object he hit, it was still under the sand.

"Bo, you really ought to go down there and get your
shovel," he told himself.

Then a lightning bolt struck not a mile away and Bo
came to his senses. "Darn fool! Don't you have enough
sense to come in out of the rain?"

He began heading back to his place, turned around
once, and saw the lightning get closer. He saw—he
thought he saw—something moving around by his
newly dug hole.

Bo moved as fast as his old legs could go, and he was too afraid to look back again until he got to his place. He tried to get his breath, standing on the tiny porch and holding the wall, watching the desert.

The lightning struck nearby and the crack seemed to rip the air apart. The brilliance lasted long enough for Bo to see that the desert was good and empty.

"Darn fool!" Bo gasped.

Body pumping with adrenaline, he knew sleep wouldn't be easy. He decided to write a letter to his dad. He did that, every twenty years or so, as a way of helping him think through a crisis. This time it seemed especially appropriate, because who else in the world would know a thing about it except his dad?

Writing was hard, because he didn't do it much and his hand bones hurt just awful, but he got most of it down, in pencil, on the back of some old phone bills.

When he woke up he was lying on the table, the letter under his head. The lightning had stopped.

Bo Janks wasn't an educated man, but he knew something about electricity. He knew that a thing made out of metal ought not to be walking around in a desert in a storm. Now the storm had passed on. If there was something in the hole he'd dug, if it were made of metal, then it wouldn't come out when the lightning was striking. It would wait until the night was peaceful again, like now.

Bo got to his feet, slipped on his boots and walked out of his place. The desert smelled fresh and clean, as if God just gave it a good scrubbing. The clouds were almost gone, the moon and stars were bright and Bo could see the desert as clear as in daytime.

There was something in the desert, walking toward Bo's place.

"Ironhand," Bo Janks said. "You really here? Or am I just a darn, senile old fool?"

He got no answer, so he sat himself down on his stoop and just watched. The hallucination came close enough to touch him with its moon shadow.

"I wish you was here, Daddy. You'd want to see a sight like this, that's for sure."

Those were Bo Janks's last words, to himself, to his daddy or to anybody.

2

His name was Remo and he was looking at the most beautiful woman in the world.

Her eyes had the sparkle of youth and the depth of an ageless soul, while her golden hair made the sun want to hide for shame. Moving with less noise than the shimmers of heat coming off the desert, she crept across dried patches of vegetation in a wilderness naked of cover, but she remained unseen by her prey. The beautiful woman hunted, but the hunt was a mission of mercy.

Remo watched from a cliff. He was hundreds of yards away, but her grace was unmistakable. Alongside this young woman the bobcat and the snake were clumsy and incompetent. The coyote she stalked was no more aware of her than he was aware of the generations of the ancestor spirits that hunted with her and smiled upon her.

When she grabbed the coyote by the scruff of the neck, it made an almost human sound of surprise and kicked at the air wildly.

The most beautiful woman in the world held the

coyote by one hand and let it kick, gently tamping in the earth with her foot around the rabbit burrow it had been digging in. She looked up to the top of the cliff and gave Remo a smile, such a smile as the earth was not worthy of beholding. Sure as shooting, Remo Williams wasn't worthy of it, but the smile was for him.

"Told you I could get him, Daddy," said the most beautiful woman in the world, Freya, daughter of Jilda of Lakluun and Remo Williams.

"I didn't doubt you for a second, sweetheart," he said.

Only after he said it did Remo realize that Freya spoke in a normal tone of voice and he answered in a normal tone of voice. It was no surprise that he had heard her clearly, but she should not have been able to hear him. The senses he possessed came of years of training in the art of Sinanju, the sun source of all martial arts. All other martial were just splinters and fragments of the greatness that was Sinanju. So much of the great abilities of Sinanju came from magnifying the senses beyond that of other human beings, to levels that modern science would have called impossible.

So how had Freya learned to hear like that? And how had she learned to breathe? Because, by all the gods in heaven and on earth, the girl could breathe like a—well, like a Master.

The one who taught the girl much of her breathing skill was walking to the top of the cliff. Remo didn't hear him. Just an old Native American with the dark, lined face that came from a life outside in the sun, as well as from genetics. He wore expensive but old, scuffed cowboy boots and he didn't pay much attention about where he put them down, one foot after the other, but somehow he managed to make no sound.

"Howdy."

Remo wasn't alarmed. "Hiya, Sunny Joe. I was on my way to visit and spotted Freya from the road."

Sunny Joe Roam chuckled. "Girl's tryin' to reform 'em."

"Reform who?" Remo couldn't tear his eyes away from her.

"The coyotes. Ever hear of such a thing?"

"Uh-uh."

"The heck of it is, she's doing it. Watch."

The young woman knelt by the burrow and her arm shot inside. She came out with a desert hare, a scrawny gray creature with ridiculous ears. It gave a few hopeless kicks. She put the rabbit on the ground and stepped on it, pinning it to the earth without crushing it, but she wasn't so gentle with the coyote. She flattened it next to the rabbit and, despite its struggles to get free, it made a greedy snap at the rabbit. The young woman pinched the thickest part of its upper leg.

The coyote went rigid and a tiny sound leaked out of it like the pitiful howl of the damned in hell.

The woman stopped pinching and the coyote snapped at the rabbit again. The nerve pinch was reapplied, harder this time. The coyote was rigid with agony.

When the pinch was removed, the coyote wanted nothing to do with the rabbit, but the young woman wished to make her point and make it stick. Holding the canine by the scruff of the neck, she dragged it to the rabbit, forced it to smell the little rodent and then pinched it again.

It must have been a very effective pinch, because the

whimpers that came out of the coyote were almost words. Then the coyote was free.

As it stood shakily, the young woman gently lifted the rabbit and offered it to the coyote. With a yipe it ran off so fast it almost left a coyote-shaped dust cloud.

"Thanks, Bugs," the young woman told the rabbit as she set it down at the entrance to its burrow. "Let me know if those beasts come bothering you again."

Sunny Joe Roam chuckled in his old, dry throat. "Want to bet that coyote just swore off hare for all time?"

Remo Williams beamed with pride. "She's a miracle."

"Best tracker the Sun On Jo have seen since my grandfather's days," Sunny Joe agreed. "You should see her track rattlers with her bare hands."

"He did, last time he visited," Freya said as she approached the cliff bottom. "I thought he was going to have a heart attack."

"You should see her hunt prairie dogs," Sunny Joe said, not without pride himself. "Rattlers are easy compared to prairie dogs."

"You should see me hunt wolves," Freya said.

Remo Williams, who was still smiling all this time, stopped.

HIS NAME WAS WINSTON, but what kind of a loser name was Winston? When you thought of "Winston" you thought of cigarettes or a gray old man in a suit and tie who lived his entire life in an office. Winston had once adopted a nickname, a true warrior's name, but hadn't quite lived up to it. Now they just called him Winner. You could do a lot worse than Winner.

Winner Smith had lived through his share of troubles. He'd grown up too fast, but didn't necessarily feel grown up even now.

The way he saw it, his life started for real on the day he came here, to the Sun On Jo reservation near Yuma, Arizona. The mess that came before, much of it of his own making, faded like a dream. Here, with the people who were his people, he somehow fit in. He learned to be at peace with the world without giving in to it.

Not long after arriving, his new life became more complete with the appearance of the sister he never knew he had. Freya was, then and now, a pain-in-the-ass brat. He couldn't have loved her more.

Lately she'd been stirring up more trouble, and when Winner Smith saw what was coming into the village about midmorning he assumed the trouble was just beginning.

"Would you just please tell me what's wrong?" Freya demanded.

"I want to see it first," said Remo Williams, who had a strange look in his eyes. Winner had seen the look before, before he'd come to the rez. It was the look of— he didn't want to even go there.

They were walking fast across the village, straight to the pit, drawing the attention of the meager population of Sun On Jos from their homes and hogans.

"First tell me why!" Freya insisted.

"First I see."

"No!" She grabbed him by the arm and made herself a boulder. It should have brought Remo to a halt. She'd pulled that move on Winner and it felt like having your arm in a vise of iron spikes.

It didn't work on the man who was their father.

Remo did something with his arm, something speedy but gentle, and all at once Freya was off the ground, spun around and held against him with one strong arm around her waist. Kind of like she does to the coyotes, Winner thought happily.

"Let go!" She dug her fingers into Remo's arm.

Remo stopped at the entrance to the pit, where a loosely woven mat covered the hole in the earth. "Freya," he said, "that hurts."

"Oh." Freya was shocked to see her fingers bloodied. There were punctures up and down the arm that was clamped immovably around her middle. "I'm sorry."

Remo toed the woven mat away from the entrance of the pit, allowing the morning sun to shine inside. He could see the shape huddled against the wall, alert and waiting. He placed his daughter on her feet, then stepped into the entrance and dropped to the earth, fifteen feet below, as easily as a man stepping off a curb. His eyes adjusted from bright sun to the dim haze, and Remo was eye to eye with the wolf.

The wolf cocked its head, appraising him, then raised its snout and sniffed at the air. At that moment Freya clambered through the entrance, hanging for a moment from the wooden beams reinforcing the roof, then dropped to the floor with a thud. She brushed dirt from the knees of her jeans and regarded them, the wolf, then Remo, and there was something wild and stubborn in her eyes.

"Young lady," Remo said, "you've got some explaining to do."

"I heard you talking about the wolves the last time you were here. Remember?"

Remo had been on the rez a few months back, when

he got a call from Upstairs. They had been watching for signs of the wolves for weeks, months. A series of savage attacks formed a trail that led onto the Fort Bliss Military Reservation in the New Mexico desert. There, in a ghost town that had once thrived on Sacramento Mountains silver, Remo had found evidence of the wolves.

Wolves weren't normally the prey he sought, but there was nothing normal about these wolves.

"I didn't talk about the wolves when I was here."

"You were on the phone with Prince Junior," Freya explained.

"How do you know Prince Junior?"

"I don't." She shrugged. "I just know you called him Prince Junior. He was the one who told you where to go get the wolves. Then the other one, Smitty, he gave you the cover to get into the exercises going on at Bliss. Later, Sunny Joe said you wouldn't be coming back like you thought you would."

"You were listening in on my phone calls?"

"When I'm standing right there in the same room it's kind of hard not hear what you loudmouths are saying."

Remo shook his head. "The dots still aren't connecting, sweetheart."

"I drove out to see about the wolves, that's all. I found this one in the desert about ten miles outside the ghost town. He was with a dead one. This one had half his flank torn off, but I managed to stabilize him and get him home."

Remo Williams was about as shocked as he had ever been, and there were so many things shocking him he couldn't sort through them all. Freya had overheard his phone call from halfway across the room, which was surprising, yes. She had gone hunting, for dangerous animals. She had penetrated the security of a U.S. military reservation. She had taken the dying creature and escaped the military without being apprehended, then nursed this beast back to health. Every fact demanded a why and/or a how.

The wolf was indeed healthy now. It walked easily across the pit with only a slight limp and thrust its muzzle underneath the small, delicate hand of Freya.

It gave a small start when Remo silently came alongside to examine the beast.

"It's small," he said. That was a good sign.

He had to be sure. He took the animal's head in his hands, held on to it and looked into its eyes. The animal panicked when it couldn't break the hold, but Freya stroked it, spoke to it, as Remo searched the glassy orbs. He didn't know what he was looking for, really, but when he let go of the wolf's head he was sure he hadn't found it.

"It's just a wolf."

Freya didn't question that strangely obvious statement. She explained, "Its pack was wiped out by a rival wolf pack. This one only survived because it was small enough to slip through the rocks into a crevasse. It was starved when I found it. The other pack was long gone, but it was too afraid to come out of the rocks."

"What about the other pack? You didn't track them, did you?"

"I tried. The trail was cold and I lost it."

Remo looked at the creature. "I didn't know there were wolves still living in the desert."

Freya's eyes lowered. "Nobody did, and they really are gone now, I think," she said. "She's mute. I bet her entire pack was. It must have been just enough of an edge to keep them from being hunted. This might have been the last free pack of Mexican Gray Wolves in the Southwestern U.S. They were lucky and clever enough to stay hidden from man for decades. For generations. But now man's finally found them and wiped them out."

Remo considered what Freya had just said as he climbed out of the pit, and as he ate his dinner, and when he lay down to sleep on his mat in Sunny Joe's home.

Freya was intuitive. Remo never told her anything about the nature of the wolves that he was hunting, so how had she come to her conclusion that the pack of wolves that wounded her pet were "man"? How had she dared to go out in search of them?

What kind of a woman was Freya, anyway?

3

James Sharma knew death. He'd seen death and delivered death, sometimes with a pen stroke, sometimes with his own bare fingers. He always thought he would recognize death when it came for him.

Three minutes before he died, Sharma was smoking a cigarette and standing at the window of his room. The cigarette smelled despicable, but it masked the stench of the city of Casablanca. Forget every preconception you had ever gotten from certain movies; Casablanca, in reality, was a hot, ugly outhouse of a city.

But some of the world's biggest business deals were conducted here. Maybe one would go down within the hour. Sharma wanted to be in on it. He had a suitcase full of U.S. currency tucked under his flimsy, lumpy mattress.

Two minutes before he died, Sharma took a call on his mobile phone. He spoke briefly in Langley-approved code words. The CIA had specific ways of delivering messages. He essentially told the operative that he was sitting on his ass waiting to hear from his contact.

One minute before he died, James Sharma spotted the biggest, ugliest centipede he'd ever seen, and it was scuttling around the floor of his hotel room. He tried to stomp it, but it shot under the mattress.

Yech, Sharma thought. Maybe that's what all the lumps were in that bed. Bugs.

The centipede emerged from the other side of the bed and started up the wall. Sharma watched it as he reached for his vibrating phone.

"Our lookout says the store is open," said his CIA mission coordinator.

"Shit!" Sharma said. "Why'd they open without telling me?"

"You tell me. We thought you were one of their preferred shoppers. Is it too late to get in on the fire sale?"

"I don't know! I'll call you." Sharma disconnected and hit the number to dial his merchant contact. What had gone wrong? He was supposed to be one of the bidders! They knew he was CIA and they didn't care—why should they? He had cash and he had a lot of it.

"Faizel?" he barked into the mobile phone. "You there?"

Faizel seemed unusually pleased to hear from him. "How are you, Jim?"

"Pissed off! What's the problem? Why'm I being shut out of the bidding?"

"Because you're dead, Jim," Faizel said happily.

Eight seconds before he died, Central Intelligence Agency Field Agent Jim Sharma felt something drop on top of him. He knew it was the centipede, and then his mind registered the fact that it was very heavy. As his phone clattered on the floor and the centipede tightened around his neck, Sharma felt the cool touch of metal.

Some kind of a robot centipede? Didn't make sense. The thing wouldn't have the strength to strangle him, would it? He grabbed it and heard at that instant the high-pitched vibration of tiny spinning motors inside the centipede. His fingers were sliced to hamburger. He yelped and snatched his hands away, then realized his big mistake.

The thin tungsten centipede legs were unbelievably strong and micromachined to be razor-sharp. As they wiggled, they slid into Sharma's flesh like hot knives into warm butter.

One second before he died, Jim Sharma felt his sweaty shirt become drenched in blood, and it smelled worse than the raw sewage on the streets of Casablanca.

4

"It's amazing." The young man shook his head.

"It's ludicrous," added the elderly man with the gray complexion. "We have mobile phones smaller than a pack of playing cards and yet this organization can't stay in touch with its enforcement arm."

"It's not a matter of technology, Dr. Smith," Mark Howard said. "You could put a microchip in his skull and he'd still find a way to disable it."

"I know," sighed Harold W. Smith, the elderly director of the Folcroft Sanitarium in Rye, New York, as well as director of CURE, the supersecret organization for which Folcroft provided a front.

CURE was tiny in terms of its personnel, which numbered exactly four. Prior to the most recent major staff expansion, when Mark Howard was added to the payroll a few years previously, there had only been three official employees of CURE. Still, the scope of the organization's activities had always been substantial. The impact CURE had on global events was incalculable.

The problem at the moment was not a new one. For

years management, which consisted of Dr. Smith and Assistant Director Mark Howard, tried to set up a system for communications with its enforcement arm. The enforcement arm didn't, couldn't, wouldn't cooperate.

"Why is it too much to ask him to carry a cellular phone?" Dr. Smith complained. "We could have it programmed to connect directly with our offices. All he would have to do is open it up."

"He says they get ruined during the course of his field activities," Howard added.

"We pay for his shoes by the gross, why not mobile phones?" Dr. Smith snapped. "What's the situation with the CIA buyer?"

"He's still waiting for a contact."

"Sitting in a hotel room getting nowhere."

"That's about the size of it."

Smith glared at the top of his desk, beneath which was hidden his new, enlarged flat-screen display. The brilliant, high-resolution images had been an unexpected quality-of-life improvement for Smith. The new image reduced the tension that Smith hadn't even known he was experiencing when he viewed his old display. That didn't make it any easier to see what he was seeing now.

"This is a failure. This should not be happening." Dr. Smith spoke with subdued anger; this was not his usual sour disposition. "Remo could be at the buyers' market right now, getting the answers, finding the stolen units, getting control of the situation. Instead our fate rests in the hands of one CIA operative who may or may not have a chance of even placing a bid."

"We could send the Yuma police to find Remo," Howard suggested.

"Remo would ignore them as he's ignored our other messages," Smith said dismissively. "When was our last call to Mr. Roam?"

"Four hours," Howard answered, glancing at his watch.

"Intolerable." Smith turned and looked out his window, where the waves of Long Island Sound crashed against the shore. He turned back. "Please get an update from the CIA while I try calling Mr. Roam myself."

Dr. Smith felt foolish as he rang the line of a mobile phone somewhere in southern Arizona. It picked up on the fourth ring.

"Hello?" The man sounded curious, and he sounded familiar.

"Hello, Mr. Roam?"

"You want Sunny Joe?"

"Yes, please, this is extremely urgent."

"Uh-huh. Hold on." The voice called out to someone else. "It's Dr. Smith-for-brains. Where's Sunny Joe?"

Smith felt cold numbness grip his hands. Who was this? Why had Remo revealed Smith's name to him?

A young woman answered, "Riding the lines."

"He's out checking fences," said the young man on the line. "Call back tomorrow."

Smith said, "Mr. Roam went out to check the fences and he did not take his mobile phone with him?"

"Yes."

"That seems unlikely."

"Oh, you think I'm lying? You've got some nerve calling me a liar after what you've done."

"Who is this?"

"Hanging up now, Smith-for-brains."

"Wait! I'm looking for another man by the name of Remo. It's possible he's a guest of Mr. Roam's."

"No duh, Smitty."

Smith breathed deeply and asked, "May I speak to Remo, please?"

"Doubt it." The young man lowered the phone and announced, "It's Dr. Strangehate from the loony bin. You home?" Then the young man said, "He says he's not home right now."

"I must speak to him—it's extremely urgent," Dr. Smith said sternly.

"Go to hell, asshole."

Smith seethed and dialed again. It rang once. "I'm sorry," said the young man when he answered again, "but the mobile phone you have called has been flushed into the septic system. Please try your call again never." The speaker filled with an intense flushing sound, then the strange acoustical muffling that came of being under water. The phone functioned for an amazing four seconds before the electronics shorted and Smith was left listening to silence.

Mark Howard entered.

"Bad news."

Smith said nothing.

"The CIA buyer was made. They murdered him in his hotel room. The Company watchers think the buy went down about the same time he was getting his throat hacked."

Dr. Smith nodded stiffly, then said. "Mark, you will please go to Arizona at once."

5

Nightmares are usually the stuff of fantasy, conjured to help the subconscious face its fears. In nightmares, one can live through the worst possible events and it makes the trials of real life seem less awful.

But Remo Williams was dreaming of the past, of events that had actually happened, and it was worse than anything his mind could have imagined.

First came the horror of Kali. Kali confronting them. Kali, the Devourer, alive inside the body of Jilda, mother of Freya.

Almost as soon as he saw her confronting him, Remo saw her dead, killed by an Asian man so small, so old, he looked too feeble to brush a spider from the kitchen table. Horror and self-condemnation dawned on the face of the little Asian man as he realized who he had just killed.

Then came the horror of Kali, the Devourer, alive inside the body of Freya herself. Remo's daughter. His little girl.

"Red One, remember me," his little girl said to him in the voice of something ageless and evil.

Then came the collapse of brick and stone, and the hours of digging in the rubble, the flash of golden hair. He extracted her little body from the ruin, a limp thing that wasn't dead—Remo would not let her be dead. Almost through his own force of will he breathed life back into her.

So it was a dream that ended well enough, as in reality. Freya survived, and she still lived, but in his dream there was a nameless dread.

The dream shifted abruptly. Now there were no great events. No four-armed inhuman beings, no speaking gods. There was just Remo and a friendly woman, who was not an enemy, in a narrow room. Somehow every item in the room clashed in color and design with every other item in the room.

The woman was a seer, and when she started laying out her cards, it looked like a bad late-night television commercial for phone-in psychics, but this woman was one of the few who could truly *see*.

This was when the dream became, once again, a nightmare.

"I see you," said the seeress. "I see your fathers and your daughters and your sons, battling one another…"

"I have one son. I have one daughter. That's all." Remo was trying to convince himself more than the seeress.

"I did not say soon," the seeress reminded him. "I did not say when…."

"When," breathed the Sonoran Desert as he awoke. It was after two in the morning and the village of Sun On Jo was silent. Remo counted the steady heartbeats in the house and felt reassured. He stood at the window and watched the desert, feeling sorry for himself.

He came to Sun On Jo more often now and found it a place where he felt peace and a sense of belonging, but this time there was foreboding. He felt like a fisherman standing on the rail on a perfectly calm sea, with no sign of heavy weather in any direction, but knowing a killer storm was moving in. The weather reports wouldn't tell him how soon or from which direction the storm would come.

He didn't know how to steer around it.

He heard a slight snuff from the pit where Freya's wolf was having its own nightmares, or maybe it was hunting in its sleep. Better not be hunting, Remo thought with a wry smile. Freya didn't approve of hunting animals for food, even by natural carnivores. She didn't eat meat and she had poor Sunny Joe packing in more vegetables than he ever ate in all his life. Remo had heard some Sun On Jos complaining that Freya was again stealing ammunition so they couldn't go out after game.

Freya, Remo decided happily, simply did not have a killer instinct.

As if that revelation wasn't enough, Remo had another. Without even being aware of it, he'd been evaluating Freya as a potential heir.

Freya, his heir? His trainee? Freya, an assassin? "What was I thinking?"

Freya embracing the dangerous, bloody existence that was the life of a Sinanju Master? Freya, placed in harm's way, by her own father? Remo could *never* do such a thing.

"Well?"

Remo wasn't alone. It was the man himself, Sunny Joe, who was Remo's own biological father, who had placed Remo on the doorstep of an orphanage in New Jersey so many years ago. This was also the man who had become the father to Remo's children, taking them in when they were in distress and in need of the comfort and care of a true home.

"Didn't mean to wake you," Remo said, turning away from the desert.

"Why were you breathing so loud, then?" Sunny Joe gave Remo a tight smile that said it was a joke—they both knew Remo was probably the most skilled inhaler/exhaler on the planet. "Let's go," Joe said, "before you huff and puff and wake the whole town."

SUNNY JOE ROAM had once been a famous movie star, more or less. Using the professional name William S. Roam he appeared in cinematic gems like *Muck Man*. He even starred in the *Muck Man* sequels, but those were uninspired efforts that lacked the passion of the original. Roam's most important role was as the symbolic leader of the village, the Sunny Joe.

They were out in the desert, walking on the rocky earth under the brilliance of the stars, and in the sandy places they left no footprints.

"You were thinking about Freya, but I guess I'm still not so sure what you meant when you said, 'What was I thinking?'"

Remo felt the night around him, and he felt comfortable in it. Sun On Jo wasn't a rich place, but it was beautiful. What some saw as a stark wasteland, Remo saw as a magnificent landscape of nature, active and vibrant. He felt at home here. He felt unpressured being here, and unpressured by Sunny Joe. The question was a probing, sensitive one, but Joe wouldn't be offended if Remo never answered it. Joe—unlike some fathers Remo could mention—wasn't the harping, nagging, complaining type.

"I'm supposed to take an heir," Remo said, without really meaning to.

"This I know."

Remo wondered how much Sunny Joe did know about him, about Sinanju traditions. The Native American tribe was descended from Sinanju, from one of the twin brothers who were Sinanju Masters centuries ago. Two Masters was a violation of tradition, so one twin, Kojong, left behind his village on the rocky coast of Korea and vanished. His fate was unknown in Sinanju until discovered by Remo and Remo's adopted father, Chiun, Master of Sinanju Emeritus. They learned that Kojong had journeyed to the North American continent and become the spiritual leader of a small tribe, who called him Ko Jong Oh.

The series of events that had occurred over the centuries to intertwine Remo Williams by blood and by training with this ancient Arizona tribe and the Korean art of Sinanju was so intricate that there was no way to rationalize it, no way to name it coincidence. The implications of it *not* being coincidence were mind-boggling. Remo preferred to not think about it and to stay blissfully unboggled.

"I didn't even know it myself, that I had it in the back of my head. You know, that maybe Freya would be the right choice to be my heir. Then it occurred to me that she was all wrong for the job, and that's when it hit me that I'd been sizing her up."

"Is that why you came here this time?" Roam asked.

"No. Just came to visit." They walked a few more paces. "Maybe. Maybe that's why I came."

"What reason do you need to have an heir now?"

"No reason. I mean, Chiun's harping on me occasionally to find somebody, but I think he just uses that as filler when he's got nothing else to complain about."

"But something makes you seek an heir now?"

They walked a long way under the stars before Remo answered. "Something makes me seek out Freya now." He smiled. "I think I wanted to rule her out. See, she was a candidate. Now she's not. She's safe."

Sunny Joe nodded. "Safe from your life?"

"Yes."

"Is your life so bad?"

"My life fits me. I was meant to be who I am. But I wouldn't wish it on Freya."

"What of Winston?"

"What about him?"

"But he is your son, in blood. Is he a possible heir?"

Remo suddenly experienced a flood of new questions. If he had come to the village with the subconscious intention of evaluating Freya, had he meant to evaluate Winner, too? If not, why not? If so, why had he decided at some level already that his son, an experienced commando with battlefield kills, would be unfit?

"I don't know, he's kind of a jerk," Remo said finally. "Plus he's like Freya—he's a Sun On Jo now. He's not a killer anymore."

"Huh." This ancient Sun On Jo word translated into "bullshit."

"He's a child," Remo added. "He's immature. He's an egotistical brat. Most Sinanju Masters do begin training when they're young, but they grow up with their training. I'd be pushing the envelope enough by taking a trainee who's already grown up. But one who's grown up and still acts like he's in junior high school? Now that would be asking for trouble."

"I think that is good thinking," Sunny Joe Roam said. "But I think one day Winner will knock your socks off. Boys have a way of surprising their fathers."

"I guess so."

They were miles away and gazing down on the village, peaceful and dark.

"Don't look like too much when you look at it from all the way up here," Roam observed.

"Looks like the whole world to me," Remo said.

"Yep."

Remo squinted. There was a flicker of light on the horizon. Car headlights, coming toward the village. Sun On Jo didn't often get visitors, let alone in the dead of night. Who would that be?

"My son."

The familiar words, said in that gruff Native American voice, caught Remo off guard and he looked at Sunny Joe Roam.

"Yes?"

"You were saying true words, that you're satisfied with the life you lead. You believe that."

"Yes, I believe that," Remo said.

"There could come a day, maybe, when you won't feel that way."

"I guess it's possible, sure."

Sunny Joe looked out at the village.

"Remember what I told those people when I showed you off to them the first time?"

Remo thought about that, trying to remember.

"That'd be the prince," Roam said, starting back toward the village as the headlights burst over a rise in the road.

"Huh? Prince Junior?"

"Said he'd get here by midnight," Roam said. "It's almost three. Thought I gave him pretty good directions."

Remo caught up and they paced quickly back to the village. "You talked to him?"

"He's been calling since 'bout an hour after you got here. You told us to hold your calls, remember?"

"Sure."

"So he finally said he'd come to talk to you in person."

"Dammit. Why can't they leave me alone?"

6

Mark Howard stopped the car amid the dark buildings. The place didn't feel abandoned; it felt as if it was ignoring him.

So what did he do now? Which house was Roam's anyway? He took out his mobile phone, feeling stupid, but there was no other way than to simply phone Roam and ask him to wave from his doorstep or something.

The phone turned to air in his hands. The car turned itself off and the lights went dark. There was something black and menacing standing outside the rental car, and for a second Mark Howard's mind conjured an irrational riot of possibilities.

"Shut up. Don't make another freaking sound. Isn't it good enough that you had to wake the whole place up?"

"Remo," Howard said. "Where the hell have you been?"

"Come on."

Mark Howard felt himself extracted through the window of the little rental car like a cooked snail being forked out of its buttery shell. His yelp was flattened behind a rough hand clamped over his face, and he struggled for a minute as the village melted away and he found himself in the desert.

Unexpectedly he was free and he crashed onto his feet. If he hadn't landed on sand he might have snapped a bone.

"Ouch! That hurt!"

"Lower your voice," Remo growled.

Howard glared at the village. "We're a half mile away."

"It's the desert. Sound carries. You already woke up everybody in town with your racket and your lights."

"I didn't see anybody."

"Yeah. They saw you and everybody was wondering who the fool was who didn't know enough to douse his lights and turn off his car when he comes into a sleeping village."

Mark Howard was getting his wind back. "Remo, look," he said angrily. "I've got about a hundred reasons to be pissed off at you right now. You refuse to stay in communication with us, you ignore our messages, you make me come down to get you in person! You know how long I've been wandering around Arizona trying to find this place?"

"Don't know. Don't care. Go home."

"I'm not going home. I came here to give you a mission briefing."

"A mission briefing?" Remo asked incredulously. "Listen, braniac, did you or the emperor in the ugly clothes ever stop to think about why I put up the Do Not Disturb sign?"

"We need—"

"It's so I won't be disturbed."

"We have a situation that requires your involvement."

Remo folded his arms on his chest, staring at the village. It wasn't just that CURE was interrupting his vacation time; it was that Sun On Jo had been violated by this intrusion of Remo's other world. "Junior, go tell Smitty I don't want a mission briefing and I don't want to be involved in any situation. I want to have some time. That's all. Just a few days of peace and quiet."

Mark Howard was fretting. "Do you know what we had to do? It was an intolerable breach in security to try to reach you through Mr. Roam."

"Speaking of intolerable, go away."

"Remo, we need you to do your job."

"I'm not a doctor, Junior. I'm not on call one hundred percent of the time, okay?"

"Your contract says you are," Howard replied.

Remo rolled his eyes to the brilliant night sky. "It does?"

"Yes."

"So what?"

"So you'll be in violation of your contract if you refuse this job."

"In three or four days, I won't refuse it. Come back then."

Howard's face became stony. "In four days the U.S. might not have a functional military."

Remo waited. Howard waited, too, and he was deadly serious.

"Do we really need a functioning military?" Remo asked hopefully.

Howard said nothing.

"Aw, crap."

MARK HOWARD was surprised to find several men gathered around his little rental car, which was sitting on its rear fender and leaning with its roof against an adobe wall, exposing its underside.

"Hey, you can't do that!" Howard barked. "You're gonna scratch it all up!"

The gathered men turned to Mark Howard with faces like dark auburn sandstone, their features sharpened by the harsh blaze of a drop-cord light hooked to the underside of the car. They began to chuckle, a low grumble.

"What's so funny?" Howard demanded.

"You the prince we heard so much about?" asked the only young man in the group.

Mark Howard didn't know how to respond to that.

"Got a message for Smitty," said Winner Smith. "Will you take a message to Smitty for me?"

Mark Howard looked desperately at Remo, who was no help whatsoever.

"What's the message?" Howard asked, as noncommittal as he could.

"Rot in hell, you pale-faced son of a bitch," Winner said. "Got it?"

Howard's brain was spinning.

"What's the matter with the car?" Remo asked.

"Bent rim," Sunny Joe Roam replied. "Oil leaking from somewhere. Suspension's whacked out of joint. You're about to lose this transmission." Roam cast a benign gaze at Howard. "You went off the road, I guess. I told you not to come out here in the dark."

"I tried to follow your directions," Howard protested. "It would help if they had road signs out here. I bottomed out in a creek bed."

There were more chuckles from the men. "Road signs," Winner said. "Why didn't we think of that? I'm going to go write my congressman right away."

"It's not driveable, is it?" Remo said.

"Some day, who knows?" Sunny Joe said. "But not now."

"Fine. We'll take mine."

Howard shimmied nervously into the precariously propped-up car and retrieved his bag as Remo quickly and quietly said goodbye to the men. Then, while Remo went into a nearby house, Mark stood there, trying to not look uncomfortable and failing miserably. It wasn't that the Sun On Jos were trying to be unfriendly—except for the jerk who didn't even look like a Native American—but it was clear to all present that Howard was an outsider and not necessarily a welcome one.

Remo emerged from the house with his luggage, which consisted of a sleeping mat rolled around some new, still-in-the-plastic shirts and pants exactly like the chinos and T-shirt he wore now.

"C'mon, Junior."

Remo Williams couldn't help notice that Mark wasn't following him. He turned and saw the assistant director of CURE standing there with his jaw hanging all the way to the ground. Mark Howard was looking at Sunny Joe Roam's house, where a small yellow lantern was illuminating the figure that stood in the doorway.

"'Bye, Daddy," she called.

"'Bye, sweetheart," Remo said, then he carried away Mark Howard over one shoulder.

"PUT YOUR TONGUE back in, Junior," Remo growled.

"Sorry. You didn't have to carry me off like a sick cat. I looked stupid enough as it was."

"Letting you stand there drooling on yourself wouldn't have raised your esteem on the rez," Remo remarked.

"Sorry."

Remo glanced over. Mark Howard's cheeks were a flaming red.

"Chill, dude."

"Remo, I didn't know she was your daughter."

"Now you know."

"I feel like a stupid teenager who just got busted peeping on the girl next door."

"You're not a teenager."

"She just kind of caught me off guard, when I saw her standing there."

"Okay."

"I mean, I was just kind of, overcome, I guess."

"You're rambling, Junior."

"Yeah, I am."

Remo could feel the red heat radiating from Howard's face.

Ten minutes passed in silence.

"This is a little awkward," Mark Howard finally said.

"Shut up."

HOWARD WAS PERPLEXED when they arrived in Yuma in amazingly quick time. "If you only knew how many hours it took me to get from the airport to the village. Next time I'll rent something bigger, no matter how much it costs." He patted the dashboard of Remo's Ford

SUV, which the commercials claimed had enough horsepower to pull frame houses off their foundations.

"Next time don't come. That's not advice but a threat, by the way. Where to?"

Howard gave him directions into the unimpressive Yuma airport, to a waiting jet, a sleek and shiny corporate charter.

"You rented this thing?" Remo said. "I guess you *are* in a hurry."

"Glad you're on board with the seriousness of the crisis," Howard said as he rushed up the aircraft stairs and inside. Remo dawdled but was inside soon enough. The flight attendant was anxious, too. She secured the doors almost before Remo had his foot through the door. The aircraft started rolling.

"Hey, you're violating FDA rules about me being in my seat with the back in an upright position," Remo pointed out.

"Let's get you in, then, before agents of the Food and Drug Administration come for a surprise inspection," the flight attendant said, not even pretending to be friendly.

Remo didn't resist as he was shoved into a seat and his belt was latched across his lap. With a brutal yank, the flight attendant tightened it further. Then she took the loose strap in both hands, braced her feet against the seat base, and put her entire body into the effort of dragging the belt as hard as she could.

"Snug enough, sir?"

"I do use the lower extremities, you know," Remo pointed out.

She came close, her eyes on fire. "Liar!"

Then she stood, smiled and asked a stunned Mark

Howard if he would like anything. Maybe a refreshing beverage?

"Just water," Howard asked worriedly. "Miss?"

"Yes, sir?"

"Do you know this gentleman?"

"Oh, yes, sir, he has flown with us in the past," she said, her smile brightening to a thousand watts. "He's a manipulative bastard who uses women then throws them into the garbage heap."

She went to get his water.

"Happens all the time," Remo explained.

The aircraft was stopped on the tarmac awaiting the go-ahead for takeoff, and yet the flight attendant still managed to stumble and spill the large plastic cup of water she was bringing Howard. She was disappointed that Remo had somehow, without her noticing, moved to another seat, and the water missed him.

"I'll get you another, sir."

"This is fine," Howard insisted as he took the half-emptied water bottle from her hand. "I don't need a cup."

She simmered at Remo and took her seat in the galley.

"Now you know why I hate flight attendants," Remo said.

"Maybe you should treat them with a little more respect."

"You don't know what you're asking. Maybe you have the time to intercourse the flight crew of every commercial aircraft in the North American commercial fleets—I don't. Let's talk, Junior."

Mark Howard felt his stomach drop as the aircraft left the ground and muscled its way skyward. "I'm sorry, Remo. How many times can I say it."

"Huh? Junior, you never once said you were sorry about any of this."

"Any of what?"

"Hello? Nice Remo taking a nice vacation, mean old Mark come and make nice Remo leave?"

"I'm not sorry about that!"

"What I want to know is, where in my contract does it say that you get to call and demand my services whenever you feel like it?"

Howard rubbed the bridge of his nose. "Remo, I don't know where and if I told you section and paragraph it wouldn't make a difference anyway. I do know there is a 24/7 clause in the contract."

Remo looked suspicious. "What's a 24/7 clause?"

"Just what it sounds like. It means you'll be available 24/7."

"Is that some sort of code for 'all the time'?"

Howard sighed. "You know, twenty-four hours in a day, seven days a week."

"This one of Smitty's sneaky word tricks?"

"It's a pretty common term."

"Never heard of it."

"It's Internet vernacular."

"Figures."

"Can we talk about the mission now?"

"Any other Internet vernacular in the contract? I want to know what other unpleasant obligations I have."

"I don't have a copy of your contract on me," Howard exclaimed. "Why is every conversation with you like arguing with a smart parrot?"

Remo grinned and sat back in his seat. "Could be worse. Could be Chiun."

"Chiun is not worse! Chiun is not as egotistical."

"Yeah, right."

"Chiun is not as arrogant."

"He's the emperor of arrogance."

"But he's a grown-up, Remo. Maybe that's what makes the difference."

"I think I'll throw a snit now and give you the silent treatment all the way to New York."

"We're going to Morocco."

"Aw, crap."

MARK ENDURED the silent treatment only so long before he said, "Look, Remo, I know I made an idiot of myself in Arizona."

Remo said nothing.

"I was just looking at her. I mean, I saw her, and she sort of took my breath away. I feel bad about it."

Remo shook his head. "You don't feel bad about it."

"What do you mean?"

"I mean I was over it before we left the village. You're the one who won't let it drop."

"Oh." Mark Howard looked at Remo seriously and said, "But you know I would never even try to—you know."

"What? Take Freya to the movies?"

"Yes. I could never take her to the movies. There's a hundred reasons why it wouldn't work, even if I wanted it to."

"Which you don't," Remo added.

"'Course not. CURE security would never allow it. Not to mention the distance between Rye and Yuma, and who knows if she would have any interest in me at all anyway, even if I did have an interest in her? Then there's the cultural differences." Mark stopped. "What kind of a cultural background does she have? Freya's not a Native American name."

"No, she didn't join the Sun On Jos until she was twelvish. Before that she was the daughter of Norse princess and the avatar of Hindu deity."

Howard said, "Okay, I deserve that."

"Deserve what? That's the truth."

"You're trying to demonstrate how you feel about me checking out your daughter."

Remo smirked. "Wrong, Junior. It's not like that. I'm not going to go roughing up guys who get interested in Freya. She's as intelligent as she is beautiful, and she's got good instincts. She can take care of herself and she sure as shitting can make her own good decisions."

Howard nodded. "Do you, you know, have a father-daughter relationship?"

"With our history?" Remo asked. "Not too much. Sunny Joe might be a different story."

"Sunny Joe's like you," Mark said. "He wouldn't dream of telling Freya how to run her life. It's not his way. That's what I picked up from him, anyway."

"You pegged him."

"And Freya?"

Remo leaned forward, elbows on his knees, and stared down. Instead of the floor he saw the golden-haired image of Freya catching a coyote in her hands in the Arizona desert.

"Freya is Sun On Jo," Remo said. "She's all the best of Sun On Jo ways rolled up into one human being."

Mark smiled, shrugged a little. "I haven't a clue what Sun On Jo is all about, so I don't really know what it says about her."

"She's taken to heart everything Sunny Joe Roam

had to teach her. I guess Sunny Joe's really her father."
Remo thought about his own words and felt…what?
Lonely? Saddened? Yes, he felt sad.

Mark got down to business. "I've got to warn you,
Remo, Dr. Smith is unhappy."

"Smitty and happy are like matter and antimatter.
They can't exist in the same room together."

"No, Remo," Mark said, "I mean he's really angry.
Like I've never seen him before. And you're the one
he's mad at."

"Because I took time off? He's out of line."

"Just warning you." Mark Howard flipped open his
laptop and dialed a satellite connection into Folcroft's
secure system, and a moment later the cabin of the aircraft was treated to the lemony voice of Dr. Harold W.
Smith through the laptop speakers.

"Is Remo with you, Mark?"

"I'm here and I'm not in the mood for your crap."

"Remo, do you know what trouble you've caused?"

"Didn't you hear the part about the crap?"

"Military components have been sold on the black
market. A CIA agent is dead. You could have prevented
these things from happening."

"Bulldookey."

"That's just the start, Remo. You've been getting out
of hand lately. You flagrantly compromise the security
of CURE."

"Do not."

"You've been raking up huge, frivolous expenses."

"You're making that up."

"And you're doing a bad job."

"Remember what I said at the start of this phone
call? Your crap. Not in the mood."

"I don't care if you're in the mood or not, I want you to be aware just how poorly—"

"What happens when I do this?" Remo asked Mark, slapping the laptop computer closed. It latched with a click.

"Remo!" Howard exclaimed. "You disconnected Dr. Smith."

"Really? That's exactly what I wanted to do. See, I know how to work a computer."

Mark Howard quickly opened the unit and didn't have to dial into Folcroft, because the line was ringing in.

"Remo, I do not appreciate this disrespect," Smith said insistently.

"I don't appreciate being treated like your errand boy."

"You have an obligation—"

"I have a life. Not much of one outside of CURE, but it is a little tiny one. How did that fit into this whole thing?"

"Not at all," Smith intoned angrily.

"That's what I thought," Remo said and closed the computer again, so fast Mark Howard couldn't begin to stop him.

"Remo!" He opened it swiftly.

"Take a letter, Junior."

"What?" The computer made a distinctly insistent and lemony beeping.

"Answer that, Junior, and I'll turn the computer off again, permanently."

Mark heard it in Remo's voice—this was not any kind of kidding around. "I can't ignore Dr. Smith."

"'Dear Dr. Emperor Smitty.' Type it exactly as I say it, Junior."

Mark Howard sighed and typed.

"'Please refer to my previously stated conditions for continuing this conversation.'"

"What previously stated conditions?" Mark demanded.

"It's not to you. You don't need to know."

"If I don't understand, I'm sure Dr. Smith won't."

"Fine. 'Conditions are as follows.' Type that. 'Conditions are as follows. Dr. Smith will give Remo no crap and Remo defines what is crap. Otherwise Remo gets off the plane.'"

"You can't get off…"

"Send it."

Mark sent it. A few minutes later an e-mail came back. "Will discuss only the current assignment."

"I don't trust him, but I'll give him another chance."

It was a cold, cold Dr. Smith who came back on-line when Mark reconnected.

"This is the situation, Remo, as of this moment."

There was a moment of silence.

"I'm here," Remo said.

"Good."

Remo could almost feel the unspoken sarcastic comment that was something like, "I thought maybe you got off the plane." Let the old fart stew.

"There has been a number of thefts in recent months that defy explanation. The targets have all been research labs for U.S. defense industries."

"Explain 'defy explanation,'" Remo said.

"I will. In four recent cases research labs in the southwestern United States have been burgled."

"Burgled?"

"Burgled. Defenses penetrated by an individual with

rather startling capabilities. These are among the most highly secure laboratories anywhere, designed to be impenetrable by an army or even a skilled special-forces unit. Still, someone broke into each of them and made off with valuable military technology."

"How?"

"We think we have a partial answer to that," Smith said. His voice had ceased being icy and was now simply frosty. "Here's how it happened. Mark?"

Mark typed on the computer and quickly brought a computer-generated graphic onto the wide screen. The pale yellow map had light brown broken lines for the state borders of Arizona, New Mexico, Texas, Utah and Colorado. There was a red dot in each state for the capital city, but there was nothing for the Sun On Jo reservation. Remo was already wishing he was back there. He felt cheated.

"What's with the slide show?" he asked. "I don't usually get the whole secret-agent briefing."

"One reason, we have time," Smith said dryly. "For another, it is pertinent, as you'll see. Mark?"

"Mark?" Remo echoed.

Mark shot Remo a dark look and fiddled with the keys of the computer, bringing up a small blinking star. "This was three weeks ago. A technology firm was hit about ten miles south of Flagstaff. The laboratory was ransacked and the company mainframes were destroyed. One hard drive was stolen, as well as test materials. Then the lab was burned to the ground."

"Somebody really hated that lab, I guess," Remo said.

"Someone was very determined to steal the technology the firm was developing for the U.S. military, and they were also determined to be sure no one else would have it. They left no usable electronic or hard files."

Remo frowned. "Didn't they make backup copies? You know, like on a floppy disc?"

"First of all, Remo," Smith said sourly, "the amount of data the company generated would not fit onto ten thousand floppy discs. The company did make remote backups of their data, but their data generation was dynamic. The material they were developing was actually being formulated using a software that combined attributes of various chemicals and their deposition technologies and measuring the theoretical results."

"Uh-huh."

"The software was the real marvel," Mark explained. "The software was what was creating the materials for the military. A software copy and a six-day-old data dump were stored off-site. The problem was that the hardware to run the software is unique and will have to be rebuilt before the software can be run again."

"I understand perfectly," Remo said. "So what?"

"The materials being developed by the firm were for stealth paint," Smith said.

"Stealth paint? To make your split-level invisible to radar?"

"To make just about anything invisible to radar, lidar, infrared, you name it," Mark explained. "It was just about perfected. The thief knew the right moment to strike. He got the coating and he left the research firm incapable of recreating its own technology for the immediate future."

"The thief also took the only test batch of the material. The older samples were poured out and ruined in the fire," Smith said. "We believe the thief then used the material as a coating when he next penetrated two military laboratories in rapid succession in a high-security complex near Phoenix."

"Okay," Remo said, hoping to hurry all this along.

"The thefts were for missile guidance systems. Old systems, outdated by current U.S. state-of-the-art but decades ahead of the systems used by most global militaries," Mark said. "They've got a lot of black market value. The last theft took place a week ago."

The screen lit up with a marker in south central New Mexico.

"This time the thief targeted a research lab operated at White Sands," Mark said.

"Wasn't the Air Force being especially careful after the first three thefts?" Remo asked. "Who did this, anyway? Who could get into a military base, let alone a top-secret compound, without being noticed? I could. Chiun could. I don't know who else could."

Remo realized he was fibbing. He did know who else could. Freya could, if what he had witnessed in recent days was any indication.

"Hey, they weren't doing any testing on animals, were they?" Remo added.

"What?" Mark said.

"Forget it."

"Interesting that you should mention yourself and Chiun," Smith said in a droll voice. "We've got some video from the surveillance at White Sands. Mark?"

"Mark?" Remo added.

Mark made an effort to ignore Remo as he brought a video onto the screen. It was a dark concrete lot, a small drift of sand swelling over it in a steady breeze. "White Sands. We tapped into their security system and found three conditions of security tape from the time of the theft. This is unaltered tape, and yet we see no sign of the intruder."

"Because he's covered in stealth paint?" Remo asked.

"Watch," Mark said.

Remo spotted the movement. It was a flash of a tiny, whirling blade and it moved outside of the chain-link fence that towered out of sight on the screen. It moved up, over and down, and the flicker was enough to attract the attention of the motion-sensitive camera. It targeted the spot, turning to bring the movement to the center of the frame.

"The camera automatically switches to thermal, senses nothing," Mark said. The image became green with bright spots, showing just a faint glimmer of something beyond the fence. "Then it switches to a white negative view, and finally back to normal vision. Sound and laser landscape measurement systems are also at work. They sense nothing."

"There's something there," Remo protested. He could see it, although the limitations of the video recording made it indefinable.

"According to the algorithms driving the security system, there's nothing," Smith said. "It watched the same spot for two hours and there was no further movement. Not so much as the rising and falling of a breathing human being."

"Then this, after two hours," Mark said. He touched a key and the camera was still on the same spot on the fence, although Remo could see a shifting of the stars in the background to prove time had passed. The camera jerked abruptly to the right, falling upon a tiny mechanical device that hopped across the concrete and froze against the fence.

"The camera decided later this was a rabbit."

"Looks like the toy from a Happy Meal."

"While the camera was distracted, the fence cut-out was opened and closed," Smith said.

The camera panned back to the fence, where the opening was now slightly askew. There was nothing behind it now. Remo had to admit that whatever went through it had moved skillfully.

"The second kind of tape we saw was deliberately distorted," Mark said, bringing up a view from within a hallway that was suddenly a sea of swimming monochrome shades. "Lasers polarize the lens. A similar sound-obstructing technology erases the sound before the security picks it up. The third kind of video we downloaded was when the intruder deliberately revealed itself."

The next scene was in another hallway, with a door to the outside. The lens polarization was there, then gone, just long enough to show the strangest thing Remo had seen in a long time.

It was a black place in the shape of a bulky foot, and the ankle disappeared into an orange silk kimono.

"Come on. You're joking."

"We're not joking."

"It looked like the elephant man in a bad geisha costume."

"It was an armored or mechanically enhanced human in a kimono," Smith said. "The kimono was put there for our benefit."

"What do you mean? Somebody wants us to think Chiun is responsible?"

"Not if they know anything about Master Chiun," Smith said. "The intruders used all kinds of techniques Chiun would never use. We think they deliberately revealed this as way of attracting our attention."

"Why?"

"To get us involved."

"Why?"

"I don't know why," Smith retorted. "It's enough to know they have an awareness of Chiun's existence. If they're aware of Chiun, they may be aware of CURE. If they're aware of CURE, then CURE must shut itself down."

"Now I get the picture."

"I wish I could believe that," Smith said.

"Junior, play back the leg scene," Remo said. The image had frozen as the door shut. Remo watched the three seconds of tape play out. "Again, Junior, but this time don't stop the tape."

Mark ran the tape again, and kept the tape rolling after the bizarre, kimono-clad foot was gone and the door closed itself. The opaque glass clearly showed a bulky figure outside, pausing for a moment, then walking out of the view. "What just happened?"

"He used a microwave device to override the biometrics security system," Mark explained. "Stolen technology, but stolen years ago. Half the world has it now."

"That's a weird suit he's wearing."

"Some sort of an armored housing covered in stealth paint," Smith explained. "Remo, do you realize how dangerously exposed CURE is now?"

"I have news for you, Smitty. CURE has been dangerously exposed for a long time," Remo said. "Lots of people know Chiun. Half the world leaders know there's a Master of Sinanju. They always have."

"And your friends on the Sun On Jo reservation?" Smith asked sharply.

"They've known about Sinanju longer than you have, Smitty," Remo said. "Face it—you're a late-comer."

"They know much more than about the existence of a Master of Sinanju—they know me!" Smith exhorted. "There was one young man who knew me by name, by voice!"

Remo furled his brow. "Hey, Smitty, take a deep breath. In. Out. You talking about the jerk on the phone? That's just Winston."

"Winston?"

"Yeah. He's a got a real attitude."

"Winston?"

"Who's Winston?" Mark asked.

"Let's move on," Smith stated, voice wavering slightly. "Mark, explain to Remo what was stolen from White Sands."

"Uh," Mark said, eyes darting back and forth between the screen and Remo, who shrugged. "Okay. You've heard of JDAM? The Joint Direct Attack Munitions is an inexpensive computer and tail-fin component that is retrofitted to free-fall bombs and turns them into smart bombs. They can then be guided with a high degree of precision to their targets. White Sands was developing a technology with a similar objective. It's called Guidance Device, Autonomous, Multifunctional."

"G-D-A-M?" Remo spelled.

"Yes."

"Guh-DAM?"

"Gee-DAM," Smith said impatiently.

"Gee-DAM is similar in concept to JDAM," Mark added. "It's a small chip with a high degree of electronic intelligence combined with a military GPS and other positional sensors, like a barometer, compass, even a tiny ultrasonic acoustical send/receive combination for positioning solid objects."

"For missiles?" Remo asked.

"For anything but," Mark said. "Anything."

"Like a car?"

"Sure, a car, but think smaller. The U.S. is developing spy planes the size of hummingbirds and ground-based insertion devices no bigger than a mouse. The Gee-DAM will serve as a one-size-fits-all guidance system for all of those devices—it can get any mobile machine from point A to point B virtually autonomously, and with an auxiliary set of instructions programmed in that are specific to the device."

"It's extremely powerful technology," Smith added.

"Sounds like something you buy in a little plastic bag at RadioShack," Remo said.

"Losing it could seriously disable the military superiority of the United States," Smith said. "One man has died already, trying to get it back for us. The item was offered for sale at an international arms bazaar yesterday and a CIA operative was on the scene to make an offer. He was found dead twelve hours ago. I'd like you to pick up where he left off. Obviously someone wants CURE on the scene. We'll just have to satisfy them."

"But I can't help but notice that we're flying away from the one part of the country where the burgles happened," Remo pointed out.

"After you pick up Master Chiun, you're heading to Morocco," Smith stated. "That's where the bazaar was held. With luck, you'll be attacked."

"Thanks."

"I mean by whoever is trying to attract our attention. Your first task will be to find out who knows what and how they learned it. Until we know that much, we're adrift. If our cover is compromised irreversibly, we'll initiate shutdown."

Smith was somber. Mark wore a distant, serious expression.

"Gee-DAM!" Remo exclaimed.

7

The house was centuries old and the great tree that had protected the house for generations was older still. These days it was just a hulk of dead wood with some green stalks jutting out here and there, somehow finding the force of will to produce a few token leaves every spring.

Sarah Slate hated the tree but clung to it year after year. After all, the Slate family was embodied in the tree. Now that the Slate family was virtually gone, she, Sarah, was the last of the green leaves. This was an idiotic and morbid outlook, she knew, but she couldn't get it out of her head, so she stayed in the house, although it was far too dark and huge for a bright young woman. And whenever the brisk breezes that gusted over the hills of Providence, Rhode Island, were not too bitter, she would take her breakfast on the small brick patio under the stark limbs of the great oak tree that she hated.

"Oh, my God," she exclaimed.

Mrs. Sanderson came out of the kitchen entrance with her hands covered in soapsuds. "Is something wrong, Sarah?"

"No. Not really, Mrs. Sanderson. Look at this." She thrust the newspaper at the woman, who had been cooking breakfast for the Slate family for more than forty years.

"My goodness," she said. "Who'd have thought it. That poor man."

"Poor man?" Sarah asked. She took back the paper and reexamined it. "Oh—I had not even read that far. I just saw the part about the sighting."

"It's an astounding story," Mrs. Sanderson said. "I'll bet no one has seen Slate's mechanical man in eighty years. It was old news when I started with the family. This poor old hermit must have gone soft in the head and forgot what year it was."

"Then killed himself," Sarah concluded sadly. "Out there, all alone in the desert."

"Alone, indeed," Mrs. Sanderson said. "You would have to be a lonely man to summon the ghost of Ironhand for company."

Tsking, Mrs. Sanderson returned to her kitchen and her breakfast dishes. Sarah read the story yet again, thinking that maybe she understood how lonely that poor old desert hermit must have been.

"THIS IS WHERE YOU get off, isn't it, Junior?" Remo asked as they touched down in Atlanta.

"Actually, I'm tagging along with you to Morocco."

Remo smirked. "Did you know your body temperature just started going up, Junior? Your pulse increased at the same time. Also, your forehead started sweating, you started doing a Rodney Dangerfield thing with your tie, and a little neon sign began blinking on and off above your head. It says,

He's Hiding Something, and there's a big fat arrow pointing at you."

Mark Howard tried to appear nonplussed but realized that he did so by darting his eyes from side to side. He tried not saying anything and found himself facing down a slightly irritated, highly smug Remo Williams. He wondered if Sinanju training included some sort of ability to stimulate a sense of extreme discomfort in selected victims or if that was Remo's special talent.

"Long flight to Morocco?" Remo asked.

Mark nodded. "Hours. Point taken."

"So? Fess up."

"I'm supposed to accompany you and help keep the mission on track."

"You're my field handler now?"

"No, not—"

"Chaperone, then?"

"Well—"

"Whatever. I've got the picture." Remo settled in his seat.

Mark and Remo had rarely seen eye to eye, but the relationship had improved over the first antagonistic couple of years Mark served with CURE. Remo had grudgingly accepted Mark as a valuable addition to the team, which meant he treated him with about the same level of disrespect as Dr. Smith. Mark knew Remo's behavior—thought he did, anyway. He didn't understand what was happening right now.

"You're not going to kick me off the plane?"

Remo looked at him. "You want me to?"

"No. I thought you would."

Remo shook his head.

Mark Howard hated being unsure of what was going

on, especially with the Masters of Sinanju. They were, after all, the most awesome, deadly and powerful human beings on the planet. Even if they were on Mark's team, he sometimes felt in deadly peril just being in the same room.

He wondered if he would ever figure Remo Williams out.

"Your forehead gonna sweat like that all the way across the Atlantic?" Remo asked.

THE JET WAS A PRIVATE transcontinental aircraft designed to get VIPs from one continent to another continent as soon as possible, in style. The pilot taxied quickly to a terminal where a bored-looking young man in ear protectors drove a set of motorized stairs to meet them. The young man chomped his gum and palmed the steering wheel of the stairs, going too fast and bumping into the aircraft a little too hard and too far to the right. When the flight attendant opened the door, the steps weren't aligned with the opening.

She waved at the operator. The young man purposely looked in the opposite direction.

"Fix the stairs!" she shouted down.

The operator chomped his gum and watched a tiny corporate jet take off. The flight attendant shrugged and went back to doing whatever she did in the galley for hours at a time.

A small cart appeared from inside the private terminal and rolled across the tarmac, the driver flinching as if he expected to be slapped every time he hit an imperfection in the pavement.

Beside him, in a brilliant display of turquoise, was a robed Asian man at least eighty years old. He had a nearly bald head, with just a few threads of yellowing hair around his ears and on his chin. He had the characteristic eyes of a Korean, but his features were almost masked in the deep wrinkles of advanced age, and his flesh seemed too thin, as if the slightest bump or scrape might rip it open.

When the cart stopped at the bottom of the stairs, the old Korean stepped out and revealed himself to be short, almost tiny. A breeze rustled the fabric of his robe, and it was as if the wind might flutter him away like a paper scrap.

But the small ancient man didn't go anywhere. He glanced at the stairs, glanced at the operator of the stairs and put his hands into the sleeves of his robe. He stood there, completely at ease, and waited.

The cart driver finished loading six lacquered chests into the belly of the aircraft and ran, not walked, to his cart, then steered it away as fast as its tiny electric engine would carry it.

The old man never moved.

"What's he doing?" Mark Howard demanded.

"I see nothing." Remo moved to a seat farther back in the cabin and read the air-sickness bag.

"Why isn't he coming up?" Mark asked.

The stewardess emerged from the galley and peered down the steps.

"He need a wheelchair lift or something?" she asked.

"I think he's insulted by the sloppy alignment of the stairs," Mark explained.

"Insulted? I thought you guys were in a hurry."

"We are. Get the pilot, please."

Remo tried to ignore it all as the flight attendant demanded to know if Mark Howard was joking, then got the pilot, who phoned the tower, who phoned the terminal management office, who eventually radioed the supervisor of the operator of the stairs.

"Why don't I just go down and carry him up myself," the flight attendant demanded at one point. "He's got to weigh less than my dog."

"Ix-nay," Remo muttered out the side of his mouth. "She'll be ed-day."

"No, better not," Mark said. He was irked, yet fascinated by the composure of the man, Chiun, the Master of Sinanju Emeritus and trainer of Remo Williams. The small man was in fact, older than he looked—he was born more than a century ago—but he was also stronger than he looked.

The fact was, Chiun was stronger than anybody had ever looked.

The young man in the driveable stairs snarled into his walkie-talkie then angrily started the stairs, pulled away from the jet, stomped on the brakes to halt it, and yanked it into reverse. He backed it into place, and the alignment with the door was only slightly better.

"Still not good enough for you, old man?" the operator demanded, loud enough for Mark Howard to hear from the jet hatch.

Chiun hadn't moved a muscle. His face hadn't ticked when the vehicle came within inches of colliding with him. He hadn't blinked when the young man spoke to him. He remained stationary, as if meditating and oblivious to the world around him.

The operator was grumbling under his breath.

Mark Howard looked desperately at his watch. "We're in a great hurry!" he called down.

Chiun smiled blissfully, as if awakening from a daze.

"Good day, Prince Howard. It is an honor to be in your presence this morning."

"We're in a great hurry," Mark pleaded.

"Ah. It is your wish that I take the steps necessary to expedite our departure." Chiun regarded the stairs. "I shall gladly correct the cause of the delay."

MARK HOWARD had a sinking *What have I done?* feeling, but they were in a hurry. He tried to decide if he should say anything more, but by then it was too late.

The Asian man strolled around the side of the stairs, to the small compartment where the operator was seated, and nudged the stairs with his sandaled foot.

The compartment caved in, crushing the operator's abdomen at the same time the stairs scraped sideways several inches. The solid rubber tires left black skid marks. Mark Howard noticed that the stairs were now perfectly aligned with the jet hatch.

Chiun put his hands into his sleeves and ascended with the dignity of royalty.

"What's all the shouting?" asked the flight attendant, who reappeared to see Chiun arrive and bow deeply to Mark. "Oh, my God, the man is hurt!" The flight attendant gestured at the sight of the wriggling, bellowing operator trapped by his crushed stomach in the driver's seat of the stairs.

"We're ready to go," Mark told her.

"We can't go now!" she protested.

"Somebody will come and help him. Let's get going," Mark insisted.

"But the stairs have to be moved!"

The small Asian man had a smile on his face that never wavered, but he seemed to kick back briefly with his foot. The flight attendant was sure she saw him do that.

Another thing she was sure of—at that moment, the mobile stairs rolled across the tarmac with a rattle of failing mechanical brakes and, going faster than they were ever designed to, crunched into the fireproof brick face of the terminal building.

"Oh, my God!" she wailed, trying to process what she had witnessed. The small kick. The crash. They *couldn't* be connected.

The steps, eleven feet high, wobbled and fell over with a clang and more shouting from the operator, which blended with the cry of an ambulance cart's siren.

"There you go. Medical personnel are on the way. They'll take care of him," Howard said.

"May we begin our journey now?" asked the old man who could not possibly have done what the flight attendant saw him do.

"Yes," she said with a stiff smile. "Please take your seats."

The old man took his seat across the aisle from Remo, and they taxied away from the mayhem as more emergency vehicles arrived.

"My son," Chiun said as he settled in.

"Little Father. Nice trip?"

"Travel is monotonous," sighed the old man, peering intently out the window at the wing of the aircraft.

"Here's a factoid that will put a sparkle into your day—these things aren't reusable." Remo held up an air-sickness bag. "Says so right here. 'Dispose after use.'"

"It is good to see you reading, my son," Chiun said.

8

The newspaper, Harold W. Smith decided, was drivel.
Ever since a reporter with the *New York Times* admitted
fabricating years of dramatic stories, journalistic integrity had gone down the tubes across the country. At least
prior to that scandal, there had been lip service paid to
journalistic integrity. Nowadays nobody even tried to
pretend. The best papers in the nation had become tabloids.

Still, Smith couldn't help but wonder at the report
out of El Paso. The wires had picked it up, then pulled
it. To Smith it looked as if somebody had tried to
squelch the article.

But the CURE quartet of computers had snatched it
out of the electronic ether before a seek-and-destroy Internet spider could remove it from the world's archiving mainframes, and had flagged it for Smith simply
because it was anomalous and was in the proximity of
his current watch zones.

An old man was dead in his shack not too far from
one of the technology thefts at White Sands. He was
found on his front porch with his head caved in against
a wooden post.

What was odd was the letter he left, to his long-deceased father and dated the day of his death. Based on the coroner's estimated time of death at between 2:00 a.m. and 6:00 a.m., that meant the letter had been written in the wee small hours of the morning. The reporter who wrote the story saw it as a sad yet hopeful last message by a man who was looking beyond his world into the next.

"'Wouldn't it be wonderful if we all had a little Ironhand in our life?'" the reporter wrote in closing. "'What better than a memory of our childhood to give us comfort in today's world, especially as we embark on our last great journey.'"

It wasn't poignant; it was pap. And the letter, Smith decided, was clearly the work of a delusional mind. After all, the man was eighty-nine years old.

He closed the screen with the article and forgot it. Or so he thought. Hours later he found his mind returning to the article from the El Paso newspaper.

THE AIR WAS STIFLING and it smelled. The fresh breeze coming in from the Atlantic Ocean was poisoned at the seaside with the fumes of rotting fish and spilled petrochemicals. Long before the breeze worked its way to the inner slums of Casablanca, it was polluted and unbreathable. The people in the Casablanca slums had no choice but to breathe it, along with the stench of their own neighborhood. They died a little with every breath they took.

"I thought it was fog," Remo commented.

"You thought what was fog?" Chiun asked, ignoring the stares he received from the locals.

"You know, in *Casablanca,* when Ingrid Bergman is

getting on the plane and Humphrey Bogart is doing his lines and there's all this mist swirling around them. I thought it was fog, but it was smog. Fumes."

"Would it startle you to learn that the movie was not filmed on location?"

"No!"

"Yes."

"G'dam!"

"Here we are." Chiun paused at the archway entrance to a partially enclosed, exceptionally dreary-looking section of the city. The man on the ground watching them smiled with a mouth full of black teeth-nubs. He briefly revealed a battered old revolver under his vest.

"No zoo-veneers," the man said in English, every syllable an effort.

The guard was astounded when the small Asian man replied to him in his own tongue—not Arabic, but a Berber dialect that was all but extinct in the twenty-first century. "We do not seek trinkets."

"You may not enter, little old man," the guard said harshly.

"Is this not where one might spend a great deal of money?" Chiun asked.

"You wish to purchase T-shirts, go to the hotel district."

"Pah! I do not wear T-shirts. Only this pale piece of a pig's ear does so."

The gate guard smiled at the insult. The white man didn't know he was being insulted, obviously. He looked bored.

"We have much money," the Asian man said in the Berber tongue.

"How much?"

"Enough to purchase our own army, if there is one for sale."

The Berber guard scowled, then shook his head. "You need an appointment, little old man."

Chiun looked thoughtful, and smiled, and his hand whisked at the guard, who slumped forward where he sat. His forehead began dripping into his lap, and his Berber dialect took one step closer toward true extinction.

"He says we need an invitation," Chiun said as they left the nodding corpse.

"I'm inviting you," Remo said, waving magnanimously at the entrance to the dank, dark slum-within-a-slum.

"I would refuse if I could." Through the archway they entered what had once been a fine courtyard, but was now a dim, evil-smelling grotto. The corners were black with filth and trash. The deteriorating cobblestones channeled some sort of evil, greasy-looking liquid between them.

"Who are you?" demanded a voice from the shadows beyond a crumbling brick divider wall. The interior of the courtyard was filled with shacks that might house an extended family.

"We came for the auction," Remo called back, scoping out the figures in the shadows. The shacks were abandoned at the moment, but there were five men in the walkway around the fringes, and they were the kind of men Remo didn't want to see any better than he could. Unfortunately he saw almost perfectly despite the darkness.

"The auction is over."

"Hey, we didn't get a chance to place our bids."

"Go away, stupid foreigner."

"I don't want to talk to you, anyway. Who's the real man in charge?"

The speaker came toward them, waving his automatic rifle. Everybody had an AK-47 these days, ever since the Iraqis stopped needing them by the hundreds of thousands and began their new lucrative export business. This one was brandished threateningly in Remo's direction. "I am in charge!"

"You? You're a twerp."

"I am the commander of all these men and you are dead!"

"Don't think so." Remo reached out, and out, and out, and the Casablancan with the AK made a spluttering noise. The American seemed to be stretching his arm to inhuman lengths.

"Actually, I'm just light on my feet," Remo said as he stood in his original position and gripped the shocked gunner by the collar.

"And in the head," Chiun added.

"You really are the guy in charge?" Remo demanded.

"No, it is not I!"

"No, it's okay, I believe you now, twerp."

The man tried to get his AK leveled between him and his assailant. This was difficult to do while hanging by the shirtfront, toes just grazing the earth. The Casablancan suddenly felt himself being shook.

His body rattled, his limbs jounced and a few blackened tooth chips joined his AK on the old cobblestones.

"Tell the Twerp Team to back off," Remo said.

"They'll kill you if you kill me!"

"Or not, I don't care. Hold on."

The Casablancan was suddenly on his own two feet. He squinted for focus and found himself staring at the tiny Asian in the outlandish robe.

"Your dwelling smells of offal," the smiling Asian said in perfect Berber. Not city Berber, but the old traditional Berber of his great-grand-uncle.

Then he saw the white man, who was moving like a sentient shadow from man to man, crossing several yards in a heartbeat, and every time he reached one of them the man fell. Then, just seconds after he had been freed, the leader found himself being lifted again in the fist of the white man.

Off to the side he heard the collapse of the last body, and he knew his army of Casablancan street fighters was no more.

"Sorry, twerp, no more Team."

"I talk."

"Yeah, you just did something else, too," Remo said in disgust, holding his captive far away where he couldn't drip on him. "Who's the broker?"

"Broke her?"

"Who sold the plans?"

"I did."

"You just hosted the auction, you didn't own the merchandise."

"No, it was my merchandise."

"You're sort of the Christie's of Morocco, hmm? Sorry if I find it hard to swallow. I think you better come clean."

Chiun smirked.

"The man will kill me if I say anything," the captive whined.

"Like I won't."

The captive ran frantically, but all the leg-pumping in the world would get him nowhere without having his feet on solid ground. Eventually he went limp.

"Barcelona," he admitted.

"Good fish in Barcelona," Remo noted.

"Arms man there. Cote. Allessandro."

"An arms merchant in Barcelona named Cote Allessandro."

"No, Allessandro Cote."

"Okay. Good. Thanks."

"So you won't kill me?" The captive's face broke into a hideous smile.

"Yes, I will. I was being sarcastic," Remo explained. "The world need arms auctioneers like I need another old bossy guy telling me what to do."

As they were leaving, Chiun said, "I forgive the casual insult because your earlier remark was amusing, however unintended. 'Better come clean.' Heh!"

THROUGH THE DOOR came the freckle-faced teenager with the dirty scrub-brush hair. He grinned and waved. "Hiya, Pop!"

"You bring in half zee desert vith you." The older man was scowling, his voice heavy with a German accent. "You know what sand vill do to my electronics?"

"Nothing, Pop, not with my weather-proofing. You could take the roof off this place in a sandstorm and you wouldn't so much as short a power supply."

The kid never stopped grinning and his father never stopped scowling, but the old man reached out and scrubbed the kid's crew cut with his knuckles.

"Hey! You nut! Cut it out!" The kid scrambled away

and made for the tiny kitchen at the far end of the low building, where he bent at the waist with his head inside the refrigerator as if he intended to remain there for the duration.

The older man peered at his screen until he felt the cool breeze reach him, more than forty feet away. "Trying to cool zee whole building?"

The kid emerged with a bag of bread covered in a rainbow of dots, a package of bologna and a half-gallon squeeze bottle of bright yellow mustard. He set it up next to his father's monitor and watched the screen as he laid out five bread slices, squeezed a thick puddle of mustard on the first four, then layered them with slices of pale meat from the package. He stacked them atop one another, putting the fifth slice of doughy white bread on top, and carefully compressed the sandwich until the mustard just barely began oozing out the sides. He took a huge bite and noticed his father watching him with unconcealed distaste.

"Train wreck," the kid said, and opened his mouth wide to display the half-chewed contents.

"Disgusting." The older man turned back to his display.

"Casablanca?" the kid asked.

"Yes."

"Find the right plane?"

"Perhaps. How was school?"

"I got a B on a science quiz."

"You are joking?"

"Nope."

The older man waited for the punch line. It was impossible for his son to get a B on a science exam. "Teacher error?"

"Yeah. I set her straight. She was cool about it."

"Cool as in not perturbed."

"Yeah. You know. Not ticked off or anything because I was right and she was wrong. She changed it to an A."

"Cool," the older man said, his concentration on the screen.

The kid chewed loudly in his ear for a full minute as they watched the stark, high-contrast video images displaying in three small windows.

"Your possibles?" the kid asked.

"Yes. This is the only aircraft I have traced so far." He tapped the small window showing the looming profile of a sleek jet. The image, like the other two, seemed to be shot from extremely low to the ground, as if someone had dropped a video camera a few paces from the aircraft and it was looking up. The legend beneath the video feed identified the aircraft as originating in the State of Florida in the United States.

The kid rubbed the tip of this freckled nose contemplatively, then tapped another window. "Let me see this one."

The older man expanded the window with the next aircraft, also videotaped from very low to the ground but from farther away. The long sweep of tarmac that dominated the image moved slightly as the camera seemed to creep slowly toward the aircraft.

"Nah. Forget that one."

"Why?" the older man asked. "You don't even know its origin."

"I think it's a Saudi jet. See this?" He tapped the blur of green on the tail. "Saudi flag, I bet. Plus, that's a Cessna Citation X, no special retrofits apparent, which means it'll cruise 1,500 nautical miles on a full tank. Not what you'd use for crossing the Atlantic."

The father nodded and used the mouse to adjust the camera, zooming in on the blurry image of the flag and tapping out a command that made the window freeze. A moment later a high-resolution digital photo of the blur of color resolved itself laboriously on the screen until it was a square of green with white Arabic letters underscored with a white sword. The image next to it was a logo or family insignia of some kind.

"Yeah. Forget 'em," the kid said.

"I agree." The older man punched out commands, then moved on to the third screen. "Not much larger than the other Saudi jet."

"It's bigger than it looks and there's a big difference in the specs, too, Pop. It's a Raytheon business jet, Hawker Horizon. It'll fly at least twice as far, for one thing, as the Cessna. Could have come from the U.S. easy."

The aircraft in the image was closer than the others. The camera seemed to be inching ever so slowly up on the right rear wheel.

"Who's the uniforms?" the kid asked.

"Airport security. Morocco is a dangerous place to leave a valuable aircraft unattended."

"There's like five of them. Seems excessive."

"That in itself means nothing," the older man said in his German-heavy speech. "It costs little to hire a small army to guard a jet for a few hours." After ten minutes, the camera appeared to have crept only a few yards closer to the wheels of the aircraft and the older man said, "Don't you have homework?"

"Done."

"When?"

"I dictated the answers into the phone on the way home," the kid explained, and stretched to one of the printers that were scattered among the vast array of electronics equipment in the big, low room. He snatched up a small stack of papers and fanned them. "See?"

"Humph."

"Gonna have another sandwich. Want one?"

"No, thank you. I want to monitor the crawl."

THE CENTIPEDE kept itself inside the channel dividing the concrete slabs that made up the tarmac on this private end of the airport at Casablanca. The terrain was broken and uneven from the perspective of a crawling creature that was no more than twelve millimeters in height, and time and again the centipede was forced to crawl out of the channel or over a crack or around a raised broken concrete chunk.

Once, one of the armed security men strolled around the back of the jet, out of boredom more than thoroughness. The chances of any mischief coming from the far side of the aircraft, across the open, empty airport runways, was small.

If he had been more observant he might have noticed the strange, dull, slate-gray thing stretched out in the gap in the concrete. He never saw it.

When the man passed on, the centipede began moving again. It came to the big wooden block, then to the right rear tire. It reared up, two inches off the surface, its activities now hidden by the tire from the view of the guards. It took the rubber in its legs and dug in.

The eighty-four tungsten legs of the mechanical centipede were like filament, no wider than a human hair but strong and extremely sharp. The algorithms that controlled their movement, computer-generated to match the movements of real centipedes, allowed it to flow easily through a natural movement. Getting a grip was the easy part; not getting too much grip, that was a challenge.

The force of each leg was feather-light, but the filament legs were so sharp they penetrated the rubber easily. The tires were new, and the heat had softened them somewhat; still, the specialty aircraft tire polymer was so tough it adhered to the tiny needles that penetrated it. By the time the centipede had crawled to the top of the tire and onto the metal strut, it had lost six tungsten legs to the tire.

That was a slight handicap, but the centipede's next task was its most difficult.

THE KID WITH THE CREW CUT grinned with his mouth full of white bread and olive loaf. "Ouch. Six legs lost. You gonna make it?"

"Please stop chewing in my ear," the older man said.

"I told you tungsten was a mistake."

"There's nothing stronger."

"Titanium thretcheth," the kid managed to say while stuffing in a huge mouthful.

"Where are your manners? I did not understood you," the father said irritably.

The kid chewed and swallowed a huge glob, washing it down with milk from a frosty glass bottle. "I said, titanium stretches."

"Tungsten is far stronger. You look like an advertisement for zee Dairy Farmers of New Mexico."

The kid grinned and dragged an arm over his mouth, erasing most of his milk mustache.

On screen, the chart of numbers updated itself dynamically and the image of the aircraft wheel well abruptly rotated and closed in.

Somewhere in the northwestern corner of Africa, the centipede was gripping the strut of the aircraft through a combination of constriction and the needle-like penetration, to microscopic depths, of its seventy-eight surviving legs into the surface of the steel, and as it did so it ascended.

All they could do was watch. The algorithms controlling the centipede made their own adjustments far too fast for manual assistance.

But seconds later the image became stationary and the monitoring window indicated the centipede was in position.

"All right, Pops!" the kid shouted, spraying milk on the older man and on his computer screen.

His father was too self-satisfied to complain. Minutes later, he was gratified to see the next centipede likewise position itself in the wheel well of the other aircraft.

The third centipede had by this time crawled away into the grass by the tarmac to hide in wait for other commands.

The older man picked up the phone on the first ring.

"Mr. Fastbinder," said a familiar voice. "I'm eager to hear about your progress."

"Excuse me one moment," the older man said, and put the phone to his chest. "Jack," he said to his grinning son, "don't you have a date with Sue Ellen this evening?"

"Not until six, Pops."

"Can't you find something else to do?" He nodded at the phone.

"Oh, yeah, sure. I'll go install those new gyroscopes in the Walkers."

When the teenager had moved across the workspace to a distant bench, the older man put the phone back to his ear and apologized. "My son is enthusiastic."

"Don't blame him, Fastbinder. What's the word out of Morocco?"

"We narrowed it down to two aircraft that arrived in zee last three hours."

"Did you get any eyewitness reports from the Barbers?"

"Berbers," Fastbinder corrected. "All are dead."

"Really? I guess I should have expected that. Wow. Nobody saw anything?"

"Our police mole says one passerby reported seeing a dark young man and an old man in a Japanese geisha outfit."

"That's it! That's him! That's them, all right!"

"As soon as I lost contact with our Berbers, I initiated zee airport activities. We'll have stowaway on both aircraft."

"And when will we know which is the right plane?"

"We'll monitor their position on GPS, simple enough," Fastbinder reported. "One of zee planes will make the flight to Barcelona, and then vee'll know."

"Yeah," said his caller. "Then we'll know! Ouch!" There was a fumble and the phone was recovered a moment later. "Scraped my foot on the carpet. Jesus, that burns! What's the spook doing?"

"Decomposing," Fastbinder reported.

"Aw, hell, did you have to kill him!"

"It did the job. Your friends showed up."

"Makes me uncomfortable, though, killing CIA agents."

Fastbinder didn't reply.

"Well, whatever. Let me know when something happens."

Fastbinder hung up, but he was dialing the phone again within five minutes.

"Already?" asked the man on the line excitedly. In the background was the sound of running water.

"They must have high-priority clearance," Fastbinder said. "My motion sensors picked up increased movement on the aircraft just minutes ago, and already it is pushing back."

"Ahhhh! Just got my feet in some water. Damn that feels good. Your bug is not gonna get squished when the wheels are pulled in?"

"Unlikely. There is enough space in zee wheel well. The aircraft is taxiing."

"Already? Can I just stay on the line and maybe we'll know right away where it's going."

"As you wish."

Fastbinder ignored the distant sounds of splashing water and sighs of contentment. "Zee aircraft is in the air."

"This the first one or the second one, anyway?"

"The Raytheon Hawker, which my son assures me is capable of transcontinental transport."

"He know his stuff?"

"Yes."

"Okay. What's it doing now?"

"Turning onto its flight path." Fastbinder was watching the GPS feed from the device and, as the wheels were pulled in, his eyes locked on the data feed. Only so much transmitting power could be packed into the miniaturized electronics in the centipede, and they kicked in as the aircraft left the vicinity of the ground-based retransmitter that had been relaying the centipede signals thus far.

All Fastbinder needed was a minuscule data stream, just enough for a GPS read. And he got it.

"Vee have them," Fastbinder reported happily. "They're on a flight path to the eastern Iberian Peninsula."

"That's where Barcelona is, right?"

"Correct."

"All right!" There was a heavy splash. "Oh shit, that hurts! Shit! Keep me posted, Fastbinder. I got a spill to clean up."

Fastbinder hung up, and only then did he realize his son was standing at his shoulder again.

"Sorry, Pops, I couldn't resist checking it out. Way to go."

"Thank you, Jack."

"But that Herbie is a real dweeb, isn't he?"

"Dweeb does not begin to describe him."

9

Chiun observed Remo thoughtfully as they took the cleanest available taxi to the Casablanca airport. After five minutes, Remo caved. "What? What did I do?"

"I was considering that you have become soft, my son."

"Marshmallow soft or down-comforter soft?"

"Complacent soft. You have lost your respect for danger."

"What danger?" Remo demanded.

"Exactly! You do not see the danger that is around you every day, every minute. I cannot be your sense of caution, Remo."

The old Korean Master spoke with such serious intent that Remo stopped to think about it. "Chiun, I am not careless."

"Careless and incautious are not one and the same," Chiun explained, his brow vaguely troubled. "While you have become Master of Sinanju, while you are a skilled and powerful assassin, I fear for you because of your lack of humility."

"I'm *careful*."

"Not careful enough."

Remo shrugged, not sure what he should say. "I'll work on it."

"It is not a matter of actions but of attitude. You are not afraid enough."

"Little Father, you taught me to master fear, to experience it and make use of it."

"Yes, but I speak now of the fear you must carry upon your person, be it nothing more than a speck of fear, a mote of fear."

"How do I get this speck?"

Chiun looked away. "I cannot teach you how to feel, only how to process what you feel. This speck is for you to find and cultivate, but heed me in this, Remo—a speck of fear will serve you well."

"YOU SHOULD HAVE SEEN the thing. It was at least ten inches long," Mark Howard said excitedly as they boarded the aircraft.

"Lucky you, you got to stay inside the nice plane. We had to go out and live it," Remo said.

"You see any bugs?"

"The bugs decided Casablanca was too dirty. They all got grossed out and migrated to someplace more hygienic, like Sierra Leone," Remo said.

Mark Howard wasn't satisfied with Remo's reaction. He had been entirely amazed by the size of the many-legged bug he had glimpsed crawling around on the tarmac. But Remo shrugged it off as if it were nothing.

Well, Remo had traveled extensively, and to some of the worst parts of the world, and had likely seen all kinds of ugly insects the likes of which Mark could only imagine. He wasn't going to make himself look like more of a neophyte by going on about it.

Still, the image of the thing stuck in his head. He wasn't especially creeped out by it so much as he was, well, bothered by it somehow.

This trip was turning out to be a huge yawn. He had been stuck inside this aircraft for most of a day since leaving Rye, New York, except for the endless few hours he was stuck inside the car lost in the Arizona desert near Yuma. The only interesting thing that had happened to him, other than the big bug sighting, was the glimpse of the young woman Freya on the Sun On Jo reservation.

Mark Howard concentrated on pushing away the image. Her exquisite face, barely glimpsed in the night; the shimmering of her golden hair in the lantern glow. Cripes, he was acting like a thirteen-year-old again, but the sight of her had intrigued him as no woman...

"Hey!"

Mark Howard was startled back to the here and now. Remo was shooting daggers at him with his eyes. "What?"

"Your neon sign is blinking again, Junior, only this time it reads, Hot-N-Bothered, Hot-N-Bothered," Remo said.

Mark Howard felt the blood rise to his face.

"You better not be hot-n-bothered about what I think you're hot-n-bothered about."

Mark Howard was mortified and humiliated and his jaw felt wired shut.

"What has caused this stir of lasciviousness in the young prince regent?" Chiun asked curiously in Korean.

"He's got a woman under his skin," Remo responded.

"And you care why?"

Remo stopped glaring at Mark long enough to glare briefly at Chiun.

"Ah. His eyes have beheld the vision of the lovely young daughter of the Reigning Master of Sinanju."

"Yes."

Mark didn't understand a word of the conversation but he knew what it was about. He wished the floor would spontaneously open and allow him to plummet mercifully to the earth.

"You cannot blame him," Chiun said. "She is comely by his standards."

"Meaning?"

"She is white, which makes her naturally unattractive, and her hair makes her appear sickly. Still, measured by the Caucasian yardstick she is quite comely."

"What's wrong with her hair?" Remo demanded.

"It is albinous. The most attractive hair color is a rich, dark brown or black."

"Hey, you look in the mirror, lately? You've been forgetting the Grecian Formula."

"My hair is the hair of an elderly man," Chiun explained patiently. "Light hair makes one appear old, beyond one's breeding seasons. Light hair on a young woman makes her appear diseased."

"Go to hell."

"This is why blond-haired women are universally regarded as unattractive."

"Really? I think I'll get you a subscription to *Maxim*."

"I mean among those with sophisticated taste in women."

"Koreans?"

Chiun smiled. "Traditionalist Koreans."

"Go to hell again."

Nobody said another word until the aircraft was over Spain.

10

The cinderblock walls had been repainted with the same high-gloss white paint every summer for twenty-seven years. When the afternoon sun angled in through the big round windows, the corridor became a sea of glaring light that forced most of the students to put on sunglasses in the late afternoon between classes. Looking west down the corridor, toward the language-arts wing, it was impossible to see faces.

A verbal alert system had spontaneously developed. Like the warning barks of prairie dogs, the high-school students up-hall began calling down-hall.

"Goodwin coming!"

"Goodwin!"

"Goodwin!"

A flock of varsity cheerleaders skipped into the nearest classroom, skirts rising just enough to reveal their school-board-sanctioned thong panties. Every freshman and sophomore flattened against the wall and stared at his or her feet. Even the knot of senior girls, furtively planning a hazing ceremony for the junior girls, hastily gave way to Goodwin.

Goodwin came, his footsteps shaking the hall, his shadow gigantic in front of him. He was vaguely satisfied with the performance of the student body. Somehow they always knew when he was angry and needed his space.

At the moment he was extremely angry, and when his eyes fell on the person who had made him angry, he became angrier.

The jerk kid was standing there talking to his girlfriend as though he hadn't even heard the warnings. He had his back to Goodwin. Nobody turned their back on Neil Goodwin!

"Hey, you! Fast!"

Jack Fast glanced over his shoulder. "Hey, Neil. Be with you in a second."

The skinny kid with the sun-bleached crew cut turned back to his girlfriend and continued his conversation. The girlfriend giggled.

"Hey, Fast Fucker, I'm talking to you!"

Jack Fast stopped and, without hurrying up about it, turned around. "What's the problem, Neil?"

"Yes, Mr. Goodwin, what is the problem?"

Goodwin was startled at the appearance of Mr. Cescepi at his shoulder. Dean Cescepi was the one guy in the entire school who could intimidate Neil Goodwin.

"This is between him and me, Dean," Goodwin explained.

"Really? The last time you told me that was just before you slugged Tom Newton in the stomach."

"You can't prove I did that," Goodwin declared.

"But I know you did," Dean Cescepi said, then gave Jack the once-over. "Mr. Fast is a little big for you, isn't he, Goodwin? Don't you usually sucker punch kids half your size?"

Goodwin simmered and clenched his fists at his sides.

"Go for it, Goodwin." Dean Cescepi smirked.

Goodwin had heard the stories about Cescepi. Cescepi was said to have killed someone, literally wrung his neck when the guy tried to steal his wife's purse in a city park. And the other guy had used a gun.

"Come on, Goodwin," the dean goaded. "You know you want to. Look at me—I'm not bigger than Fast."

Neil Goodwin felt the urge. He did want a piece of Cescepi. That prick had been giving him grief for three long years….

"Holy smokes, you guys! There's no reason to get into a fight."

Neil Goodwin and Dean Cescepi turned to Jack Fast, who was wearing his goofy smile on his freckled face. "You jokers! You're just putting me on with all that tough talk."

Dean Cescepi grinned. Fast was inane. Some sort of idiot savant. Faced with that level of sunshiny dorkiness, who could stay angry?

"That's right, we're just putting you on. Aren't we, Mr. Goodwin?"

Goodwin shifted from foot to foot. "Yeah. Just jokin'."

"Carry on, gentlemen," the dean said, and he wandered down the corridor just far enough so he could keep an eye on the situation.

Neil Goodwin sneered at Fast, aware that the dean's footsteps had not carried him far off. "You the dean's pet now, Fast Fucker?"

"What can I do for you, Neil?"

"We need to talk about what you did in calculus today."

"I give up. What did I do?"

Goodwin snorted. "The test. Remember the test?"

"Sure."

"You aced it."

"Yes."

"Don't act stupid, Fast. Those tests were graded on a curve, and you threw it all off. I failed the test because of you!"

"Oh, give me a break!" interjected Nancy Fielding, Fast's girlfriend. She was extremely attractive, a curious combination of retro clean-cut and sexy. Her tailored linen blazer was worn over a silk halter top that exposed a vast span of beautiful stomach. How the hell did Fast rate a piece of hot ass like that?

"This is the thing," Goodwin said. "I fail calculus and I won't have the GPA I need to get into the old man's fraternity. One more F is all it will take."

"Sorry to hear it." Fast was still grinning.

"You're not getting the picture," Goodwin insisted.

"Oh, we all get the picture, Neil," Nancy declared loudly enough for everyone in the vicinity to hear her, and everybody turned to stare. "You're pissed off because Jack won't stoop to your level of stupidity."

Then she laughed. Up and down the hall people saw Neil Goodwin being laughed at by the most hottest babe in the entire school.

Goodwin's face was on fire.

"Why, you're turning red as a cherry, Neil!" Nancy exclaimed in delight, and Fast just stood there smiling like some dork from the cover of the June 1955 issue of *Boy's Life*.

Goodwin exerted all his self-control in an effort to not put his fist in both their faces.

"I think we need to talk again, Fast," Goodwin growled. "Tonight. On the football field."

"Okay, Neil. How does 6:45 sound?" Fast said. He turned to Nancy. "We'll still have time to make it to the movies by 7:30."

"Sure." Nancy rewarded Fast with an adoring smile. "See you then. 'Bye, Neil!"

They were gone. Neil Goodwin was pretty sure he hadn't intimidated them as he had intended to.

Tonight he would show that slick piece of shit and his prissy slut just how intimidating he could be—and they sure as shit were *not* going to make the 7:30 movie.

SOMETIMES Dean Alain Cescepi wondered if Jack Fast was for real. The kid lived in a different world. He was some sort of an intellectual genius but he came across as utterly naive, too. He was the only student Cescepi could remember in twenty years who used the word "gosh."

And yet Fast had something going for him, on top of the perfect GPA. People gravitated to him. He was the certified nerd who somehow managed to be cool. Not to mention he had managed to rope Nancy Fielding, the most delectable barely legal in the history of Larchwill High School.

Dean Cescepi didn't know what to expect at the scheduled meeting between Jack Fast and the designated big dumb bully of the current graduating class, Neil Goodwin. Fast was a mystery. Goodwin was powerful and egocentric and stupid enough to kill somebody.

No matter what, it would be interesting.

Cescepi was crouched in the announcer's booth at

the top of the bleachers at 6:30 when Goodwin showed up with his loose-knit gang of buddies from the football team. There wasn't an average IQ in the lot, but most of them were smart enough to be nervous. After all, they were all seniors, all bound for college on nonacademic merits. And even sports scholarships required that you actually finish high school.

Two decades of high-school administration and you got to know what kind of kids there were and how they would behave in a given situation. Cescepi knew this bunch was on the verge of doing something that even they knew was stupid. But why had Jack Fast agreed to this meeting? Jack Fast didn't fit into any easy classification.

Hell, Cescepi thought, Fast would not show at all if he was *really* smart.

At 6:43 Jack and Nancy pulled into the nearby lot and came into the football field. She was clinging to his arm and they were laughing like lovers on a moonlit stroll.

Goodwin was standing on the fifty-yard line, looking stern. "This ain't no laughing matter, Fast Fucker."

Nancy Fielding giggled at Goodwin, and Cescepi saw the kid stiffen.

"Oh, dear, you're getting all red, again, Neil!" Nancy cried. "Did Neil tell you about this afternoon?" she asked his gang of buddies. "He was red as a cherry!"

Goodwin bellowed, "What do you think we oughtta do about this situation, Fast?"

"About you getting embarrassed whenever Nancy is around?" Jack asked innocently.

"About the damn calc test! I can not fail another damn calc test!"

"Maybe you should study," Jack suggested.

Cescepi knew Goodwin had no intention of negotiating with Fast. He was simply psyching himself up to attack the boy. Eventually, Goodwin raised a fist.

"Knock it off, Neil! There's no need to get into a fight about this."

Cescepi shook his head, amazed. That kid was still smiling as if he didn't know what was about to hit him.

Then Goodwin struck. Nancy screamed. Jack Fast raised his own arm to defend himself, but his arm moved extraordinarily fast, knocking Goodwin's punch back the way it had come.

"Aw, gee, I'm sorry, Neil," Fast said.

"You broke my fucking arm! You son of a fucking bitch, you broke my fucking arm!"

Cescepi couldn't quite believe his eyes. Goodwin's right arm was indeed wobbling at an unnatural angle. He was on his knees on the artificial turf, holding it.

"Oh, that's terrible," Fast said. "It's an elbow break, too."

"You're hyperextended," Nancy pointed out helpfully. "The whole joint failed. You're going to need to have the joint replaced."

"Huh?" Goodwin grunted, confused and in pain.

"They can work miracles with stainless steel," Nancy said. "Three or four surgeries, maybe eighteen months of physical therapy, and you'll be able to write your name again."

"I guess you're not gonna get that football scholarship, though," Fast said regretfully.

Goodwin looked as if he had been slapped, understanding dawning in his mulelike eyes.

Of course. No college was going to give a football

scholarship to a kid who couldn't play football. Even if he could pick up a ball again in eighteen months, there would be no place to play, so he'd never get a chance at another scholarship.

Neil Goodwin's future had been crushed and ruined along with his elbow joint.

Goodwin launched himself at Jack Fast, rising off the turf with a bellow that was part pain, part rage, and his ruined arm flopped at his side while his good arm sought Fast's throat.

Jack Fast blocked Goodwin, just as he had before, but the forearm blow was so powerful it sent Goodwin's arm flying around his back, shattering most of the bones of his forearm and wrist. Goodwin collapsed, moaning.

Goodwin's friends were getting agitated.

"Maybe one of you should call an ambulance," Nancy suggested.

The boys looked at one another, then one of them remembered his cell phone. He yanked it out, then looked at Nancy questioningly. Actually, he was looking at the slight scoop in the very low front of her low-ride jeans.

"Nine," she suggested.

He looked up at her face, then at his phone, nodded and poked a button.

"One," Nancy said.

He nodded again, poked the phone, looked at Nancy.

"One."

"I already did one."

"You need to do another one."

"Oh."

He poked it and began conversing with the emergency dispatch. Goodwin's moans were becoming sobs.

"That was a pretty good block, Jack," said one of Goodwin's buddies.

"Thanks, Larry."

"Maybe you should have played football."

"Aw, jeez, thanks, but I'm not that good."

"Okay," said the boy with the cell phone. "Thanks a lot. No, no hurry." He closed the phone and looked triumphantly at Nancy. "They'll be here in a while."

"How long?" Goodwin gasped.

"I don't know. They've got some real emergencies to get to first. Not like you got anything else to do— for the rest of your life."

The boy guffawed and gave Nancy a thumbs-up. She rewarded him with a smile that he never forgot, then Jack said, "Sorry we can't stay. We've got a 7:30 movie to catch."

"JACK, wait!"

Dean Cescepi jogged up as they were getting into Jack's car.

"I was up in the booth. I saw what happened."

"Oh, Christ," Nancy Fielding exclaimed. "You're not going to get all legal on him, are you?"

Cescepi smirked. "Ms. Fielding, Jack was only defending himself from Mr. Goodwin's assaults, as I plainly witnessed. But I have got to know, Jack—" Cescepi was grinning conspiratorially "—how'd you do it?"

Jack smiled. "East German judo."

Cescepi's grin faltered.

"Freedom-fighters in East Germany developed it in the 1960s. My dad taught it to me."

"East German judo?"

"OKAY, HOW DID YOU *really* do it?" Nancy asked when they were driving away.

Jack held out his right arm. "Pull off my sleeve."

Nancy pulled the sleeve of his windbreaker off and gasped. Jack's arm looked artificial, smooth and plastic and swollen to twice its normal girth.

"What is it?"

"Human amplification technology. I found the plans on the MIT Web site."

Nancy stroked the arm. "Pneumatics?" she asked.

"No. Too slow and bulky. It's magnetic fibers in flexible resin. Electrical currents make the fibers constrict. You bunch them together to imitate muscles."

"Wow," Nancy said, enjoying the feel of the arm. "What other kinds of human amplification can you do with this stuff?"

"Any kind," Fast said, but it took him a few seconds to see where she was heading. "Oh!"

They never made it to the 7:30 showing of *Charlie's Angels in the Matrix.*

11

They were on their final approach into Barcelona when Mark Howard said to Remo, "I've been thinking about what you said, about how Freya had learned so much from Sunny Joe Roam."

"Yes?" Remo didn't look away from the window. He wasn't keen on revisiting this topic again.

"She said goodbye to you. You know what, she was really saying goodbye to her dad. Really."

"Yes?"

"Don't you see, Remo? She wasn't faking it. You're her dad and she knows that and she believes it in her heart. Sunny Joe is her grandfather and maybe her mentor and maybe even her adopted father in some ways, but you're her dad. You could hear it."

Remo tried to think about the rather mundane event of leaving the village of Sun On Jo. He had gone in and kissed her goodbye and then she'd come to the door. "'Bye, Daddy!" she'd said, while Mark Howard stood there seeing little red hearts and stars.

Now that he thought about it, it sounded very true. He smiled.

Remo Williams felt happy. Despite all the weirdness and horrific events that had brought Freya to where she was, despite Remo's absence from so much of her life, she saw Remo as her dad.

What could be better than that?

MARK HOWARD deemed it worthwhile to make himself useful. He drove the rental Mercedes, easily finding the way to the home of Allessandro Cote.

"He's a well-known arms distributor, working mostly through legitimate channels," Dr. Smith informed them after he researched the name briefly. "He's known to have been a primary benefactor of the flood of arms out of Iraq after the last war. At least a thousand Kalashnikov rifles went through his system to end up in the hands of street gangs on the West Coast, mostly Los Angeles. Another five to eight thousand AKs are suspected to have been shipped into Colombia on both sides of the conflict. On the other hand, he's done enough legitimate trade with enough legal entities around the world that he's created a safety net. Not many people seem eager to prosecute his occasional indiscretions."

"I am," Remo said. "But he's a reseller, so who did he resell the Gee-DAM to?"

"Watch your language when speaking to your emperor and his regent," Chiun warned.

"What I don't understand is why he bought the plans in Morocco at all," Mark Howard added. "I mean, the Gee-DAM was stolen by a professional arms trade outfit, we assume. Cote is also a professional arms trader. What did they need with the bazaar in Casablanca?"

"That puzzled me, as well," Smith said over the

speakerphone. "The answer is that they would not. It was clearly a ploy, maybe designed to give them adequate warning of your arrival in Barcelona. They may have an ambush in mind."

"Their trap will fail," Chiun declared.

"They obviously know something of our activities," Smith pointed out. "You saw the videotape, Master Chiun?"

"They know one of us wears a kimono. Who doesn't?" Remo pointed out. "Remember the press conference in Washington a few months ago?"

"We locked it down. We know of no media feeds made public from that event," Mark said.

"Yeah, but did you notice that there were maybe forty reporters on the scene? They'd remember a guy in a kimono. That's just the latest public appearance by the Man in the Silk Pajamas. He's a tough one to miss in your average crowd of non-kimono-wearing Americans."

"Enough!" Chiun snapped. "I dislike being discussed as if I am not present."

"I'm just saying, is all." Remo shrugged. "You've been spotted, taped, broadcast and publicized. How many times I can't even guess."

"My garments, perhaps, but my face is still unknown," Chiun insisted.

"Thousands of people have seen you over the years, Chiun," Remo said. "Face it, you attract people's attention. Now somebody remembers seeing you, and maybe he has decided you work for some sort of a government agency, and is trying to draw you out."

"Shush, imbecile!"

"I'm afraid Remo may be correct, Master Chiun," Smith said.

"This conversation is designed to intimidate me into giving up my traditional garb," Chiun said accusingly.

"No," Smith said, but he allowed the word to linger a little too long. "This conversation is intended to warn you to a possible danger in Barcelona. We do not know what they know, but it appears they have baited us here for some reason."

"We'll stay frosty," Remo assured him.

"I shall not stay frosty." Chiun glowered.

"You'll stay grumpy."

"Fah!"

The neighborhood Allessandro Cote called home dated back at least two centuries. The homes were small castles erected on vast estates looking out over the Mediterranean Sea.

"I guess selling murder is good business," Remo said. "Or was he born to the wealthy parents and sells guns as a hobby?"

"His father was a bus driver in Madrid," Mark explained as he drove them along the manicured, semiprivate drive that meandered behind the seafront estates. "He bought the house from the government after the owners went bankrupt."

"We'll call you when we need a ride home," Remo said.

Howard was about to ask where they wanted to be left off, but heard the brief thunk of car doors and realized that he was alone. He had never even slowed down. He looked in the rearview mirror and never saw Chiun and Remo, but he knew they must have entered a nearby decorative row of Mediterranean trees.

He rolled down the window and continued driving down the isolated road, enjoying the fragrant semitropical breezes.

THE OLD BRICK HOME looked like something medieval, like an old church, but it had been augmented in recent decades with a white stucco addition the size of a small shopping mall. The walls were freshly whitewashed. The clay-tile roof would have been quaint if there weren't acres and acres of it. The addition had probably tripled the square footage of interior space in the home, and it descended with the mountainside, halfway to the shore below.

The pair of shadows, slipped among the cultivated gardens of temperate-climate plants with less noise than the salt-laden breeze.

Chiun, Master of Sinanju Emeritus, smelled the fragrant salt air and the gentle sea breeze and became cold inside.

"Nice digs," Remo said when he and Chiun stood unseen in the shadows of a palm tree grove adjoining the structure. "Let's move here after we kick out the Boomstick Baron."

Chiun said nothing.

"What's with you?" Remo asked.

"Have you embraced your speck, Remo?"

"What speck?"

Chiun pierced him with a glare.

"Oh, my fear speck," Remo said. "I haven't forgotten what we talked about, Little Father."

"Good."

"But I don't know what these creeps could throw at us that we can't handle."

"That is right, you do not know," Chiun snapped. "And yet, wicked men are innovators in the ways of poison and torture and murder. Most of their efforts are no more dangerous than the rocks lobbed by baboons, but we do not know what is in this house."

Remo was getting worried now. "Chiun, this isn't like you. Do you know something I don't know?"

Chiun shook his head. "There is something. Perhaps." He held out his hands, as if warming them at a campfire. "It is strange."

Remo frowned and held out his hands, too. He tried to feel whatever it was that had upset Chiun.

He shook his head and opened his mouth, to say he felt nothing, and then it was there, like a flicker of movement just outside his vision.

"You felt it?" Chiun asked.

"I felt something. I don't know what."

"Yes."

"Seems sort of familiar. Sort of like a pressure shift or a temperature change or something."

Chiun nodded. "But not those things."

"I don't know. It came and went so fast I couldn't get a taste of it." It wasn't often that he and Chiun ran up against something foreign to their experience, and now he was worried. "You'll be pleased to know I found the speck."

Chiun didn't look pleased.

ALLESSANDRO COTE PACED through the ballroom where once the aristocrats of Barcelona had met to dance and make merry. The aristocrats were dead. Their progeny had failed to sustain their wealth or dignity. They were back among the rabble as they deserved to be, surrendering the symbols of prestige to those who had earned, rather than inherited, a place of importance in the world.

"This won't do," Allessandro Cote complained. His accent was British with effeminate Spanish undertones. "Jenkins!"

The impossibly gaunt man who came through the servants' entrance at the rear of the ballroom was dressed in a butler's formal coat and tails. He could not have looked more uncomfortable in the get-up.

"Yes, Mr. Cote?"

Normally, Cote would have relished the perfection of the performance. Gomez had done an admirable job of learning his new role, as much as he had complained about it.

"Ring Fastbinder for me, will you, Jenkins?"

"*Sí.* Yes!" Gomez swallowed the mistake and put back on his supremely bored face. "Certainly, suh, I'll ring him at once." Gomez/Jenkins walked slowly and deliberately to the rear of the room and through the servants' entrance.

"I'll have to dock the old git's wages if he can't learn to speak properly," Cote complained, sipping his tea, which was actually coffee.

Jenkins relaxed into Gomez when he was out of the ballroom. He, too, was muttering to himself, words of encouragement and self-recrimination, all in his native Spanish. "You can do this. It's just playing a part. You've played tougher roles than this." He took the antique phone, sterling silver with ivory inlay, and lifted the original metal dial to expose the touch-pad that had been retrofitted into it. He poked out the number for Fastbinder in the United States and got the kid instead.

"Hiya, Jenkins," said the kid. "How's the butler bit going for you these days?"

"Fine, Master Jack. May I have your father, please?"

"It's for you, Dad! He'll be here in a minute, Jenkins."

"That will be fine."

"You know, you need some sort of a gimmick to complete the image, Jenkins."

"A gimmick, Master Jack?"

"You know, Oddjob. He had the hat that sliced people's head off?"

"I don't have much call for slicing off 'eads."

"There was Jaws, you know, the big guy with the steel teeth? Or there was the one movie with the babe who was into pain."

"I fear I am not following you, Master Jack."

"Point is, Jenkins, all the bodyguards have some sort of special feature or trick."

"Yes?"

"So I started thinking about shoes. What if I gave you shoes with dart guns in them? It'd be real easy. All we'd need is a compressed-gas cartridge in the sole of the shoes and a series of firing tubes in the soles. Maybe make one a long-distance, high-accuracy projectile, one a fast-acting poison, maybe pack the others with fléchettes. You know, little barbed suckers that would bury themselves into skin?"

"I don't see this as truly necessary, Master Jack."

"It's no trouble. Then we'd have a series of switches inside the shoe. A certain combination of toe work would turn off the safety, then you could fire at the enemy as needed."

"Listen, kid, cut me some slack, would you, *por*

favor?" said Jenkins, dropping the act and becoming a sad-looking Gomez. "I'm going loco trying to play the British-butler routine as it is. I don't think I could pull it off if it got any more complicated."

"Read you loud and clear, amigo," the kid said, just as cheerful as ever. "You ever change your mind, you let me know. I'll work up some nice offensive footwear weaponry for you."

"Sounds great," Gomez said.

"Here's Dad."

Gomez wrenched himself back into the Jenkins persona when Fastbinder came on the line. "Allessandro?"

"No, suh. One moment, suh."

"Gomez, do not tell me he has you serving up the phone."

"Yes, suh. Exactly, suh." Jenkins had the receiver on a silver tray with a starched white linen doily. He carried the tray to the servants' entrance, trailing the cord for the phone behind him. The cord was eighty yards long—it had to be to reach from the small servants workstation to the far side of the ballroom.

"Hurry it up, at least, will you, Jenkins?"

"I am proceeding swiftly, suh."

Gomez the Spanish street thug, murderer and occasional actor had endured a number of trials as he learned to become Jenkins, the English butler for the formal British household of Mr. Allessandro Cote.

He knew Allessandro Cote was really just a piece of Madrid street trash no better than any other piece of Madrid street trash. He started as beggar, became a nightclub bouncer, became a small-time gun-runner, and lucked into a big-time arms distribution deal. Along the way he'd managed to make friends with every organized crime figure west of the Basque region and, somehow, earned himself the nickname Captain Goat Fucker. Gomez/Jenkins had heard only the faintest whispers about the origin of the nickname. Spreading those rumors was a crime punishable by death. Gomez/Jenkins didn't need to know the story. The nickname was pretty self-explanatory.

Fucking goats was something Gomez could understand. After all, Spanish goats were among the most attractive and spirited goats in all of Europe. It was Cote's infatuation with all things British that Gomez found puzzling.

But he was willing to play along. Every time he started getting fed up with the British-butler routine he'd get another paycheck and all his doubts would be swept away.

"I could get myself a genuine British butler, but I need somebody who can handle himself in a tough situation," Cote had explained, apparently entirely unself-consciously. "I've seen you handle yourself on the street, Gomez. I know you've got the soldier skills I'm looking for. You speak excellent English. I've also seen you perform. You were quite good as Oberon."

Gomez was flabbergasted. None of the street toughs in his loose-knit Madrid gang of drug dealers and protection racketeers had ever seen him act.

"Thank you, Mr. Cote!"

Still, Gomez hadn't understood. It took days before he really grasped the scope of the role he was to play.

"This will be a formal, aristocratic British household, and I need a formal British butler to run it. I have a consultant coming from London to train you if you take the job."

When Gomez heard the salary, he took the job. Weird as was, it wasn't too weird.

The consultant turned out to be a seventy-six-year-old butler who had served most of the British royal family during his long career. At their first session, the old man, who never went by any name other than Robert, dressed Gomez in his stiff butler uniform and stuck a slender, dried meter of wood down the back of his shirt.

"Stand straight, don't break it."

Within minutes Gomez broke the wooden stick. Robert emotionlessly replaced it with another.

Robert taught Gomez how to stand stiffly, how to walk at half his usual speed, how to maintain a droll and emotionless demeanor at all times. By the end of the week Gomez could walk around for hours without breaking the stick in his shirt. He knew he could do this job.

But acting a role and actually living it, day after day, was taking its toll. He was horrified to discover that Gomez was going away and Jenkins was becoming the dominant personality.

He didn't know how much longer he could stand it before he either gave up and became Jenkins, the living, breathing cliché role to last a lifetime, or flee Cote and his formal British household and his extravagant paychecks and go back to distributing heroin in shantytowns around Madrid.

There was a lot to be said for shantytowns.

JENKINS MADE the deliberate and lengthy walk across the ballroom with the silver platter and the antique telephone, as if it were a crown on a felt pillow he were presenting.

"Mr. Fastbinder on the line from America, suh," he intoned to his employer.

"Ah, terrific." Cote snatched up the receiver lying on the doily aside the phone. "Fastbinder, how *are* you, old man? Fastbinder? Oh, bloody hell, he rang off."

"Allow me to get him on the line again, suh," Jenkins said, turning back for the servants' entrance. Inside he was screaming—the walk was six minutes round trip, not counting the time it would take to get the kraut on the line. He didn't know if he could stand it.

"Bugger it!" Cote blurted, snatching a mobile phone from his pocket, pressing a button and getting Fastbinder in seconds. "There you are, old man! Where'd you run off to then?"

"Your grasp of British frippery is excruciating, and I find your whole act repulsive," snapped Fastbinder. "Please don't make me a part of your fairy tale."

"Hang on, old chap." Cote lowered the phone. Jenkins took his cue.

"Will there be anything else, suh?"

"Not right now, Jenkins, thank you."

Jenkins turned and began pacing back to the servants' service room.

"All right, Fastbinder, I'm as ready as I'll ever be. So where's our little ducks, eh?"

"They landed thirty-six minutes ago and had a car waiting for them," Fastbinder reported.

"Is that all?"

"That's all I know," Fastbinder said.

"That's all you know? What happened to all your whiz-bang technology you've been going on about?" Cote demanded.

"Surveillance isn't my specialty. Besides, Spain is

your realm, not mine. What have your spotters reported?"

"My spotters couldn't find their arseholes even if you stuck a lit signal flare up in 'em," Cote exclaimed. "They somehow managed to miss seeing who it was that got off the aircraft and into the car."

"We've been told these men are fast and elusive."

"Poppycock! What I want to know is when the bastards are coming here."

Fastbinder tsked. "Really, Allessandro. Poppycock? Did anyone ever really use the word?"

"When, Fastbinder? When?"

"Soon enough," Fastbinder said. "You're drinking far too much coffee today."

"I'm drinking tea."

"I can see the tea service, Allessandro, and I watched your poor imitation butler brew coffee."

Cote swore silently. He'd forgotten Fastbinder had the place set up for intense data gathering, including audio, video and a scattering of other sensors he couldn't begin to understand. "It's not the coffee, it's the whole bloody setup. I don't even know how much risk there is."

"Very little."

"So you say."

"You get the Gee-DAM schematics as a reward— you'll make millions, Cote. Besides, it's too late to back out now. Everything is in place."

Cote said, "Yeah." He stood in the middle of his ballroom and slowly walked in a circle. He saw wooden panels painted in the late eighteenth century. He saw stained glass and a polished marble floor. There wasn't a hint as to the location of Fastbinder's equipment.

"How can I be sure your mechanical contraptions won't mistake me for one of your special agents?"

"You've got your pocket watch?" Fastbinder asked.

Cote withdrew the old, gold-plated pocket watch provided him by Fastbinder and his son when they'd outfitted the great old Spanish house just days before. It supposedly served as a beacon that Fastbinder's equipment could sense. As long as he had the watch, he wouldn't be targeted—in theory.

"What I said was, how do I *know?*"

"Little late to be asking now," Fastbinder replied.

Leaving Cote not at all reassured.

12

Jorge Portillo was finally getting some use out of his AK-47 after all these weeks. Actually, it was only the bayonet that came in handy. He was scraping mud out of the treads of his boots with it.

"What's this all about?" Pincay hissed.

"Shut up. We're supposed to stay silent," Portillo said. He looked around to make sure no one was within earshot. There was just the grassy lawn, the sparse patches of garden that couldn't possibly hide an attacker and the glimmering sliver of the Mediterranean off down below.

"But why does Allessandro think something is going to happen today?"

Portillo shrugged. He didn't believe anything would happen today, but it was a nice day for standing outside.

"Why don't we have a real plan for defending the estate?" Pincay demanded in a whisper. "He's got us scattered all over the place."

"I don't know," murmured Portillo. The only bad

thing about today was spending it with Pincay, who refused to keep his jaw from flapping.

"We're sitting ducks."

"You are not worthy of being called a duck," said a new voice.

By the time Portillo looked up, the owner of the new voice had silenced the voice of Pincay permanently. The throat had been cut most of the way through, including the spinal column, so that Pincay's skull flopped backward on a skin flap and the back of his head hit between his shoulder blades. The exposed neck column was a spurting fountain of blood until the corpse collapsed amid a pair of jade trees.

"A duck," explained the killer, "has value. You do not."

The old man slashed at him so fast Portillo never saw the knife, but he saw his own severed hand jump into the grass still holding the detached bayonet.

"Poke," said someone else entirely, and at that moment Portillo felt the unbelievable sensation of a steel spike penetrating his skull case and driving deep into his brain tissue. He heard and felt the squish deep between his ears and then the lights went out.

Remo leaned the one-armed corpse against the wall and whacked his knees into position just hard enough to fracture the bone and jam them there. With a little creative balancing he managed to get the dead man to stand where he was, head against the building to hide the drain hole Remo put there.

FRANCO WAS VERY contemplative for a hit man. He was intelligent, but not the kind of intelligent that turned him into a brilliant student. He was more the kind of man who pondered life and nature and even ethical questions. He could have been a philosopher if not for all the school that a fully licensed and accredited philosopher required.

So instead he killed people. Being a philosopher, he pondered deeply the ethics of murder, especially the innocent victims. It was always easy to shrug off annihilating a rival in the drug business, but a lot harder to come up with a rationale for killing, say, the pretty young teacher who kept taking the drugs away from her fourteen-year-old students who just happened to be dealers for Franco's boss. So after he killed her, which was after he did other things to her, Franco went into a long period of contemplation. At breakfast the next morning, after he was reading about the grisly murder in the paper, he happened to turn to the television listings and, like a message from heaven, his answer came to him.

Conan the Barbarian was on. Not the cartoon show, but the original Schwarzenegger masterpiece, which did suffer somewhat when it was dubbed in Spanish using the same actor who also did the voice for the dubbed Urkel. But it wasn't Ahnuld that Franco remembered from the movie; it was the philosophy that was presented as the theme at the beginning of the movie. "That which does not kill us makes us stronger," said the badly photographed Spanish cue card at the movie's beginning.

So, killing someone was a way of making them stronger, right?

So it followed that killing someone was beneficial for all mankind because it strengthened the human race as a whole by increasing the vitality of the pool of human beings. Obviously, anybody Franco tried to kill but couldn't kill was strong enough that they deserved to keep living. Not that Franco had ever failed to completely murder anyone when he tried to, but it might happen someday.

His conscience entirely eased, he'd moved on to a stellar career as one of the most reliable and effective killers on the entire Iberian Peninsula.

"I'm good at my job because I love my work," he would tell his prospective employers. "I love my work because I know I am benefiting all of mankind."

Even the crime bosses of Spain didn't buy into that, but who cared when he did such a great job?

Franco was now attached to the Cote organization, serving as a security consultant and keeping himself sharp with the occasional hit.

But he wasn't as sharp as the thin man in the gray chinos, the fine leather shoes and the inappropriate undershirt. The thin man came around the front of the building and took out the guard detail fast, his arms slipping through the air and snatching up heads like a pair of frog tongues snatching up buzzing flies. Then the heads came together so hard they were crushed together into a single mass. The pair of corpses flopped onto the granite tile of the circular exterior entranceway to the house, still joined.

"An undignified technique," Franco observed.

The guard detail had been three men, with Franco stationed in the hedges twenty yards away. The third man raised his automatic rifle and squeezed the trigger, only to find his hands empty. The rifle clattered in pieces on the granite. Before the third man could say the Spanish equivalent of "Hey, you jerk!" the thin man flicked him in the nose.

REMO FLICKED HARD enough to send nose cartilage and some of the bony nose bridge careening into the man's head, cutting a path through the brain tissue. The third man slithered silently to the ground.

"Very skillful indeed, but also quite reprehensible."

Remo looked at the guard who was covering him with a whopping big machine gun.

"Shouldn't that be mounted on a Hummer or something?" Remo asked distractedly, eyes on the building.

"Usually, but I knew you were coming," Franco noted.

"Oh, yeah, what do you know?"

"I know you are a killer of immense skill. You are an assassin who moves like a bird or a shadow. But you are also a man who does not respect death."

"Say what?"

"I should say, you do not give your customers a respectful death."

Franco couldn't help but notice that the American was hardly paying attention, focusing instead on the front door.

"You are not even listening."

"Sorry, did you say something?"

"I'm talking about respect for death! Do you know about respect?"

"R-E-S-P-E-C-T. What is inside of this place, anyway?"

"I will tell you nothing."

"You don't know what's in there?"

"Of course I do!"

"Liar."

"I do know, but what I don't know is what kind of a man you are. Imbecile? Moron?"

"Guess I'm such a moron I don't know if I'm an imbecile. I've been called both a hundred times, just since breakfast. Is there some sort of a secret laser weapon in there or something?"

Franco frowned and shook his head in disappointment. "Put these on, please." He tossed a pair of self-locking manacles to Remo—extra-heavy-duty, meant for veterinary use on terrified zoo creatures like gorillas.

"No, thanks," Remo answered, and tossed them back.

Franco saw them flash at him like a yellow fluorescent bolt of lightning. They twisted around his wrist and the machine gun like a bolo, but driven by such force that they wrapped themselves with crushing force.

Franco staggered, tried to shake off the machine gun that was now a part of his arm, then the excruciating pain hit him. Why, of course there would be pain. The arm was all but smashed flat, with bloody gore extruding through the trigger guard.

He was opening his mouth to scream and was aware that the killer was standing in front of him. He must have moved impossibly fast.

Then Franco's good hand was closed into a fist and inserted into his open mouth, just in time to cork the scream.

"With all due respect, sir," Remo said, and stuffed the fist in even further.

Remo let the goof wander around the football-field-size front yard while he wandered on, his concern mounting. None of the guards on the outside seemed to know what was happening inside, and all the weapons they had were conventional. Maybe whatever was in there wasn't even a weapon, but now that he was this close to the house, he felt the strangeness unmistakably. It was a black wave of static that reached out and numbed him....

Another pod of dimwits with AKs stood at a side entrance, near the big section of the structure in the middle. Chiun was just finishing up with the final dimwit when Remo joined him. Chiun was barely paying attention to the job at hand, his emerald-green eyes locked on the oversize section of the building.

"It is familiar," Chiun said.

"But still strange," Remo added.

Chiun simply nodded slightly. "We go into the unknown."

"Every day, every minute we venture into the unknown, Little Father."

Chiun gave him a rare and sincere smile, although it was a little one.

They went back to the front door and walked in without knocking.

"THE FRONT DOOR? Don't tell me it's them? Coming in the bloody front door?" Allessandro Cote was livid. "That's just wrong!"

"Perhaps one of our men entered mistakenly without keying in his PIN, suh," Jenkins said hopefully.

Cote jogged to the keyboard at the bank of monitors. There were only thirty keys or so, all dramatically oversize. They were lighted, too, and when Cote began pressing them they made tiny electronic mews and burps.

"Where'd that overpaid monk go to?" Then one of the monitors switched to an image from the front yard, and there was Franco.

"Jesus, Mary and Joseph!" Cote exclaimed.

Jenkins gasped. There was Franco, all right, with one arm sunk into his mouth up to the elbow, the other squashed and bloody and somehow adhered to his weapon. The man was staggering to the road that ran in front of the house, maybe looking for a passing ambulance. He dropped to the grass, never to rise again.

"Suh!" Jenkins said, and indicated another monitor. One of the guards in the video feed lay on his back, his severed head wobbling nearby.

"The front door must have been them, suh. The killers."

"All my goons are dead? Every bleeding man jack of them?"

"I suggest you power up the defenses, suh."

Allessandro Cote stood up straight, looked down his nose at his butler and tightened his lips. "Quite right, Jenkins," he said, fully in control once more. "These—" he waved at the screens "—were just extras, anyway."

"Of course, suh."

The picture of British reserve, Allessandro Cote strolled to the next oversize control panel. There were three chunks of jagged, unpolished quartz crystal set into the panel, each one the size of a teacup. Cote placed his hand against a hard, cool crystal—the purplish one on the end.

The door on the far end of the ballroom burst open.

"IT'S STRONGER, Little Father," Remo said.

"I feel it in my bones," Chiun said.

They had moved fast through the endless, opulent rooms of the old section of the ancient mansion, but the strange sensation was intensified now. Remo felt his limbs becoming heavier.

"How far?" Remo asked, realizing his sense of direction was askew.

Chiun yanked open a door that was hand carved, the figurines around the door latch smoothed by centuries of contact with human fingers. "Beyond the next door," Chiun stated.

Remo wondered how Chiun could sound so sure of himself when Remo's own disorientation was escalating and this room looked just like all the others, musty and packed with a lot of well-polished antique furniture.

"How many freaking parlors do you freaking need?" Remo demanded.

"This is it," Chiun announced at the next set of extra-wide double doors. He looked at Remo, and Remo saw the old man thinking hard. "I shall enter alone."

"No, you won't."

"You shall remain here and assess the nature of this anomaly."

"No way in hell."

"It is foolish for both of us to walk into danger!"

Remo cocked his head. "Right you are, and I decide who."

"I am the Master Emeritus!" Chiun stamped one foot, but it was a gesture without vigor.

"I'm Reigning Master and what I say goes and I say I go."

He never gave the old Korean time to reply before he bashed his shoulder into the doors. They squeaked open and the sensation increased to a shrill pitch. Remo imagined he heard some sort of supersonic sound that assaulted him, drained him of vitality, confused his thinking. It was all he could do to hold himself upright and walk with feigned energy across the huge, open room.

The ceilings were high and set with iron-filigreed frames around frosted glass, and the floor was ancient, polished wood planks. The walls were decorated with bigger-than-life-size murals of Spanish royalty, the paintings separated by red-velvet-upholstered panels.

The room was entirely empty except for flashing, multicolored banks of electronic controls and screens on the far side of the room and the pair of formally dressed men who stood watching him.

"Sorry. Didn't know it was black tie." Remo felt that he had to shout to be heard above the chaos that was attacking him. The pair in the money suits seemed unaffected.

"May I ask who you are and what business you have?" asked the younger man.

Remo's confusion grew. Was he mistaken, or was the man trying to force a hackneyed British accent on top of his native Spanish accent?

"Which of you is Al Cote?"

"I am Mr. Cote. And you are?"

"Annoyed. Remo Annoyed."

"Not as annoyed as I am, to be sure," the younger man said. Remo realized the acoustics of the room were allowing them to speak normally despite the distance between them. He seemed to be having trouble walking at a normal pace.

"Which old movie set did you steal, anyway?" Remo asked. "Was it *Logan's Run?* Now, that was a stupid-looking computer."

Cote looked as if he was trying to stifle an outburst. "Not science fiction! Think secret agent."

"Huh?" Now he was really confused. The movie crack had been just that—a crack, a joke. "You mean, like James Bond?"

"Exactly!" Suddenly Cote was beaming.

"You mean, you really did model your little command console after something out of a James Bond movie?"

Cote looked like an excited corgi about to go walkies. "Not just this, but all of it! Look around you!"

Remo stopped where he was in the middle of the room, hoping a pause would restore some of his waning strength. He looked around the empty old room, trying to make sense of what Cote was saying.

"What?"

"Think about it! Think about what this would look like if we were in a motion picture right now."

Remo was trying to follow the thread. "Like, a James Bond movie?"

"Yes!" Cote was ecstatic.

"So this is like, the big set where the climax takes place?"

"Yes! Yes! You are exactly right!"

"Uh-huh." Remo's mind chewed on this, looking for a nugget of logical filling. If he were thinking straight, would this sound just as stupid? "So you're like the evil genius, right?"

"Yes, precisely!" He was so worked up that Cote actually started coming toward Remo as if to shake his hand.

Then Cote stopped, stiffened and pulled down on the vest of his three-piece suit. "And now, Mr. Annoyed, I think it is time I give you the welcome you deserve."

Cote's hand was resting on a big purple chunk of crystal that was pulsing from a hidden light. When he depressed it, the quartz began to glow steadily and the knob recessed into the control panel.

The red-velvet panels around the room shifted, making unnecessarily loud servomotor sounds, then each door began to lift, each on a pair of heavy pneumatic cylinders.

Remo realized he was still standing there and he didn't think he could move another step. There was a black cloud seeping around the edges of his vision....

Whatever it was behind the doors, which were taking forever to open, how would he be able to run from them, let alone defend himself?

"Hey, Blofeld, laying it on a little thick, aren't you?"

"*Au revoir,* Mr. Annoyed. Or perhaps I should say goodbye."

Remo Williams looked around, found he couldn't take it all in at once, and concentrated on a single hidden chamber as the doors halted in a fully raised position. He still didn't think he was seeing it correctly. Was he hallucinating?

It was a man in a wheelchair. The man was silver, grinning easily with a massive chrome grin. Its head rotated ninety degrees left, then right, before turning to face Remo Williams. Red lights came on in its eye sockets.

"Allow me to introduce my dear friend," Cote said grandly.

"Mecha-Stephen Hawking?" Remo asked.

"I am Mr. U.," said the thing in the wheelchair.

"Mr. Who?" Remo asked, trying to make his feet function, trying to make his vision clear, trying to think.

He looked at the next open space in the wall. Inside was…a rocking horse. He squeezed his eyes, forcing his tunnel of vision to focus itself, and then saw it was a mechanical jumble with legs bolted to a small tank tread on either side. It still resembled a rocking horse. Its surface was composed of dull gray metal shingles and its doglike head ended in a nose with a gun barrel jutting out of it. In the next cubicle was a steel rack mounted with four wheeled devices, like aluminum bread boxes with many long needles sticking out of their skin.

There must be fifteen or twenty open doors, and if Remo could trust his vision, each one of them contained its own unique glowing, blinking contraption.

"Now, Mr. Annoyed, you die," said Cote with well-rehearsed understated flair.

"Mr. U. die or you die?" Remo demanded.

"You die, I said," Cote retorted.

"You?"

"Not me, you!"

"Him?" Remo pointed at the wheelchair droid with the red eyes.

"Shut up!"

Remo couldn't help but smirk. "Sorry if I'm not playing the right part in your little scene."

"You will act out the most important part of the scene, have no fear," Cote said and, almost casually, he depressed the next pulsing crystal, the pink one.

There was a whirring of multiple small motors and Remo saw a connection on a mechanical arm separate from the back of the chrome-toothed Mr. U. The same connection was severed from every cubicle as all the devices were freed of their umbilicals, and at that moment Remo felt the debilitating sensation—stop.

It didn't fade, it didn't decrease, it just stopped. Whatever had caused it had been turned off when all the devices were released from their umbilicals. Remo watched his tunnel of vision expand, felt the current of life surge into his limbs.

Mr. U, came at him wearing a wicked smile, and Remo moved out of its path. Now he saw it more clearly and found it was a sort of battering ram on wheels, a sculpted chrome demon head perched atop a mass of steel arms and claws. The shivering floor attested to its great weight.

Regardless of Mr. U.'s huge mass, it moved fast on its wheelchair, and when Remo moved, Mr. U. altered course to intercept him. Remo moved faster, pushing his wobbly legs, trying to force them to recover faster. Cote and his butler were just standing there, so who had the joystick?

Mr. U. stopped where it was and turned in a circle, rotating, and raised its palm. An inch-wide barrel opening appeared, and Remo braced himself.

Mr. U. fired its weapon and a tiny rocket screamed in Remo's direction on a tail of blue fire. It wasn't even a bullet. It was slow. He could dodge this thing. A rocket was just bullet, and a bullet was just a rock, and anybody could dodge a rock.

Remo moved fast on legs of rubber, judged the approach of the missile, judged his own speed and knew he wasn't going to make it. He pushed harder and lurched into a violent, ungraceful twist.

He felt the heat, and then the rocket was gone. He heard the small burst and turned too slowly to see what was hit, but he knew it was one of the other robots. By the time he had his head turned there was nothing except some collapsing mechanical rubble, enough to fill a bathtub.

Remo didn't know what the deal was, but he had a pretty good idea that all the rolling, buzzing, whirring doohickeys were of the injury-causing variety. He needed to buy himself some time to get his strength back, then take them on.

"What is all this, Cote?" he demanded loudly, hoping to get the supercriminal wanna-be talking again. "I don't get it."

"These are my tools of domination, Mr. Annoying." Cote was now sitting in a throne that looked like a big aluminum champagne glass with a doughnut cushion. The slender stem disappeared into a slot in the floor.

"World domination, I assume."

Cote was wearing his smuggest look yet. "Perhaps not *world* domination. I do know, of course, that Remo Annoying is not your real name. What is your real name, pray tell?"

"Hell if I know. So, why not world domination?" Remo could see Cote's interest was piqued. He had to play this guy's game for a while—and Cote was more than willing. Cote relaxed against the back of his chair and tried not to reveal the fact that his hands were working a tiny joystick on the side of the doughnut cushion. The chair moved, with a whirring of motors under the floor, carrying him to the front of his banks of obnoxiously bright and flashy controls.

"I don't know if I am prepared yet to dominate the planet. Someday, perhaps. For now I'll settle for Europe."

"With these guys you want to conquer Europe? Mr. U. is cool-looking and well polished and everything, but does he have what it takes to defeat whole nations?" Remo's eyesight was restored fully and he turned casually right and left, taking in the vast array of mechanical creatures that surrounded him, all poised as if to strike. The always-smiling Mr. U. adjusted its position by the millimeter to keep the aim of its distended armlauncher locked on Remo.

Remo had guessed Cote right. He was into his spymovie super villian role, and the last thing he wanted was for it to be over within a blink of an eye. Cote began explaining the self-replicating properties of the various autonomous vehicles in his menagerie, and Remo put on his best shocked-and-awed expression while he evaluated his body. He felt much better, but he didn't feel he was back to one hundred percent yet. Maybe it would take hours or days. Maybe he was scarred permanently.

But did he have what it would take to fight off the mysterious Mr. U.?

How good were these contraptions anyway?

"They might be able to replicate themselves in body, but not in mind," Remo asserted. "You don't have robots to build Gee-DAMS."

Cote's sonorous speech, delivered in a booming stage voice, faltered at the interruption and his face clouded. He advanced on Remo, but the last feet of track was not aligned well and the chair began to shimmy as the mechanics ground together under the floor. Now Cote was even angrier, his face flushing as he grabbed onto the sides of the seat and held on until the chair managed to come to a halt, tipping a little to one side.

Remo chuckled.

"What is so humorous?"

"What isn't? Cote, you're about as much a supervillian as I am George Lazenby. You're a clown."

"What?"

"Look at you. You're a clown. A stupid fake. You've got everything wrong. You don't even know what stupid game you're trying to pretend at."

"What do you mean?"

"I mean, what's with the British accent? Most of the supervillians weren't British. They were Eastern Europeans or whatever. So what are you trying to do, be the British secret agent and the supervillian at the same time? Can't play both sides of the fence, Cote."

"I know what I am doing," Cote retorted.

"And the accent sucks anyway. I mean, I've heard junior high-school kids from Detroit doing Monty Python skits and they're way more genuine than you."

"My good man—"

"Also, what's with the retro look? I mean, okay, if you've made the commitment to be a pseudo-supervillian, and you've already committed some horrific crimes—and you have—and you've got a few million in disposable cash to outfit your new supervillian stronghold, then why in God's name would you go retro? It makes you look stupider than you already look."

"You're wearing my patience, Mr.—"

"Even if you ignore all that, you forgot the most important part of being a supervillian."

"I forgot nothing!"

Remo shrugged. "Fine."

"What? What did I forget?"

"You forgot that every supervillian fails," Remo said.

Cote applied the smug British smile to his sweaty Spanish face. Remo could see, from maybe thirty long paces away, that the man's respiration was slowing again, his heart rate becoming steady. He was relaxing in a moment of self-confidence. Now was the time to make his move, with Cote's reflexes slowed. "That is where I have revamped the character, whoever you are," Cote explained.

"Sorry, old chap." Remo smirked. "You're nothing but a Dr. No and away you go."

Remo charged.

But he attacked Cote as Cote had never been attacked before. Instead of running him down in a flurry of flying legs, Remo Annoying seemed to slip and slither and glide across the ballroom with more grace than any dancer had ever moved, and faster than any human being was capable of moving.

Cote had been told to expect extraordinary skills and speed, but this was inhuman. He stabbed at the nearest control, a fat orange plastic square, and across the room one of the automatons shot into motion. Mr. U. was already activated and it rotated quickly, its body quivering as if it had a bad case of nerves, but it was actually the minute and precise maneuverings of the aiming mechanism—and yet Mr. U. failed to lock on to its target.

Remo Williams slipped around the room in sporadic fits, but he closed in on Cote fast. The man yelped in astonishment when something clamped on to his neck and he became a statue, frozen in his seat. He could only watch what happened around him.

Remo circled the laughably huge computer and zipped out the other side to find Mr. U. bearing down on him. He felt the pressure waves of the next igniting rocket even as it shot from the barrel in Mr. U.'s palm.

It was a different projectile, slightly stubbier, and as he moved out of its path, it moved to intercept him. He stopped, watched it burn the air directly at him, then nodded his head forward when it was just inches from crashing into him.

There was a powerful scream from the second robot, an eight-legged spider of jointed brass legs, and for a moment Remo had an ugly flashback.

But this wasn't *that* mechanical spider, just a bunch of hollow tubes for legs, pneumatic cylinders for muscles and tiny discs positioned on every square inch, spinning fast, creating a drone like the buzzing of steel bees. This spider specialized in wasted motion but it still came fast, clattering on the wood, and the sharpness of its tiny rotary saws was made evident by the cloud of sawdust it raised.

The little rocket managed to recover itself before crashing into the walls or floor, spinning wildly in the upper air of the ballroom, then veering into a dive. Remo ran at the spider robot, which turned to catch him by reaching out with four front legs. Remo faked it out by going low, then jumped over the whizzing tubular limbs, and the spider reared up in a vain attempt to tag him.

Remo hit the ground and glided back the way he'd come, under the raised spider legs and around the rear of the spider, moving too fast for the spider to match—but not too fast for the motion-sending rocket, which homed in on Remo without knowing or caring what was in its way. The spider was still balanced on its rear end when the tiny rocket slammed into it as Remo fell and rolled. The explosion was an intense pressure burst, and Remo exhaled fully and let it roll over him.

When he got to his feet he was pleased to see that the spider had been splatted and another nearby automaton was damaged, the pair of round cylinders that made up its body shifting on positioning motors while its wheeled feet adjusted like a circus clown on a ball, trying to get balanced.

Remo stepped up and gave the thing a nudge with his foot, and the two-tank robot raced across the room at Mr. U., who was lining up to fire again. Mr. U.'s grin became less cheerful when it swung away fast to avoid the impact.

It wasn't fast enough and the twin-tanked robot broadsided Mr. U., toppled on its side and spritzed a yellow liquid out of its mangled barrels. A stream of it tinkled on Mr. U., enough to start smoking.

Whatever was in those tanks was dangerous stuff. Another nearby honeycomb rack of blinking, small-winged robots was coated with it. They and their metal rack began to collapse in on themselves.

Mr. U. ignored its ruined plating and spun on Remo, only to find Remo gone. It spun left, then right, then did a complete circle before its sensors located the movement that had to be its target.

Allessandro Cote was as miserable as he could have ever been. To fail was despicable; to fail like this, paralyzed and helpless, was disgraceful.

"Please, I can't move!"

"Here you go," Remo said. He took Cote by the hand and squeezed his fingers around the tiny joystick on the chair. Then he fiddled with Cote's neck, looking for the correct nerve combination.

Cote twitched, face and body and fingers, which sent the track-mounted chair flying backward while spinning fast. The chair reached the end of the track and halted abruptly, then Cote's body twitched again, violently, and he found himself flying the other way.

"Hey, Mr. U., let's see what you've got!" Remo shouted.

Cote tried to make a noise, but he managed nothing more than a squeak that became a grunt as he twitched and jolted and spun sickeningly. Amid the chaos, he was terrified to see the flash of a rocket, which brightened in his vision, only to vanish as another violent twitch of his nerves sent him spinning and veered away.

Remo led the small rocket like a fox teasing the hounds, leading it through high-powered figure eights. Remo steered it directly into the next robot he came to, then stepped into a conveniently vacated wall cubicle for cover.

The explosion sent mechanical parts raining in all directions, and Remo was now feeling ready to take on the big Mr. U. himself. He eased out of the cubicle as the chrome automaton fired another rocket and ran into the open to give the little missile an easy target, stepping aside just before it slammed into his chest. Then he took hold of the rocket.

"Bet you didn't think I could do that, did you?" Remo called to Mr. U. as he held the hot little thing in two fingers, shaking it like a match to extinguish it.

Mr. U. couldn't seem to figure out what had happened or what he should do next.

"Does not compute, huh?" Remo asked it. "Here. Think about this."

Remo flicked his wrist and sent the tiny rocket back

to its sender, sent it faster than the little solid-fuel engine could ever have propelled it, and Mr. U. didn't have time to get out of the way. The rocket shot underneath Mr. U.'s deck and hit the floor, detonating and lifting Mr. U. on a destructive pressure burst that burned it up the center. When Mr. U. landed, it was split up the middle all the way to its chrome skull.

Mr. U. wasn't dead yet. It jerkily distended its arm and fed power to its drive system, its two halves lurching about in search of its assailant.

Somebody tapped Mr. U. on the shoulder.

"Here I am."

Mr. U.'s grinning face spun 180 degrees to find its assailant standing right behind it, and its programming sent it into its last-ditch, close-combat defense protocol. With a savage lunge it bit down hard. Its programming assured it that its assailant's forearm had just been amputated.

Its programming could not account for the bizarre nature of the disparity in its sensor position, which told it that its head and its body now moved independent of one another.

"Heads. You lose."

Mr. U.'s visual sensors saw its own torso rushing at it very fast.

By the time Remo had pounded the droid skull into a much smaller round metal lump, Mr. U. was nonfunctional.

"You're a mess," Remo said to Cote, who had by this time vomited on himself repeatedly, the rapid gyration of the chair spreading it everywhere. Remo picked his way through the puddles and brought Cote to a halt with a swift kick that jammed the chair in its track. It began smoking slightly. Cote toppled out.

"Disgusting," Chiun observed, now standing outside the splash zone.

"You okay, Little Father?"

"I have recovered, my son. I assume I am now allowed to come out of my room?"

"It would have been okay a long time ago. Like when I was being shot at with missiles and so on."

"I saw you playing with your toys and did not want to interfere. Did you break all your toys as a child, as well?"

"Didn't have any," Remo said with a shrug. "What's that?"

Chiun held up a handful of cables attached to quarter-size glass devices. "Ask the man with the digestive instability. They were in his wall, observing your frolics. I removed them while you were amusing yourself."

"Well, Cote, what are they?"

Cote lay on the floor, heaving, stinking, twitching, wishing he could die. Remo gingerly touched his neck and Cote's body was working again, sort of. He sat up and nearly fell over again from the dizziness.

"Cote, answer the question."

"Video pickups, what do you think?"

"Him? Not much of anything," Chiun explained.

"Can it. Okay, Cote, we want some real answers now. You're too stupid to have planned this whole scheme on your own. Who did? Where are they? What are they up to? Why were they watching us?"

"Go to hell, miserable bleeding bastards."

"I've got to hand it to you," Remo said. "You're dedicated to your fairy tale. Let's see if this will convince you to not stay in character."

Remo touched Cote's neck again, and Cote began

panting and whimpering, racked with unbearable pain. He snapped in mere seconds.

"I'll talk. I'll tell you everything."

13

The audio feed still worked even if the video was out. They heard Allessandro Cote say, "I'll tell you everything."

"Way to have an iron will, Cote," said the crew-cut teenager, rolling his eyes to his father. "He's a dick, Dad."

"He may be an unpleasant man—"

"Not to mention nuttier than a fruitcake."

"He may be delusional, as well, but he has kept you and I well provided for," Fastbinder said.

"That money well is running dry as we speak. Can we take him out?" The boy's blue eyes were bright with anticipation.

"Yes, I suppose we must."

"Can I push the button?"

"Go ahead. Push the button."

The teenage kid leaned back in his chair and reached for one of the many computer terminals scattered around their small work area. He tapped a few keys and grinned broadly.

"'Bye-bye, dick," the kid said. "I just wish I could see it go down."

COTE LOOKED WILDLY AROUND as the ballroom filled with the whirs and buzzing sounds of more automatons coming to life.

"What's happening?" Cote shouted.

"Remo," Chiun asked, "did you accidentally lean on any buttons?"

"No way, uh-uh."

"That son of a bitch!" Cote exclaimed.

Remo and Chiun put themselves between the advancing mechanicals. The attack was spearheaded by a rotor-driven airborne device that was as big as a garbage can, and it swept down on Remo, firing high-velocity rounds from an air gun. Remo dodged the rounds and tried to draw its attention away from Cote, but the machine had a one-track mind. It ignored Remo, gunning for the arms merchant, until Remo ran up underneath it, jumped twice his own height and snatched it by the bottom-mounted gun barrel. It came down with him, still firing, rotors buzzing to their maximum speed in a bid for freedom, but Remo used it to sweep at the wave of rolling, plodding robots that came after it.

There was a series of rolling, rodentlike robots that turned to flee but were chopped up by the spinning rotors, then the tread-mounted doglike robot was smashed and it collapsed on its side, treads spinning uselessly.

Remo dropped the ruined helicopter and simply began disabling machinery by hand. First he plucked a quartet of V-wing gliders out of the air as they attempted to impale him on their needlelike noses, which dripped poison. Remo reached around the needles just as each wing was about to drive into him, crushing the wings and dropping them on the floor one after another. The rest of the automatons were rolling or walking, and they surrendered their vital parts without much more effort. Chiun appeared with an armful of mechanical heads. Behind him a few of his victims still rolled or stomped in circles.

"Starting a collection?" Remo asked.

"I do not understand this," Chiun said, peering at one of the apple-size robot skulls.

"What's to understand?"

Chiun pressed his finger into the dull black metal. "Iron?"

"So?"

"Hand forged. There are the marks of a blacksmith's hammer. It is very old."

"Look who's talking. So what?"

"Must you always act like an idiot? You are no better than the imbecile who thinks he is a powerful villain from a Hollywood film!"

Cote, curled on the floor in his own filth, began sobbing quietly.

"Come on, Chiun, that's not true. I do not walk around pretending to be stupid."

"You cannot possibly be that *genuinely* stupid."

"Listen, just because I'm not following your brilliant deductions, it doesn't mean I'm an idiot. You are obviously a much better detective than I am. We're all very impressed by your powers of observation, Matlock, now cut the crap and tell me what's so effing important about an old robot."

Chiun put the iron robot head into his sleeves with his hands and said nothing.

"Wait a second. Why's there a robot with a head made by a blacksmith?" Remo asked. "Even I know they didn't have robots back in the horse-and-buggy days. Did they?"

Chiun might as well have been a stuffed display for all the reaction he offered.

"Fine. Hey, you, Cote. Why do you have robots with forged-iron heads."

"They were made that way," Cote said through sobs. "They're antiques. That one was from 1908."

Remo sighed. "You know what, I don't even want you to explain that to me." He grabbed the Spanish crime boss by his amazingly unsoiled hair and lifted him to his feet.

"Come on. I know a couple of nerds who'll appreciate it more than I do anyway."

"WHOA!" the kid said, cycling through the windows. "Every dang one of them knocked out of commission!"

"I am aware of that, Jack," Fastbinder said unhappily.

"And they did it in like a minute!"

"Yes, I know."

"Pops, we can't let them take away Cote. He'll blab. We have to hit them with the rest of Cote's munitions."

Fastbinder sighed. "I don't think it will do any good, but it can't hurt. Cote's already paid for them." He grimaced. "Power them up."

"Yeah, Pops!" Jack leaned back in his chair and poked at another keyboard. The system came to life, opened a connection that circled the globe from New Mexico to the Mediterranean coast of Spain, and began communications with a master override system that Fastbinder and his son always built into every device they sold.

Just so, when they wanted to, they could make use of their precious creations and restorations.

"Charging up," Jack exclaimed.

"Let's hope they stay around long enough," Fast-binder muttered.

REMO'S MIND AND BODY seemed to become ghostly, his energy gushing out of him, his vision collapsing. Cote sprawled on the floor where Remo had dropped him.

"It's come back, Little Father!" he gasped.

"Remo!" Chiun's voice sounded like the scratched, plaintive cry of a squeeze toy. Remo as if he was dying on his feet, but his mind rallied with fear for Chiun and he tried to make his eyes work to find the old man. This was like being disgustingly, sickeningly drunk, from what he remembered, but not as fun. Not fun at all.

He twisted his head and spotted a colorful blur, a blur that was lowering slowly to the floor.

"Chiun!" Remo leaned and staggered at Chiun. He felt the tiny body of the old Master, encased in the silk kimono, come into his arms. Remo felt a pang of worry about how frail and slack the old Korean felt, but it was weight enough to nearly pull him down.

"Stand, Chiun!" Remo slurred instead of shouted. "We go down, we'll never get up."

Chiun moved, seemed to look up at Remo, and maybe it was his own altered vision or maybe Chiun stared at him with the eyes of man descending into the void.

"Chiun! Walk! This way!"

Remo steered himself and Chiun away from the source of the weakness. Whatever it was, it was behind them, no longer in the ballroom, but coming from the front part of the house. They had gone through there and not seen anything.

Remo felt Chiun's legs working, and that gave him strength. He steered them both toward the dancing brown square of the rear double doors until the door jumped out at them, slamming into them. Remo's skull vibrated, but the pain stimulated him. His hands flopped when he tried to make the latch work, and then the door opened on its own.

"Evening, suhs." It was Cote's butler. "Departing so soon? I must insist you enjoy more of our hospitality." The butler insisted with an AK-47, which he held as though he knew what to do with it.

"Help us out of here," Remo said. "I'll make it worth your while."

"I am afraid that is out of the question, suhs."

Remo did what he had to do. He released Chiun and pushed himself, with all his energy, into the partially open door. The butler took a step back and watched the men fall. First the lifeless old Asian slumped down, then the white man collapsed.

But the white man kept going, rolling, taking Jenkins by surprise when he collided with his shins. Jenkins felt himself going over and swore at himself. Bloody fool! Oddjob would never have allowed himself to be bested like this! This was the kind of performance you'd expect from a second-rate supervillian—think Herve Villechaize as Nick Nack.

Jenkins refused to loose the rifle but pushed out one hand to cushion his fall. The man who knocked him down now began rolling, scrambling, clawing on top of him, grabbing Jenkins's clothing and using it to drag himself forward, heaving with every effort. Jenkins battered the man with the AK.

The man collapsed on Jenkins's chest but reached for his throat. Jenkins butted the rifle into his jaw, and the fingers closed on Jenkins's throat with only a feather touch.

Then Jenkins experienced pain so undignified and excruciating he sat up barking like a wild dog. His attacker flopped onto the floor, and Jenkins found himself looking at the little Asian man, who seemed on the verge of simply kicking the bucket from old age. Still, he had an iron grip on Jenkins's gentleman parts, and it made Jenkins see stars.

Jenkins kicked the Asian man, who crawled away like a crippled, miserable beggar, and Jenkins held on to his most impolite region with two hands, riding out the agony.

He got to his feet to find his attackers were fleeing down the rear corridor where the old section of the home adjoined the new wings, and they were gone before he could gun them down. But they weren't healthy. They must have been tagged by one of the poisons.

Allessandro Cote seemed to be begging for his life. Now, what was that all about?

"Good gracious!" Jenkins exclaimed.

Only half of Mr. Cote's collection of automatons had been wiped out in the ballroom. Now, somehow, the other automatons stored in the hidden cubicles in the front of the house had been activated. That was odd, since only Mr. Cote had the pass codes.

These units had come to the ballroom, and they were, so to speak, on the hunt. But surely they should not be hunting Mr. Cote! Jenkins knew for a fact that they were programmed to never, ever put Mr. Cote at risk.

What Jenkins didn't know, what Allessandro Cote didn't know, was that Fastbinder and his son had executed the KTA routine.

The KTA routine was the surest way of eradicating their enemies, because the KTA routine called for eradicating *everybody*.

If you Kill Them All, you're bound to kill the right ones.

Jenkins soon realized that the collection was on a spree, for whatever reason. Allessandro Cote was blasted with cyanide darts from a lighter-than-air gunship even as a rolling keg of gasoline spurted a tongue of fire at his legs. A ninety-year-old mechanical cannon that looked like an end table on wheels, and was actually constructed largely of wood, belched black smoke from the deck-mounted gun. It blasted half of Cote's abdomen away. Allessandro Cote's corpse was then sliced to ribbons by an old-time gas-powered tree trimmer, almost eight feet long and counterbalanced on a hat stand that was itself mounted on a power mower deck.

The alligator rolled into sight, just outside the door, and Jenkins knew he was dead. Buck up, old chap, he thought, the alligator will be a quick death, clean and neat. Certainly better than the dragonflies.

Nothing could be worse than the dragonflies, right?

The bronze alligator put on a burst of speed and its head rotated sideways, then its hinged jaws snapped open, revealing 140 teeth made from stainless-steel blades salvaged from an abattoir. Very effective, indeed, Jenkins thought, as the massive jaws slammed shut on pneumatic pistons, biting his legs clean off just below the knees.

The alligator backed off. Jenkins collapsed to the ground but didn't feel it. He saw his bloody feet still standing there, and the neatly severed calves tumbled out of the creature's maw when it opened its jaws and spun its head in a full circle, first this way, then that. The gears clanked and rattled in its neck.

Now free of obstruction, it came at Jenkins again, closing its jaws on his torso and arm. Not very neat, Jenkins thought. There was a big mess of torn tissue when the alligator pulled back. Very messy.

Very painful, too.

But better than the dragonflies.

14

The strange phenomenon that leeched their energy stopped. Their strength came back. Remo and Chiun felt their vigor seeping into them again, step by step, as they descended through the levels of rooms that clung to the hillside. Finally they came to an elegant sunroom that was all glass, walls and ceiling. The Mediterranean Sea was golden in the lowering sun, and long shadows cooled the lawns outside.

There was no one in the sunroom.

There was no one outside.

They were halfway through the room when they felt it again. Still stumbling with weakness, Remo felt his knees buckle almost immediately, and he grabbed for a wicker chair back to hold himself up.

He didn't have the strength to be as angry as he wanted to be.

"Shush," gasped Chiun, giving him a warning look, adding in Korean, "Act natural."

"There are more of them coming, Chiun," Remo insisted.

"Then this phenomenon will cease and we will deal

with whatever weapon materializes," Chiun said. "Meanwhile, we are being watched."

Remo tried hard to stand up straight, as if the reason he had stopped was simply to watch for whatever danger would present itself. What Chiun called a phenomenon had been slightly different with each experience. Now it was as if there were many, many small sources, maybe hundreds, and they came from the very earth outside the sunroom.

Then it stopped.

Once again Remo felt the intense relief as the energy began to elevate rapidly into his body, but he wasn't fooled this time. He wasn't free of it. Not yet.

"Must we stand here and await an attack?" Chiun complained in English, obviously wanting their voyeurs to hear.

"Nice place for it," Remo said. His recuperation was slower than it had been previously. Would he get his strength back before the attack came? Would he get it back ever?

If they ran for it now, weakened and exhausted, they wouldn't get far.

A tiny shadow passed over the window. A pair of dragonflies darted about one another just outside the glass.

Another pair.

Then the dragonflies began billowing out of the bushes, forming a storm cloud of insects that seeped over the glass until they were thick on it, hovering outside, waiting.

Thousands of them.

Remo moved closer to the glass, fascinated. "They're mechanical. They're freaking robots."

"Yes."

"Think they're poisonous or something?"

"No poison," said the tiny voice from a small, wall-mounted speaker. "But they nip."

Remo looked around the room, finding the small black speaker grille and the shining glass eye of a lens. "They nip? Sounds downright disagreeable, Mr. Who-ever-the-fuck-you-are."

"Look at it as being pricked with a pin." He spoke English with a thick German accent.

"Not even worth a Band-Aid."

"Think about being pricked with four or five thousand pins, one after another. A drop of blood here, a drop of blood there."

"I get it," Remo said. "It adds up until you run out."

"Exactly."

"Unless the batteries run out," Remo said.

"They won't."

"Sure, they will. I don't care what you've got in there. Duracells. Everreadys. DieHards from Sears. No battery lasts forever."

"There are no batteries, Mr. Remo Annoying. Your name is apt, by the way. They have electric power cells that provide any amperage needed for an extended period."

"What's your name anyway?"

"Stalling for time worked on that idiot Cote but it won't work on me."

"Are you sure, idiot?" Chiun asked.

"I am sure, Korean. It is I who have been stalling you. As you can see, the swarm is ready to break in."

Remo and Chiun cast about until they noticed the swarm cloud grow blacker directly overhead, then the dragonflies dived in a steady stream at the window, their tiny, sharp needle heads hitting the glass and bouncing off. The number was so great it was like the sound of serene rainfall.

The pace of the onslaught increased. Every tiny bug removed just the tiniest chip of glass and yet it was enough to erode the pane in seconds.

"If we stay here, they shall eat us alive," Chiun remarked.

"Ditto if we go out there."

"Remo," Chiun said somberly, "I will not get far."

"Don't give me the feeble-old-man shit, Chiun. I'm in sad shape myself. But I think running is better than staying."

"Run if you like," said the voice from the speaker. "They'll chase you all the way to France."

"Chiun," Remo whispered in Korean, "I bet those bugs can't swim. We can. Maybe."

Chiun nodded and said, "Race you to the water."

At that moment the pane of storm-proof glass had been worn so thin it began to spiderweb under its own weight, and as Remo and Chiun emerged from the rear of the sunroom, the glass fell in and the dragonflies began swarming inside, while thousands more descended on the Masters of Sinanju from above, and Remo felt them began to nip at his flesh. They dived at him, swarmed over him, touched him like raindrops and then fell away.

He was too weak to outrun them or to harden his flesh against them for long. Another ten minutes, maybe, and he could have simply run away, or let them prod him incessantly without penetrating his flesh.

Even as he felt stronger every second, he felt weaker

every second, exhausted from his exertions. The blood was dappling his skin, then it became a sheen of red underneath the smokelike swarm of dragonflies. He tried waving them off but it was like trying to shove away the incoming tide.

He knew he was running because his legs screamed, but it seemed they had made no progress. The air was so thick with the bugs it clouded the vision. How far to the ocean's edge?

His skin felt raw, his legs heavy, but amazingly his breathing became invigorated. He was recuperating from his weakness even as that weakness allowed him to succumb to the bugs.

Then Chiun was gone from his side. Remo stopped, retreated, waving furiously at the swarms and his returning breath gave him the strength to wipe them away long enough to spot the fallen figure of Chiun.

Remo blundered to him, grabbed the small body and turned back to the ocean.

"Breathe, Chiun," Remo said.

The dragonflies seemed to form a solid wall in front of him. He would never see it when he reached the edge, and now his flesh was screaming. He was been skinned alive. He felt one foot come down on nothing and he drew back.

"Breathe, Chiun!"

He felt nothing, not even a breath, from the small figure in his arms.

"We're going in," Remo said. He launched himself and Chiun out into space, and dropped. Sixty feet of emptiness separated the edge of the land and the Mediterranean waters, with a thin beach at the bottom.

Remo inhaled, knowing his lungs weren't right. The

dragonflies fell away suddenly and for a moment the world was clean and bright. Then Remo saw how much blood there was on Chiun, on himself. Every exposed inch of flesh was flayed, and here he was putting them in salt water.

"This," he said to himself, "is gonna hurt."

He hit the water and realized just how correct he was.

15

Mark Howard knew he was doing the wrong thing, but he did it anyway, driving across the lawn of the Cote estate just as soon as the clouds of—whatever were they?—drifted away and vanished. He knew they might come back at any second, and if they had effectively forced Remo and Chiun to run for their lives, they would surely kill Mark Howard.

He had a Beretta handgun, and he could use it, but he knew that cloud of stuff wouldn't be slowed down by a few 9 mm rounds.

He jumped out of the rental car and ran to the wooden stairs, glancing down briefly when he felt something crunching under his feet.

Dragonflies?

Dead ones were everywhere. Remo and Chiun had been attacked by dragonflies? He stooped and snatched one off the ground as he ran, examined it for a moment, then stuffed it in his pocket.

Automatons. Aerogel construction with some sort of oscillators for wing movement. Somebody had constructed thousands of them.

He practically fell down the wooden stairs to the small beach. He was looking at the cliff edge to the right, looking for corpses adrift in the surf, and his attention was so focused he almost didn't see the man sitting in the sand.

He had his back to Mark and water was still dripping from his hair, but his clothes were steaming slightly.

"Remo? It's me."

"I know."

Mark Howard felt a curious coldness in his stomach as he walked around Remo and stopped dead.

"Jesus!"

Remo's face and arms wore a sheen of raw blood, making his eyes into a wildman's white eyes. His T-shirt was tattered and soaked with blood. Caked to him, virtually every square inch, was gritty sand.

Chiun looked worse. Flat on his back, mouth slightly open, he was a mask of thick blood that oozed and dripped into the sand.

Mark looked at him. Remo touched the old man's blood-painted skull and dropped his hand as if lifting it was an effort. Mark didn't even want to speak.

"Remo, are you okay?"

Remo winced. "My face hurts."

"It pains all who look upon it."

Mark grinned. "Chiun! You're okay!"

"Chiun is not okay." Chiun crawled painfully to his knees, then to his feet. "Chiun is distantly removed from 'okay' or any word bearing a resemblance to 'okay.' I have been sent running about like a schoolboy on a scavenger hunt, subjected to dangerous radiation, then pecked nearly to death by insects, and at the moment of my greatest discomfort from this terrific torture, I have had salt rubbed literally in my wounds."

"You're welcome," Remo said.

"And as I was drowning and suffering the most enormous pain from this series of events, as my life is fading into the oblivious, with what am I assaulted? The most vile profanity!"

"It hurt like hell," Remo said.

"You did not hear me cursing."

"You were drowning, remember?"

"The sea life fled en masse. This coast will likely be barren for years."

"You calling me an environmental catastrophe?"

"Environmental is but one of the many types of catastrophe you embody."

"Enough!" Mark Howard blurted. "Stop bickering. We've got to get you to a hospital."

"He'll live," Remo said.

"His wounds are superficial," Chiun added. "Several layers of bandages wrapped around his head and face will help, but it is vital that they be tied tightly and left on for a minimum of ten days."

"Har-dee-har-har."

"And the worst thing is…" Chiun pursed his lips into a white line on his blood-smeared face. "The worst thing, you broke my iBlogger."

"How can you break an eye booger?" Remo asked.

"No," Chiun said. "This!"

He removed his hands from his sleeves and thrust a small white electronic box at Remo. There was a multicolored piece of fruit inlaid in the plastic and a miniature keyboard beneath a dark screen.

"What is it?"

"Read it!"

"iBlogger."

"See?"

"Oh, now I understand."

Mark Howard's joy at finding them alive was replaced with almost instant annoyance. He trudged up the stairs without them. Remo started up after him.

"It is an Internet device," Chiun said. "It is a way for people to share their diaries with others."

"Huh?"

"*Huh*? What is *huh*, Remo? What word have I used that escapes your understanding?"

"I understood all the words, I just couldn't make sense of the way you put them all together," Remo said. He called up, "Hey, Junior, what's an iBlogger?"

"Internet gizmo for teeny-boppers. Why?"

"Not just for tiny-boobers," Chiun insisted. "The blog has become a mass medium for the sharing of one's lives." He waved his plastic box for emphasis and Mark took it curiously when Chiun materialized at his side with the device.

"Yep, that's an iBlogger. See, people all over the world use the Internet to post their personal journals. This thing shows them."

"Why?" Remo asked.

"Well, it started out as a gimmick for teenage girls, you know, like the electronic equivalent of passing notes in class. But Chiun's right—other people are doing it now."

"It allows the average man or woman to tell his or her story to the world," Chiun explained. "It allows one to share one's life with the entire world, everything from mundane day-to-day events to great moments of joy and sorrow."

As they reached the car, Remo understood. "Like a soap opera."

"Yes, but real," Chiun said as they entered the rental car. "These are genuine human lives, genuine human personalities. Some are unlikable, some are vain, some are petty, some are sad."

"All real winners, huh? Aren't any of them just boring?"

"Of course, but those blogs I do not visit. I only go to sites written by truly interesting personalities. One of my favorites is a woman in Wyoming, an attorney by the name of Caroline Trough, who takes three new lovers each week."

"Wait a second—that's her real name? This isn't anonymous?"

"Some are, some are not. There are some brave souls who make their diaries public and allow the blog to become not just a report of the events of their lives and their feelings, but it becomes a factor in their lives, affecting the events."

"That's brave? I call that advertising," Remo said. "You're telling me this babe goes onto the blogger and tells the world how she takes a new sex partner three times a week? There must be guys lining up to get their share."

"That is but one example. There are hundreds of others," Chiun said enthusiastically.

"All right, so you've been picking bloggers," Remo said. "Guess it can't be worse than Mexican soap operas."

16

"What is this thing?" Jack asked, nodding at a sand-crusted jumble of wires sitting on the table.

Fastbinder glanced up from the papers spread before him. "Sensor pod of some sort. I had Ironhand extract it from an unmanned VTOL that was undergoing repairs at the air base."

Jack brushed sand away, then whistled appreciatively. "Gee, Dad, they sure stuffed a lot of junk inside. Have you figured out what it's for?"

"Not yet," Fastbinder replied absently, his attention on his paperwork.

"A sensor set in a drone VTOL," Jack said to himself. "This the only control system?"

He repeated the question when Fastbinder failed to answer.

"Yes," Fastbinder answered impatiently. "Whatever the aircraft was for, the answer is in that sensor pack."

"Mind if I have a go at it, Pops?"

"Yes, yes, please," Fastbinder said, waving Jack away and already concentrating on his reading again.

They were both, father and son, unsettled by the events in Barcelona. They had been told how fast and unusual the pair of assassins were, but they had never expected what had happened at the Cote mansion.

The defense system Allessandro Cote had installed was huge and powerful. He had paid millions for it, and Fastbinder had given him a huge variety of the best defensive and offensive automation devices ever created. You could have defended Baghdad with that setup.

So what went wrong? Why had all those systems failed to stop two men, even extraordinary men? Had the two men been stopped at all. There was no real guarantee that the pair was dead....

Jack Fast dropped his backpack and flipped on a telescoping light, immediately losing himself in the mystery of the electronic device in front of him. He grabbed a soft-bristled brush designed for sensitive electronics, using it to remove most of the sand. Underneath he found a plastic shell encapsulating most of the electronics. That was good news and bad news. It meant the sensors and chips should still be intact, but they would be extradifficult to get at without damaging them. The encapsulation meant the thing was designed for harsh environments, which really only made sense if they were flying the Vertical Takeoff and Landing unit at a very low altitude over the southwestern deserts. Once you got out of the reach of the airborne sand, you wouldn't need this level of environmental protection.

"Check it out! ORNL!" he exclaimed suddenly as he spritzed the device with canned air and uncovered an engraved logo.

"Hmm," Fastbinder responded, not looking up.

The Oak Ridge National Laboratory was one of the Department of Energy's national laboratories, and researchers there routinely came up with advanced technologies. Their developments regularly ended up in military hands.

Jack pondered this as he sorted out the connections. The unit had been extracted forcefully from the drone VTOL unit, wrenching apart the connections. Figuring out all the dangling cables and connectors was a little like a veterinarian trying to figure out the nature of a new species of animal, having only the dragged-off head to evaluate.

Jack Fast, however, was in his element. There was nothing he loved more than solving a technological mystery, especially when it was new, possibly top-secret technology.

Painstakingly he removed the insulation from the cables, identified those he could, and spliced them into good cables that linked into a computer terminal. The computer pulsed the unknown connections with the tiniest electrical signals that strengthened incrementally, looking for feedback.

Jack Fast rubbed his neck and was surprised to find himself alone. His father had gone to bed. He had been working three hours.

When he looked at the clock again it was after one in the morning, and the computer had identified the nature of the last of the connections. It helped tremendously that the unit's control system was the current generation of Gee-DAM, giving him a big head start. The computer was now feeding data into the unit and determining a command structure based on the Gee-DAM protocol, gaining control of the sensors. Jack

Fast now knew how to control the device—if it were attached to its autonomous helicopter.

But what did the thing *do*?

He began running it through a simulated flight. The sensor bank fed readings to the terminal, but the readings were nominal. He waved his hand in front of it. Nothing. He pointed it at the light bulb. Nothing. He bent over the pod and shouted, "Hey!"

Nothing.

He picked up the sensor pod and looked at it, then lifted it overhead, trailing the cables and connectors, and the screen jumped.

Jack grinned, but couldn't make it jump again. He waved the sensor bank around the room, so the readings jumped again, and by narrowing his sweep he homed in on a dark shape tucked under one of his father's workbenches.

Jack Fast yanked the flexible light so it would shine on the dark object.

Under the bench was a genuine, antique Flexible Flyer children's wagon. It was one of the first ones ever made, worth thousands to some toy collectors, especially with pristine original paint like this one.

Inside the near-mint wagon was a compact smart bomb, stenciled with the letters:

UNEXPLODED ORDNANCE
TOP SECRET
PROPERTY OF THE U.S. GOVERNMENT
Possession of this ordnance is extremely
dangerous and will result in the immediate
incarceration, military trial and conviction by
the Terrorist And Potential Terrorists Isolation

Division (TAPTID) of the Department Of
Homeland Security (DOHS).

Jack Fast was not surprised to find live, classified
ordnance in his home. He waved his sensors at it, waved
it away, waved it back.

"Cool!" Fast said. "Hey, Pops, wake up!"

He was waving it around when Fastbinder emerged
from his tiny bedroom cubicle in his boxers. His head
was wild, his legs were scrawny, and he was scratch-
ing his chest drowsily. He was not a pretty sight.

"What's the problem?" Fastbinder grumbled.

"Aw, jeez, Pops, the turtle's poking out his shell."

Fastbinder adjusted his boxers. "Better? Now what's
the problem?"

Jack was waving the sensor array around the workshop. "Look at the screen. I figured out what this thing
does. And it does it really well."

Fastbinder, his curiosity aroused, leaned into the
monitor. As Jack waved the sensors, the screen took a
reading of something.

"What?"

"Ordnance."

"Ordnance." An ordnance sensor was definitely
nothing new.

"Now watch." Jack waved the sensors at the wall.
The screen jumped.

Fastbinder thought about what was behind the wall.
Nothing. Twenty feet of empty dirt. Then the a storage
house, heavily shielded.

The sensors were seeing through it, registering some
of the odd bombs Fastbinder was keeping there.

No sensor should be able to see into that building.

If this sensor could see through bomb-proof shielding to find live ordnance…

"Just think what it could do!" Jack Fast exclaimed.

Fastbinder was wearing a look of rapture. "Yes. Just think!"

17

The old fairy tale was that anybody could grow up to be President of the United States. Not true. Sure, anybody could run for President. Even women. Even African-Americans. Jews. Muslims. Hindus. Great Danes named Hal. Ross Perot. Anybody could run.

The truth was that any male WASP American could grow up to be President. Being rich and socially connected was strongly recommended.

Herbert Whiteslaw was all those things. Fifty-one years old, Caucasian, very middle of the road in terms of his political views. He came from old San Francisco money and had no publicly known skeletons in his closet. He was a four-term state senator from California and had kissed political backside in every federal building on Capitol Hill.

His constituents liked him but he never seemed to get in tight with his peers. He never seemed to get the important party people excited enough to gain their support for a run at the presidency.

What he needed was internal party support, and he knew how to get it: blackmail.

Extorting support within his own party would be a fine first step, but that wouldn't guarantee him the White House. What he needed was an extraordinary level of support from the most unlikely sources.

"Picture this," he told his former campaign manager. "I get the party nomination—"

"Too late for that," Phil Mein interrupted. "You may have read in the newspaper that the primaries are over. We're just months away from the election, Herb."

Whiteslaw nodded and stuffed in a forkful of shrimp and angel hair pasta. "Yeah, but the nominees might step down. What's the replacement process?"

Mein frowned. "I don't know. What leads you to believe the nominees would step down."

"Hypothetically, they do. And, hypothetically, I get the nomination."

"Herb, think about it. You haven't been actively campaigning for this election. If a party nominee did step out of the race, there are five or six replacements waiting in the wings who've been promoting themselves for more than a year. You're an unknown. But, if by some quirk of politics you did get the party nomination, you'd be the underdog in the general election for sure. You'd never unseat the incumbent."

"I think I could."

Mein was twirling his *pasta carbonara* despondently. When Whiteslaw called him into this meeting he had been excited to think that the senator was beginning to plan his strategy for the next Senate race and, simultaneously, the White House race that was still four years off. Mein didn't like the direction this conversation was headed. "Let's talk about the next election. You know, four years from now. You might stand a chance."

"If I were to get the party nomination, and if the current administration were to suddenly become mired in scandal, what then?"

Mein looked at Whiteslaw, saw the man's eyes glimmering. He swallowed, and swallowed hard because the mouthful was mostly unchewed pasta.

"What do you know, Herb?" Mein asked.

"I know something big, Phil," Whiteslaw said.

Mein couldn't speak again because the waiter appeared to pour more wine into their glasses from the bottle on the table. When the man left, Phil urged, "Tell me!"

"No way in hell." Whiteslaw was still smiling. "You know my rules, Phil. Trust no one."

"Come on, Herb, give me a hint! You know something so big it will bring down the administration?"

Whiteslaw nodded. "It's guaranteed impeachment."

"Wow!" Mein grew cautious. "You sure?"

"Listen, Phil, I've got the goods on the President. The only way he'll escape going down in flames is if he retires first."

"In your opinion."

Whiteslaw was exasperated. "Listen, Phil, there's my public opinion and there's my real opinion and this is so strong it's not even an opinion—it's a fact."

"Okay, Senator, don't get excited."

"I have knowledge of the President of the United States authorizing intelligence forces to flagrantly violate constitutionally protected rights of freedom and privacy and due process."

"It's called the Patriot Act and it's really not a secret."

"No, *way* worse. We're talking hired assassins who target U.S. citizens. Got it?"

Phil nodded. "Okay. Good. Do you have proof?"

"Getting it now."

"Proof that will pass the TV test?"

Whiteslaw smiled. "High-quality video. H.D. fucking TV."

Phil Mein smiled and leaned back in his chair. "Okay!"

"You on board with me so far?"

"So far."

"Now listen to this," Senator Whiteslaw said, pushing his unfinished supper aside and leaning in. "Say I prove the President is culpable, but I don't have evidence to spread the blame throughout his party. Say I'm up against him when the revelation is made. This is what I want to know, Phil—what are my chances?"

Phil Mein considered that. He raised his tapered hand and raised one finger. "Okay, first, you get the party nod. That means the current nominee goes down and all the other guys who were trying to get the party nomination are bypassed. Sounds ugly. Not knowing how you intend to make that happen, Herb, I have to know—how ugly will it be?"

"Behind the scenes or in the eyes of John Q. Public?"

Phil made a sputtering noise with his lips. "Who the fuck cares about behind-the-scenes? Political reality is only what the people see."

Whiteslaw smiled. "John Q. will see nothing but smiling faces. The current nominee drops out for health reasons and I get one hundred percent support from him and everybody else. Perfectly unugly."

Phil Mein waited for more, then raised a second finger. "When do you step in?"

"Whenever the timing is just right," Whiteslaw said.

Mein raised a third finger. "When does the incumbent go down in flames?"

"Again, when the time is right."

Fourth finger. "How can you be sure somebody else won't make use of the scandal before you can?"

"I'm the only one who knows."

Phil's hand dropped heavily on the restaurant table. "Sounds too good to be true, Herb."

"It's true," Whiteslaw insisted. "But you haven't answered my question. Taking all that into account, what are my chances?"

Phil Mein shook his head, slightly awed. "Your chances are excellent. If you can deliver the goods like you say you can, I'd suggest we take care of getting you in the nominee seat ASAP. Then we hold off for a while and strike at the current administration close to the election, don't give them time to get another candidate up and running."

Herbert Whiteslaw rolled his wheelchair back from the table. "My feet still hurt like hell but they've been healed for weeks. Would a dramatic stand-up-and-walk scene help with the image?"

"Jesus, yes. The gullible masses never get tired of that shit." But Phil Mein was concentrating on the wineglass in his hand. "You asking me to run this campaign, Herb?"

"You've put me in the senator's seat four times. I have faith in you, Phil."

"But you don't trust me all the way. You have to look at this from my point of view, Senator. What you're promising is the most far-reaching scandal in the memory of the American public—"

"What about the debacle over the Florida votes in 2000? What about that twit who diddled the intern?"

"Ancient history. That's retro-politics. Anyway, from what I remember, those weren't major media scandals. What you're planning is going to be major, if you really can make it happen. Herb, I need to know more."

Herbert Whiteslaw fidgeted. His eyes got beady. "Look, my plan just might call for me to break a few laws myself."

"So?"

"There might be some 'unethical behavior' involved."

"This is politics. Ethics have no meaning in politics."

"I'll let you in on this, Phil, but only if you're on board with me. Are you on board?"

"Senator Whiteslaw," Mein said in a level voice, "if you can do what you say you can do, then you *will* be the next President of the United States of America. I want to be in on that."

Whiteslaw nodded appreciatively. "Okay, Phil. Listen to this...."

18

The blue phone did not ring this time. Instead, a blue phone icon popped up on the crystal-clear screen below Dr. Smith's desk, telling him he had an incoming transmission from the field. Namely from Mark Howard, who was chaperoning Remo on board the chartered jet, just to make sure the Reigning Master didn't go wandering off somewhere.

Mark Howard gave him a succinct report as they were driving back to the airport, giving Smith time to perform some research before they called in from the chartered aircraft for an in-depth report.

"They claim they're fine," Mark said. "But they don't look fine."

"We cleaned up real nice," Remo insisted. "What were those things we went up against there? Smitty, you have any idea?"

"Offense/defensive robotics," Smith replied, his fingers snapping over the keyboard. "None of the designs you mention are surprising."

"Oh, yeah? I was surprised," Remo said. "What about that Mr. U.? What's the deal with him?"

"Mobile Intrusion, Termination and Reconnaissance Unit," Smith said. "Nothing more than an autonomous weapons system. The prototype was stolen from a DOE-funded lab in Oregon in 2003. He was said to have been fitted with a metal skull to house the electronics and the DOE was considering using the head in the actual models for its psychological impact. The design was proven substandard in battlefield mobility trials and the project was shelved before the theft even occurred."

"I got news for you—it worked well enough," Remo said. "Running on a smooth surface, anyway. What about the dog and the big spider?"

"Both designs that have been tested within the United States. You've seen mechanical spiders yourself. It is the insects that interest me most," Smith said. "They exhibited sophisticated insect flight replication technology, down to replicating the structure of the wing muscles. One pair of wings is powered by a contracting capillary group replicating the top-to-bottom thoracic muscle set, another by an end-to-end muscle group, also on the thorax. It's better than what the U.S. had developed thus far."

"But do they have the little Gee-DAMS inside?" Remo asked.

"They don't," Howard said. "I've dissected three of them. These are remote-controlled devices with no Gee-DAM chips. I'll bet there was a heat-sensitive control device in the vicinity. Once it locked on to its targets, Remo and Chiun, it simply relayed flight patterns to the swarm. Inefficient, but there were so many of them they nearly succeeded in killing them."

"So we did not get the Gee-DAMS," Smith intoned unhappily.

"Listen, Smitty, there's something more important we need to talk about. What the hell was it that Cote was using to power up all this stuff? That's what worries me the most."

"And I," added Chiun.

"I agree. We'll be looking into that aspect of it. It's as mysterious to me as to you," Smith admitted. "Especially because it seems to have been a side effect. Remo, you're convinced Cote did not even know what he was doing?"

"He was clueless. As soon as the figurines unplugged themselves from the wall sockets, the bad feeling went away. If he knew he was doing it, he would never have let me chat him up while I regained my strength. Can you send in some pocket-protector types to dismantle the place and figure it out?"

Smith pursed his lips. "That's impossible. The villa ceased to exist within minutes of your last report. The fire department says the entire structure burned to the ground, even the stone. The place must have been rigged with thermite charges."

There was a moment of silence. "Nope," Remo said. "Otherwise it would have happened a lot sooner than that. I'll bet one of those animatronics was programmed or remote controlled to set those charges. Whatever, it's just what Cote would have wanted—a big blast of an ending."

"Who ran the remote controls?" Smith demanded.

"Whoever is really behind this thing," Remo said. "It wasn't Cote the cartoon supervillian. Somebody who was tied into the security system at the Cote house and spoke like a German."

"Any indication who it was, though?"

"Some super-*duper*-villain, I guess," Remo said.

In the privacy of his office, Smith closed his eyes, imaging he felt true physical pain. What he wouldn't give to have a truly professional-*acting* enforcement arm.

"Somebody who likes robots," Remo added helpfully. "He likes them so much he dredged up one of them that was a hundred years old."

Smith almost allowed that one to pass by, like much of what Remo said, but somewhere a light glowed in his head. "What are you talking about?"

"You know. Ironhand."

"That news report from El Paso was in one of the data feeds you sent over," Mark Howard explained. "I was asking Chiun if he remembered reading the books."

"Because I am so very old, you see," Chiun announced loudly.

"Ironhand was fiction, Remo," Smith explained.

"Not according to the letter. The old man said his father saw the real Ironhand at a World's Fair."

"A century ago," Mark Howard said.

"So?"

"There were a number of Victorian-era fakes like Ironhand," Smith said. "They were sort of a rage for a while. Some were electromechanical, some were steam powered. Remember *Metropolis?*"

"I'm sure Superman fought robots," Remo said, "and that was later than Victorian era, wasn't it?"

"The silent-era film, *Metropolis,* in 1919," Smith said. "Regardless, there were many fake robots before anyone created anything like a true automaton," Smith insisted. "Ironhand was turned into pulp fiction."

"Worth checking out, though," Remo said.

"Do not heed his ramblings, Emperor," Chiun called.

Smith could picture him sitting far away from Mark and Remo, his eyes locked on the wing out the window. "He is as delusional as the poor hermit who died alone in the deserts of Newer Mexico."

"What's the harm in looking?" Remo asked.

"Remo, think about it," Smith said. "Ironhand was supposed to be more than seven feet tall and made out of steel. Not a likely configuration if you want to get into a highly secure military base, is it?"

"Why not? One of them was good enough to work for Cote. Chiun, cough up the iron robot head."

"It is of no consequence," Chiun answered dismissively.

"Chiun! Give me the effing head!"

There was a muttering, then Smith heard the sound of something hard hitting something else hard.

"What was that?" Smith asked.

"It's a robot head, Smitty," Remo said. "It was made of iron, by a blacksmith, and I bet that makes it pretty damn old."

"Mark?" Smith asked.

"Mark?" Remo added.

"It is an iron skull, Dr. Smith," Mark Howard reported. "It looks like a doll's head."

"It tried to kill us."

"We'll look into it," Smith said dismissively. "Mark, send me some photos and specifications."

REMO SULKED. Nobody cared, but that was okay because he was sulking for his own benefit, not theirs.

Mark Howard didn't seem to notice that Remo was no longer a part of the conversation until he cut the connection with Dr. Smith.

"Well, we're going back to Folcroft while we figure out the iron head. What's the matter with you?"

"Only that I am so old as to be on death's door," bemoaned Chiun, who was also sulking, but without a good reason. He was miffed Remo made him give up his iron robot head.

"He was talking to me," Remo said.

"Yes, it is just as well that I should be ignored."

"Okay, fine."

"If I see any icebergs below us, I shall ask the pilot to descend so that you may drop me off."

"Sounds good," Remo said. "Junior, look something up for me, will you?"

"In the dictionary?"

"The Internet. Wherever it is you're always going to look things up."

"I'm always going everywhere to look things up, and the last time I looked something up for you I got my behind in a sling with Dr. Smith," Mark said. "What in particular are you interested in knowing about?"

"Ironhand."

There was a loud snort.

"I thought we agreed you were going to stay quiet," Remo accused.

"That was my death rattle," Chiun retorted.

"Keep it to yourself. Go, Junior."

Junior glared at him. "You know, Remo, most eight-year-olds can look up stuff on the Internet these days."

"There are no eight-year-olds on this flight, so it's up to you."

"I could show you some computer basics," Mark insisted.

GET FREE BOOKS and a FREE GIFT WHEN YOU PLAY THE...

Just scratch off the silver box with a coin. Then check below to see the gifts you get!

SLOT MACHINE GAME!

YES!

I have scratched off the silver box. Please send me the 2 free Gold Eagle® books and gift for which I qualify. I understand I am under no obligation to purchase any books, as explained on the back of this card.

366 ADL D34F　　　　　　　　**166 ADL D34E**

FIRST NAME	LAST NAME

ADDRESS

APT.#	CITY

STATE/PROV.	ZIP/POSTAL CODE

7	7	7	Worth **TWO FREE BOOKS** plus a **BONUS** Mystery Gift!
🍒	🍒	🍒	Worth **TWO FREE BOOKS!**
♣	♣	♣	Worth **ONE FREE BOOK!**
🔔	🔔	🍒	**TRY AGAIN!**

(MB-04-R)

DETACH AND MAIL CARD TODAY!

The Gold Eagle Reader Service™ — Here's how it works:

Accepting your 2 free books and mystery gift places you under no obligation to buy anything. You may keep the books and gift and return the shipping statement marked "cancel." If you do not cancel, about a month later we'll send you 6 additional books and bill you just $29.94* — that's a saving of over 10% off the cover price of all 6 books! And there's no extra charge for shipping! You may cancel at any time, but if you choose to continue, every other month we'll send you 6 more books, which you may either purchase at the discount price or return to us and cancel your subscription.

*Terms and prices subject to change without notice. Sales tax applicable in N.Y. Canadian residents will be charged applicable provincial taxes and GST. Credit or debit balances in a customer's account(s) may be offset by any other outstanding balance owed by or to the customer.

If offer card is missing, write to: Gold Eagle Reader Service, 3010 Walden Ave., P.O. Box 1867, Buffalo, NY 14240-1867

BUSINESS REPLY MAIL

FIRST-CLASS MAIL   PERMIT NO. 717-003   BUFFALO, NY

POSTAGE WILL BE PAID BY ADDRESSEE

GOLD EAGLE READER SERVICE
3010 WALDEN AVE
PO BOX 1867
BUFFALO NY 14240-9952

NO POSTAGE
NECESSARY
IF MAILED
IN THE
UNITED STATES

"Honestly, do you want me touching your computer?"

Mark couldn't help but agree that he did not. His fingers flew and he rotated his computer to show Remo what happened.

"What's a Google?" Remo asked.

"Search engine. See this. It knows of 346 pages on the World Wide Web that make mention of the word 'Ironhand.' Some of them look like they're rock band Web sites. This one's porn. This is porn. Porn, porn, porn. But here's some that look like they're about the robot from the 1904 World's Fair and the pulp fiction books—maybe a third of them."

"That many?"

"Sure. This one looks promising."

Mark clicked, and his computer screen filled with a new window displaying a busty nude woman in an extraordinarily lewd posture who mewled, "I want to feel that iron hand of yours."

"She's from 1904?" Remo asked.

"Sorry," Mark said, clicking the window closed in a hurry. "I guess that one was porn, too." He tried another link and said, "Okay, here we go."

Remo saw a small line drawing of a crude metal head, alongside a list of book titles. *Ironhand Defeats the Savages, Ironhand and the City of Gold, Ironhand's Polar Quest.*

"The books's copyrights are expired, so they have them on-line now for anybody to read," Mark explained. "Criminy, there's almost 140 of them."

"Trash," Chiun interjected.

"All written between 1902 and 1931. They must have been mass producing these suckers," Mark noted.

"Penny-a-word hacks can be prolific."

"This is not what I want," Remo interrupted. "Show me about the real Ironhand."

Mark moved to a small table of contents and brought up a page of the same Web site, this one dedicated to the Ironhand exposition at the 1904 World's Fair. There was a photograph of the robot standing under a banner proclaiming him to be *The Amazing Electro-Mechanical Man*. A somber man stood next to him in a suit and vest, smoking a pipe. The caption read, "Ironhand wowed visitors to the 1904 World's Fair in St. Louis, MO, where his inventor, Archibald Slate, offered a hundred-dollar reward to any man who could prove Ironhand was a fake. The hundred-dollar prize was never claimed."

Under the caption was an extended description of the fair and the Ironhand bag of tricks, which included walking, talking and shooting a rifle. Remo read all the way down to the bottom and noticed a link called "The Ironhand Rumor Mill."

Mark Howard was on a trip to the washroom, so Remo carefully moved his finger across the flat place on the computer that moved the little blinking doohickey on the screen, then tapped the clicking thingamajig.

The computer, to his surprise, did not disintegrate, detonate or go black. It showed him, of all things, a page called "The Ironhand Rumor Mill."

"I'm on to something," he told Mark, who looked alarm when he saw Remo had touched the computer. "Don't worry, it's fine. Look. 'Ironhand's participation in a U.S. geological survey of Alaska and the Arctic. Ironhand's career in the U.S. Army. Ironhand fights in Mexico and in World War One.' These are reprints from newspaper articles from the nineteen-zeros and the nine-teen-teens."

"They sound like they're taken right from the books," Mark noted.

"Look at how many," Remo said. "This guy who collects them says Ironhand sightings were a phenomenon, like UFO sightings."

"And just as believable," Mark insisted.

"Well, for years the common folks saw the B-1 bomber and called it a UFO. Finally we fessed up and said yeah okay we've got this really-bizarre looking jet bomber."

"The UFO sightings didn't stop," Mark pointed out.

"But those who saw it were right all along, weren't they?" Remo insisted. "They said they saw an unidentified flying object. They said they saw something amazing and new in the sky. They were right. Maybe the Ironhand sightings were like that."

Mark considered it, then shook his head. "I do not seriously believe there was any sort of a mechanical man walking around a hundred years ago that could do more than walk and wave his hand," Mark insisted.

"Why?"

"We can barely do that with today's robotics."

"Every generation assumes it possesses the epitome of mankind's learning, huh, Little Father?"

Chiun turned his head away from the wing, smiling broadly. "That is so, Remo. You have been listening!"

"Yeah, kinda. Repetition is everything. I still know the words to 'You Light Up My Life,' too, even though I don't want to. Chiun, what's the name of the stone dog-faced boy in the attic of the Master's House. Is it the Oracle of Anubis?"

Chiun's smile was enormous. "Yes! I have not even thought of it in years and yet you have found the perfect example. I am proud of you, Remo!"

"You're gonna hurt your face if you keep doing that, Little Father," Remo warned. "So the Oracle of Anubis is really old. It's a statue of a guy, life-size, made of rock, and he has a face like a greyhound or some other skinny dog. The oracle was made for the public library in Alexandria, Virginia."

"Alexandria, Egypt. The library of Alexander the Great," Chiun corrected.

"Yeah. Anyway, it's old."

Mark Howard was speechless.

"And when the library was torn down or fell down or whatever, the oracle was removed."

"And it survives to this day?" Mark asked. "You've seen it?"

Remo blinked. "Well, yeah. Actually, I own it. It's in a box in the attic, in Sinanju. But what is important is this, Junior—it's an effing robot. What's more, it's an effing vending machine! You put in a coin and it answers your question by pointing its finger at the answers on the stone tablet in front of it. I know it's a cheap carnival trick by today's standards, but think what it must have been like hundreds of years ago."

"Thousands," Chiun corrected.

"Thousands of years go," Remo continued, on a role. "And I don't mean what it was like to use it, I mean what it was like to invent it. He had to be some kind of a genius to think of that stuff considering he never saw anything like it before."

Mark nodded. "No frame of reference. I see your point."

"So why couldn't somebody one hundred years ago have come up with a robot that could do genuinely amazing things? If he was brilliant enough?"

Remo tapped the screen, on the picture from the World's Fair, on the face of Archibald Slate, creator of Ironhand.

"Why not this guy?" Remo asked.

19

It should have been impossible, but it was true. In the one brief moment Remo Williams had been using Mark Howard's laptop computer he had somehow commanded it to dedicate all its hacking resources to downloading the vast library of video and photography from the Web site with the shameless lady who said, "I want to feel your iron hand."

"Eight thousand JPEGs, six full-length AVI movies, holy Toledo," Mark said.

"All with the same woman?" Remo asked. "She wasn't that hot."

The flight attendant must have been waiting for her cue, because she walked into the passenger area and sneered, "You wouldn't know a hot woman if she buried your face between her breasts. Here—"

She reached for Remo's head and tried to illustrate her point, but Remo was out of there. The flight attendant thrust an un-asked-for glass of water at Mark and retreated to the galley. Remo emerged from the aircraft washroom to find Mark Howard absorbed by a new screen of data.

"I like it better when there were pictures," he told the assistant director of CURE.

"Remo, listen," Mark said. "Archibald Slate, indentured to the United States Army, 1905. Released 1928."

"Indentured?"

"This is government stuff, still classified after all these years," Howard said. "Nobody is supposed to know about this. Whoever *is* supposed to know must be long gone."

"But does it say what he did?"

"No. These files are sparse. He served in an engineering capacity, to be expected, since he was an engineer. Says he succumbed to dementia and retired. He was memorialized in August 1932."

"Meaning?"

"A memorial service, for the dead."

"Shall I be remembered when I am dead?" wailed a pitiful old man in the back, whose pride and joy in Remo had been short-lived.

"Maybe, but not in a good way," Remo said. "So did he die then or what? Why didn't they just say he died?"

Mark searched again. "Birth and death records, Providence," he explained. "No death certificate on file for Archibald Slate."

"But there's a lot of other Slates," Remo noticed. "Look at them all. Look at how many lived at the same address. I bet she still does."

He pointed to a birth record. It was just a name, Sarah Slate, born twenty-one years ago.

"Hold on," Mark said, then did some key pounding and window swapping. "That's the address for Archibald Slate in his military file in 1905."

"Family house. Maybe they still own it."

"Hold on. Yes, Sarah Slate's address is the same."

Mark looked at Remo. "I'll call Dr. Smith and let him know we're diverting to Providence."

"I have to go to the bathroom again," Remo announced. He'd had enough of Harold Smith for the time being.

20

The homes in Providence, Rhode Island, felt old. They dated back a few hundred years—new construction compared to the ancient buildings in some parts of the world. But in America, this was ancient, and it felt ancient. Every forgotten year from the Colonial era to the twenty-first century seemed to weigh heavily on these buildings, no matter how fresh the paint.

"No wonder a lot of people had this address," Remo observed. "It's a big house."

"It is also quite open," Chiun noted.

Remo looked down the street, where a number of fine big Colonial homes stood proudly, side by side, just a few feet separating them. The Slate house was different, a vast red-brick home on several open acres.

"Hello!" said the woman in the apron when they rang the bell. "I'm so pleased to meet you!" When she got a look at the guests she was taken aback. They had faces that were reddened and marred, as if both had recently been in an accident with a sandblaster.

"Ms. Slate?"

"Oh, no, I'm Mrs. Sanderson, the housekeeper.

You're Mr. Remo Dexter, right? Hello. And you are Moses Chiun! So happy to have you here. We get visitors so seldom these days."

Mrs. Sanderson ushered them through a parlor to a living room, where the air smelled musty and aged despite a fresh breeze through the open window.

"This is Sarah Slate," Mrs. Sanderson said as the woman rose from her chair.

Remo expected her to look twenty-one, not seventeen. At the same time she seemed old, weary, as if in mourning. She was somehow graceful beyond her years. Her long brown hair was tied carelessly in a ponytail in a red band. She had tossed on her peach sweater and faded jeans. She wore no makeup, but she was stunning.

"I'm so pleased to meet you." She took Remo's hand, and if she noticed his unusually scarlet complexion she didn't show it. Remo enjoyed the sensation of her skin, but she pulled away and nodded to Chiun, who nodded curtly and strolled to the wall to examine one of several hundred framed photographs.

"Holy moly," Remo said. "Look at them all." He stepped up to one of the pictures and found himself staring at a faded image of an airship. "Franklin Slate/Agnes Slate, 1909," said the neat pencil legend.

"I guess that explains why you need all the yard space," he mentioned. In the picture, the airship was tied up outside the house.

The next photo was of a man on a mountain, his beard ice encrusted. "In 1954 Orville Slate Successfully Scaled Mount Everest, Dying Whilst Descending."

"Are all these pictures of your family?" Remo asked.

"Of course," said Sarah.

"I knew of a Slate," Chiun said in a singsong of realization. "Randolph Slate was known among the royalty of the British."

"Yes," Sarah nodded. "He was an uncle."

"He claimed to have many famous exploring siblings and ancestors," Chiun recalled.

"Yes. A lot of good it got them," Sarah said. "There were thirty Slates a century ago. Now the line is all but wiped out because of their foolishness. I'm all there is."

Remo looked around the room with fresh eyes. "All these people?"

"Almost all of them died on some ridiculous venture or another. Airships, mountain climbing, polar exploration, deep-sea exploration. But I don't understand—don't you know this? If you have not come to write about my family, what have you come for?"

"We're not reporters. We came to talk about Archibald Slate," Remo said. "Your great-grandfather."

Sarah Slate smiled again, looking sadder. "You came to find Ironhand."

"Well, yeah. Is he home?"

"Of course not. Are you from the government?"

"Yes, but the government hasn't been keeping really good records, believe it or not," Remo said. "Fact is, some of us aren't sure if Ironhand ever existed. I mean, if he ever existed as a real walking, talking robot. We know only that Archibald Slate was employed by Army as an engineer."

"He was enslaved. He was imprisoned. It was despicable what America did to that man."

"Why'd they want him so bad?"

"You know why."

"No."

She sat back in her chair and looked at Remo as the housekeeper came in with a tea set, pouring three cups. Remo took his. Chiun, who had never bothered to sit down, left through a back door.

"Very insecure around women. He is habitually rude to those he finds attractive," Remo explained to Mrs. Sanderson, who blushed crimson and hurried out.

"What agency?" Sarah Slate demanded. "DOE? FBI?"

"MYOB."

"Washington has got to have records on my great-grandfather Archibald."

"Just name, rank and serial number. If they ever had anything in-depth it must have been misplaced. One of our people is trying to unearth it."

"Why?"

"Well, it might be, just might be, that Ironhand is being used again. He might have been used to kill somebody. Normally the federal government couldn't care less, you understand, but this time, he killed somebody after he stole military secrets." He looked at her. She smiled. "You already knew that."

"Read it in the paper. Tell your person in Washington to not bother. I've got all of Archibald's notes. Right here. In the house. Including his notes on Ironhand. Drink your tea."

21

Mark Howard was surprised when Remo Williams answered the door of the big brick house in Providence.

"Hey, Junior, have I got something to show you."

They went downstairs immediately, seeing no one else, and Mark was assaulted with the mildew smell of an ancient cellar. When Remo flipped the switch, thirty-five bare light bulbs set in the ceiling illuminated over seven rows of shelves crammed with boxes of paper memorabilia.

"It's a museum!" Mark exclaimed.

"Sarah calls it a morgue," Remo said. "Supposedly, this is all the documentation of a whole dynasty of suicidal dimwits named Slate. Half these boxes haven't been opened since the family got mostly killed off in the 1930s. They've been sort of on the decline ever since. Sarah's the last of them. Anyway," Remo said, shrugging, "have at it."

MARK HOWARD SPENT fifteen minutes wandering up and down the rows in a stupor, looking at more intriguing names and trinkets than he could process. Then he started at the beginning, looking for the thread of the organizational system that had obviously eluded him the first time.

"What a mess."

"Yes, it is."

Mark Howard spun.

"Sorry. I'm Sarah. You're Howie Wyrd?"

"Yes," Mark said, shaking her hand but looking as if he were biting something bitter.

"Don't worry. I know the name's fake. There is no organizational system down here, by the way. All this stuff used to be stored in the house. On the day my trustee turned over control of the estate, I had most of it shoved in crates and brought down here, out of sight."

"You honestly don't know what's in here?"

"I know the nature of it," she said, as if it was sad to think about. "These are the documented ravings of glory-hunters, irresponsible thrill-seekers and irrepressible egoists. The cellar is all they deserve. Dinner's almost ready."

Mark was wandering the rows again when she returned and informed him he had ignored the call to the evening meal.

"I have to find Archibald in all this," Mark insisted.

Sarah sent down a plate and a glass of iced tea.

"Sit. Eat."

"I need to keep looking."

"Howie."

"Please, call me Mark."

"Sit down, Mark."

She touched him, on the shoulder. Mark Howard had barely been paying attention to her until that moment. When she guided him to the folding chair, he couldn't begin to resist.

He sat down, thanked her for the plate of hot food and began eating it, thinking about the young woman. He ate the entire meal without knowing what he was eating; when the meal was done, he was startled to read on the box label in front of him: Archibald Slate.

She had seated him directly in front of the box he was seeking, and it only took him fifteen minutes to figure it out.

22

After dinner they met around the fire in the circular great room whose cornerless walls were covered with old framed photos, daguerreotypes and tintypes of dead Slates. It was the four of them. The housekeeper, Mrs. Sanderson, had departed with tears in her eyes when Remo and Chiun refused to eat her roast.

"It's the first big meal she's had the opportunity to prepare in months," Sarah Slate chastised Remo. "Would it have killed you to at least try it?"

"Sorry," Remo said. "We don't swing that way."

"So, where do I start?" Sarah asked when they were all seated in the vast but somehow cozy great room—all except Chiun, who popped up from the floor time and again to examine one of the ancient pictures. "What do you know about Archibald Slate already?"

"All we know is the public record." Mark Howard took out a steno pad and flipped it open. "Born in 1849 in Rhode Island in this house. Earned a reputation as an eccentric engineering genius while attending Brown University, right here in Providence. His reputation was enhanced when he left the university and was granted a multitude of mechanical patents, but he became a celebrity in 1899. That's when Ironhand was unveiled for the first time." Mark looked up and smiled warmly. Sarah smiled warmly in return. "How am I doing so far?"

"Wonderfully."

"Fickle," Remo said.

"Huh?" Howard asked.

"Go on," Remo added impatiently.

"Uh, let's see. Archibald Slate stages a series of Ironhand exhibitions. He writes engineering papers but they're turned down by the more prestigious journals of the time. Archibald becomes a laughingstock in some circles and promises a dramatic series of exhibitions to prove Ironhand's capabilities.

"That's the same year he and Ironhand trek two thousand miles across the Canadian-Alaskan tundra, including making a dangerous passage through the Canadian Rockies. In 1903, Slate and Ironhand spend several months in the Four Corners region of the Southwest, rounding up a slew of wanted men. They head next into South America and explore many hundreds of miles of the Amazon during the dry season.

"All these events were highly publicized, but they never achieved the goal of legitimizing Ironhand. Every eyewitness account, every photo, was derided as fakery. To his detractors, Slate went from being a pitiful source of amusement to being a symbol of every profitmongerer eager to make a buck off the public fascination with the new world of technological marvels."

Mark looked up suddenly. "I'm sorry to be so blunt, Ms. Slate. This is what my research shows. I don't mean to insult your ancestor."

Sarah smiled openly. "Not at all. I've heard much worse, Mr. Howard."

"I'm Mark, please."

"I'm Sarah."

"I'm impatient," Remo added.

"You're also rude. And illiterate," Chiun piped up. "And disrespectful. And careless and lazy and impertinent and a poor dresser and physically repulsive and scandalously uncultured."

"I'm not a poor dresser."

"You wear undergarments in public."

"T-shirts are practical. Keep reading, Mr. Howard."

Sarah Slate watched the pair of Masters with ill-concealed amazement before turning her attention back to Mark.

"In 1904, Archibald Slate was said to be despondent over his inability to convince the world that Ironhand was the singular representation of several mechanical and electrical breakthroughs, so he paid handsomely to sponsor his own exhibition at the 1904 World's Fair in St. Louis. This, he promised, would be a scientific exhibition in which Ironhand's secrets would be revealed. The exhibition was a flop with the scientific community, but it was a big hit with the public, and within a few months the first Ironhand novel, came out. *Ironhand and the Cherokee Marauders*. Supposedly based on Ironhand's true adventures in the West in 1903. This was followed up by *The Machine Man on the Dark Continent*. The series was published for years, culminating with Ironhand #136, *The Amazing Electro-Mechanical Man Conquers the Orient* and #137, *The Robot Probes under the Earth*.

"Who in their right mind would want to read 137 books about the same guy?" Remo demanded.

"Archibald Slate was credited as the author, but in reality he seems to have retired to a life of idle inventing and occasional consulting work with the U.S. Army's transportation research. Helped design the early armored vehicles. But by 1918 he was beginning to show signs of anxiety, and became senile. He wandered away from his convalescent home, here in Providence, and was never seen again."

Mark looked at Sarah Slate, who seemed lost in memory. "Did I leave anything out?"

She laughed, briefly, an unhappy sound. "Yes."

Mark smiled encouragingly. Remo waited. Chiun's eyes tightened, ever so slightly.

"In 1904," she continued, "my great-grandfather began planning his World's Fair exhibition, in which he would demonstrate the technology in Ironhand and display the diagrams of his technology on posters. He would give the technology away free to anyone who would make use of it. Surely, he thought, someone would see that what he had created was truly wonderful and ahead of its time. Somebody would surely take a chance on his inventions and see how successful they were.

"Three weeks before the Fair was to begin, the United States government illegally appropriated Ironhand from Archibald Slate. They gave him the choice of joining the government research project based on Ironhand automation technology, or being entirely excluded from the development. He had to join the government. He had no choice. The Ironhand exhibited at the Fair was a cheap tin copy—even that fake Ironhand was extremely advanced for its time. The books were a ploy by the government. They wanted the public to have no doubt that Ironhand was and had always been a cheap sideshow attraction. Victorian-era robots were a dime a dozen, all fakes, and Ironhand was cast as just one of the crowd."

"You're saying the government saw the advanced nature of Archibald's engineering and appropriated it?" Mark Howard asked.

Sarah nodded. "With the Army, Archibald created a series of new robots but none had the capability to operate autonomously like Ironhand. When war broke out Archibald and Ironhand were sent to the front. This field testing proved disastrous. Ironhand disappeared in October 1918, after destroying a German gun that was causing massive destruction in France.

"Archibald came back from France a broken man. His efforts to recreate Ironhand failed as his mental faculties waned. The Army sacked him. Being in the family home seemed to aggravate his paranoia and agitation, so we bought a local nursing home to care for him. Then as you say, Mark, he walked out of his nursing home and vanished."

Remo was grinding his gears. "Back up. What do you mean by *autonomous*?"

"Ironhand wasn't computerized, but he did have what was probably the world's first remote-control system. My great-grandfather, you see, was an acquaintance of an engineer named Jameson Davis. Over brandy in a British club in 1897, Davis began describing the extraordinary achievements of his cousin in the field of radio telegraphy."

"Marconi?" Remo asked.

"Yes." Sarah nodded.

Chiun stared at his protégé. "How could you know such a thing?"

"I have the test answers written on my arm."

"Archibald Slate licensed the rights to radio telegraphy directly from Guglielmo Marconi. Slate and Marconi agreed to keep the license a secret to protect their mutual patents, and the Slate payments were made through Davis. As Ironhand was being built, between 1897 and 1899, Marconi's radio telegraph was having its first field successes."

"So Slate could send simple commands to Ironhand using electrical pulses?" Mark asked.

"A series of relays inside Ironhand received the radio telegraph signals. At first, my great-grandfather started with relays in series. Sending one pulse would snap the relay to switch position one, for example, which controls the right lower leg, sending two pulses activated the right upper leg, and so on. When he had activated the correct system, a longer pulse closed the relay in that position. The next set of pulses would move the selected system incrementally. One pulse would bend the lower leg five degrees, two would bend it ten degrees."

"Sounds like it would work, but it would take an hour just to take a few steps," Remo said.

"It did—at first. Then Archibald began designing some of the first logical, practical-use switch systems ever created. In other words, he programmed Ironhand."

"Not with a computer?" Remo asked.

"With series of relays," Sarah said. "Electromechanical switches, using electrical coils, but no one had ever configured them like Archibald did. The switches turned certain functions on and off, one after another,

in such a way that Ironhand could perform a complicated task, like take a step forward, with one simple
command. Archibald even constructed interconnected
relay strings, which made use of nested routines, looped
the commands, even perform if/then operations."

"Cripes," Mark said. "He was doing analog
programming—in 1899."

"Yes. By the time Archibald took Ironhand to
Canada in 1902 he had added directional control using
a compass and a gyroscopic self-balancing system.
After being blackmailed into serving the U.S. government, he was forced to steal technologies developed by
others. In 1917 he was one of the first to use Ernst
Alexanderson's selective tuner for radio receivers. In
the field, Archibald himself operated Ironhand. Nobody else was capable of learning the immensely sophisticated control patterns needed to make Ironhand
actually work. In France, Archibald perched in a low-
altitude balloon and monitored Ironhand through binoc-
ulars. He directed Ironhand across a field of small-arms
fire, that killed seven men. There was a premature explosion, killing Ironhand's guard detail. Ironhand vanished and was called a loss.

"That night, Archibald returned to the battlefield
alone, and against orders. Archibald desperately tried
to get a radio signal to Ironhand, hoping it was laying
out of sight in a ditch or some weeds. He ordered Ironhand to stand up."

Sarah Slate swallowed and sipped her lemonade, as
if remembering an event from her own experience.

"He saw nothing. For minutes he saw nothing. Then
the earth moved. At first he was terrified that it was one
of the battlefield victims who had been declared dead

and hastily buried. But what he saw was a hand of steel that shot up from the ground.

"Someone else saw it, too. A German officer was hiding under cover nearby, and when he saw the metal hand emerging from the earth he ran onto the field of battle, scanning the night with his own telescope. He got a fix on Archibald Slate and began firing his rifle. Archibald was forced to retreat."

"Just so I'm clear on this," Remo said, "when the German guy runs out, he's not shooting at the robot hand that suddenly popped out of the ground?"

"Correct, Remo," Sarah said in her formal manner. "That German probably was the one who buried Ironhand, then stood watch over the area in case the Americans dared come back and try to take it. And that was the end of Ironhand, for Archibald Slate."

"But it wasn't the end at all," Remo said. "That German got him. And put him in the basement for ninety years and brought him out again."

"Yes," Sarah said. "But who?"

23

Chiun lay in the darkness and felt the past all around him—the memories of the house and the memories of a long-lived Master of Sinanju.

These Americans, he was convinced, allowed their old homes to acquire the patina of age because they possessed so little that was truly old, so little with the reverent nature of real history. But why did age have to be a dreary thing to these befuddled Americans?

This house was filled with ghosts and regret. He, Chiun, was not that kind of aged creature. Of course he had regrets, but he did not allow the sorrows to fester. This house seemed to breathe and creak and moan every moment of the dark night, as if in eternal mourning.

Chiun slept, on his mat on the hardwood floor. Remo's breathing across the room was boisterous and annoying, but Chiun had learned to live with it.

Then he awoke. Little time had gone by.

"Chiun? You awake?" Remo asked.

"A specter tapped me on the shoulder, Remo."

"I felt it, too. But it wasn't a spirit."

"It was what then?"

"Wait."

Then it came, a flutter. Remo was on his feet. "It's the same thing we felt in Barcelona," Remo declared.

"Yes. But this time it moves toward us. It has tracked us down."

"Don't think so. It's coming to find the same thing we're looking for."

Remo raced down the hall and pounded on the bedroom door of Sarah Slate, then floated to the main floor and into the cellar, where he knew Mark Howard would still be awake and at work. He found Mark standing in a sea of paper, row after row of it. He was in the midst of some large-scale organizational effort.

"Heads up, Junior, company's on the way."

"What? Who?"

"Who knows? Call Smitty and tell him to have reinforcements waiting."

"Reinforcements?"

"Hey, do you remember what happened in Spain? We got the shit kicked out of us. Whatever is coming closer to this house has got the same sort of energy-sucking beams pointed at us."

Sarah was waiting for him at the top of the stairs.

"Get in the car and get out of here," Remo ordered.

"No, thank you. I want to see it."

"I can't keep you safe."

"I wouldn't assume you could."

"Thanks for the vote of confidence. It's your funeral."

Sarah sighed, "That would be a fitting end."

"Oh, jeez, lady, get over it!"

THEY STOOD IN THE darkness of the large side yard, waiting for something to happen, while Sarah and Mark Howard played cribbage on a table in the large living room, the interior lights blazing in the night.

The feel of the bizarre, energy-robbing phenomena had ebbed and flowed menacingly but distantly, never quite growing to a painful level. Then it had stopped, and there was nothing for a while except the sounds of Providence.

Then Remo felt the shaking of the ground beneath his feet, and the shaking intensified and whatever made it came closer.

Something black came through the night, avoiding the lighted places, and stepped through the line of bushes that served as the property's back fence. It moved slowly, with extreme deliberation, but every step seemed to disturb the earth. Remo found his eyes trying to slide off the thing, and yet there was nothing translucent or invisible here. It was simply very, very black.

He heard and felt the well-oiled actuation of gears and chains and mechanical drives, reminding him of his fascination with the mechanics of a greasy old carousel from a charity carnival that once came to the orphanage that was his home as a boy. He also saw the glimmering electronics inside the black pits of its skull, and he felt the electronic eyes as they swept constantly in all directions, alert to threats.

But Ironhand didn't see the Masters of Sinanju in the darkness. It read their body heat, but the thermal signature was far outside any of the parameters it classified as human. It couldn't hear their breathing because they did not breathe.

When it stepped from the lawn to the patio stones,

there was a click of metal on rock, enough to awaken the exterior lighting. The twin porch lights blazed to life, a single steel arm smashed them out.

But the stealth paint must not have worked too well in full illumination, and in the second when the light was on they all saw Ironhand, clear as day.

It was a metal monster eight feet tall. Its heavy, chunky torso and limbs were of forged steel, constructed a century ago in a blacksmith's shop. Its head might have started out as a heavy-duty stovepipe, then augmented with welded accouterments such as a hard-forged mouth and heavy-steel eye reinforcements. Ironhand walked on massive steel feet that were center hinged. At every exposed joint Remo glimpsed black-painted copper coils and clusters of electronics that were definitely not original equipment in 1904.

Mark and Sarah jumped to their feet and Sarah came to the twin French doors onto the patio. She opened them, stood in front of the thing.

"Ironhand."

Remo really hoped the thing didn't answer, "Hello is all right." Instead it said, "Yes, Slate."

"Who is running you, Ironhand?"

"Archibald Slate III."

"Liar!"

Ironhand turned away from Sarah Slate, casting its eye-mounted visual sensors over the lawn. It scanned left to right, clicked something in its skull and scanned right to left, then completed its 360-degree turn to face Sarah.

"Archibald Slate III requires documentation from Archibald Slate I." He spoke in a synthetic, clipped voice, but with a German accent.

"You lie."

"Ironhand is incapable of lying."

"You're just a computer, aren't you, Ironhand? I know computers aren't supposed to be able to tell an untruth and I know that is bullshit. A computer does what it is programmed to do. You're programmed to say lies."

"Give me documents of Archibald Slate."

"No."

Remo moved fast as Ironhand raised its arm. He wondered if Ironhand was outfitted with the same sort of firepower as Mr. U. Not that it mattered, since any sort of gunfire from such close range was going to be a killer.

He floated over the lawn and brought his fist down hard on the arm, finding its weak spot and breaking it open in one flash of movement.

Ironhand sensed the attack in a microsecond and turned on Remo, intending to crush with a savage blow of the arm it now understood to be damaged.

Chiun floated out of the night and caught Ironhand off guard again, befuddling its sensors, and the old Korean probed the gaping eye socket, yanking out components.

Ironhand swung at Chiun, found nothing, searched until it found any anomalous heat signature, and triggered.

Remo saw the barbed fork come at him in a halo of crackling blue electricity and stepped aside effortlessly.

Sarah Slate screamed and Ironhand spun to face her. Remo didn't know what was in those electric barbecue forks exactly, but it couldn't be good. He couldn't let Sarah get fried.

"Hey, Robby! This way!" He waved his arms, and

Ironhand spun back at him, fired again, and Remo stepped aside. The projectile was like three wicked barbed daggers welded together at the base and electrified until they trailed static lightning. The air burned from their passage.

Before he could strike again, Ironhand began the rapid recharge of its electrical system. There was a tiny whir of the generator.

Remo crashed to the earth as if he'd been hit with a big truck.

IT WASN'T ELECTRICITY. It was just the opposite for Remo Williams. Instead of being jolted with current, the life energy was suddenly sucked out of him, so hard and fast he didn't have time to think. He just went limp.

Ironhand thrust one arm directly at Remo Williams and triggered another forkful of voltage.

But just as rapidly as he was drained of power, Remo felt it surge back—partially. He twisted and heard the thunk of the trident imbedding in dirt just inches from his shoulder. Remo was already launching himself off the ground and lashing out with one far-reaching leg.

The mechanical man shifted to ward off Remo, wisely using its nonfunctional hand to absorb the damage, and Remo's foot slammed through it hard enough to tear the steel plates around the rivets. The arm slammed across Ironhand's chest, then dangled from its shoulder socket by a few steel tendons.

Remo stepped up close, detached the arm with a yank, then melted away as another trident sizzled the air above him.

Where the hell was Chiun?

Remo collapsed again, hard, as Ironhand recharged

its systems. The paralyzing weakness passed in a heart-beat, and Remo found himself staring at another bolt, aiming at his head. He tossed the separated arm, which deflected the trident with a shower of sparks. When the arm thumped to the earth, it was stained with black scoring.

"Aaeei, trash can!" Chiun danced in front of Iron-hand, making a garish spectacle that even a robot would be distracted by, and Remo took advantage of it. He floated in.

Ironhand was unbelievably fast, but no discarded pile of factory equipment was faster than a Master of Sinanju. Remo cracked the good arm at its shoulder joint before it could fire. Ironhand spun with the attack, but its reaction time was a fraction too slow to save the arm. Remo hung on, Ironhand gyrated with a wild singing of servomotors, and the arm came off in an uncontrolled flash of blue lightning.

Ironhand's systems would never need to discharge the power burst again, not without a firing mechanism, but the systems automatically began the generator anyway. Remo slammed to the ground and saw Chiun wilt and collapse.

It was like being dead, just for a moment, and each of those moments felt endless. But the moment faded and Remo pushed himself to his feet, vaulted to the robot, forced himself to clamber up the steel monster despite the lethargy in his limbs. Remo stood on its steel shoulders, easily keeping his balance regardless how Ironhand spun in both directions.

"You'll never shake me, hunk of junk," Remo said. Then he kicked Ironhand in the face, blow after blow, listening to the parts inside snap and crunch. Ironhand plodded across the yard, slammed through the shrubbery and careened into the street.

"Your rock-'em-sock-'em days are over," Remo panted, his legs like lead. His nerves felt singed. Ironhand was gaining speed on the street, every step like the crunch of a dropped wrecking ball.

"Hey, Nick Chopper, give it up," Remo said, and his next kick nodded the massive head back. Remo found himself staring down into the cold, electric eyes of the robot. Ironhand never slowed as its rampage carried it into a parked car. Remo jumped lightly just before the impact, which collapsed the door of a Ford sedan all the way through the driver's half of the interior.

The armless robot lurched into the street and tried to make its head work, but the motors hummed in vain.

Remo, dangling from a nearby tree, stepped back on the thing's shoulders and stared down into its cold face.

"Not a scratch on you. I bet you get good crash-test safety ratings. But now it's recycling time."

Remo slipped his fingers under the rim of the steel neck, felt for the weakness in the metal and pulled, but Ironhand put on a burst of speed, veered off the road and crashed through a wooden fence. There was nothing underneath it for almost seventy feet.

Remo stepped back onto solid ground as easily as if he were stepping off an escalator, while Ironhand did what would normally be expected of a ton of steel that had just gone off a cliff edge.

Remo blinked, squinted, trying to make his eyes see in the blackness. His breathing was still labored and his faculties remained diminished. The crash, though, should have been louder.

It wasn't so much a cliff he was standing on as a

steep hillside, and below was a mass of vegetation. The path of ruin showed where Ironhand went through it.

Remo didn't take his eyes off the overgrowth, even when he heard Chiun approach behind him. "My son, are you injured?"

"Just catching my breath, Little Father. You okay?"

"Yes," Chiun answered shortly, and Remo knew well enough that it wasn't the truth. He could hear Chiun's heart beating too quickly and he could sense Chiun willing himself to control it.

"Personally, I feel like hell," Remo said. "Whatever this shit is, it's bad shit."

"I know whatever this shit is," Chiun said.

"You do?" Remo wanted to ask more, but at that moment a squad car careened into view, roared in their direction and screeched to a halt.

"Let us go," Chiun said.

"I have to go down there."

"You are too weak," Chiun insisted. "As am I."

Remo wouldn't drag his eyes away from the place below him, even when the pair of Providence cops ambled up.

"Hey, buddy, you the driver?"

"No," Remo said.

"Hey, buddy, you want to look at me when I'm talking to you?"

"It wasn't a car."

"Motorcycle?"

"Not a motorcycle," said the second cop. "You saw what happened to that Ford up the street."

"Big Harley maybe," said the first cop. "What was it, buddy?"

"Robot."

"Hoo-kay, buddy, you want to step away from the edge there? We'll have a little chat."

Remo knew precisely where they were, so when he reached behind him with both hands he grabbed them exactly where he wanted to grab, not an inch too low.

The police officers found themselves hanging by the belt buckle over the edge of the big hillside along North High Street.

"Shut up or I drop you," Remo informed them. "Now watch." Remo tossed both of them into a 180-degree spin and grabbed them again, this time by the belt in back. They were now facedown.

"Look," Remo said. "Tell me what you see."

The cops craned their necks and went rigid when they saw the thing that walked out of the weeds. It was armless, head skewed as if its spine was broken, but it was huge, glimmering with sparks of electricity, and the metallic clomp of its footsteps was like barbells crashing in a noisy gym.

"See that?" Remo demanded.

"We see it!"

Remo replaced them on solid ground, never taking his eyes off the robot.

"Was it Terminator?" one of them asked in a quaver.

"More or less," Remo replied.

"Will he be back?"

Remo stopped and met Chiun's eyes. The cops had never even seen the old man standing in the darkness. Chiun looked, what—sapped?

"Yeah," Remo said, feeling tired, too. "He'll be back."

Then Remo saw Ironhand's friend pushing through

undergrowth but didn't quite believe what his eyes were telling him. "You gotta be effing kidding me."

"What is it?"

Remo turned as if noticing the cops for the first time. "Hey, when you were kids did you guys get the 'Space Monkey Cartoon Roundup' show out of Jersey?"

The first cop was suspicious about where this was headed, and being hung by the crotch was insulting to his dignity. "Yeah. So what?"

"I loved that show when I was a boy," enthused the second cop.

"You remember the robot on that show?"

"Yeah," said the second cop. "So?"

"I remember!" the other cop said. "He was big and round, right? With a round head?"

"And sorta faggy for a robot," the first cop added.

"Would you know him again if you saw him? Because there he is."

"Really? Let me see!" The enthusiastic cop squinted downhill. "Oh, Stan, it's him! It's Clockwork the Robot!"

"You're nuts, Charlie." Stan looked hard. "It c-can't be!"

Remo said, "Sure looks like Clockwork to me."

"But that was years and years ago," Cop Stan said.

"Somebody just kept him around, Stan, and now he's alive again!" Charlie answered excitedly.

Clockwork was indeed a big round ball of patina-aged copper, more than a yard in diameter. Its tubular metallic arms were set in ball joints at the shoulder and elbow. On a tubular neck perched another round ball, the size of a soccer ball but also made of copper, green with age, with bright spots where the patina was scratched. On its head was Clockwork's signature tin bowler.

"His hat! His hat! He still has his hat!" Charlie exclaimed.

"But I never knew he had treads for feet," Stan said. "On the 'Space Monkey Cartoon Roundup' they never showed Clockwork below the waist."

As the armless, limping form of Ironhand emerged from the weeds Clockwork rolled on steel treads to flank it, escorting it across the street.

"Is that other guy the robot from *Destination: Earth?*" Stan asked.

"Are you thinking of *The Day the Earth Stood Still?*" Charlie asked.

"Nah, that one was all smooth and shiny. This is kinda like a life-size battle bot."

"Without the arms," Charlie said.

"Yeah, well, whoever he is, he's a lot less fruity than Clockwork. Remember Clockwork used to always get knocked over by that mean orange monkey and then he couldn't get back up?"

That was when the headlights appeared. Ironhand continued across the street as Clockwork paused on its treads and rotated on the pedestal that attached them. Its arms raised defensively.

"He's gonna get turtled by a Corolla!" Stan taunted.

Remo didn't think so. He thought he should get down there and help the occupants of the honking Corolla, but his knees were rubber.

The Corolla driver never really stopped. He slowed to a mile-per-hour roll and kept honking. Whatever he thought he was seeing, he didn't believe it was really a big dopey spherical robot on treads.

When he came within five feet of Clockwork, the arms lowered just enough, then the fat-fingered hands dropped off the wrists on hinges and dangled. Each wrist expelled a flash of light and the sound followed a fraction of a second later.

"Guess Clockwork's grown a thicker skin over the years," Remo commented.

"Jesus, that sounded like shotgun rounds!" Stan blurted as the Corolla's front tires went flat. The driver's door opened and a man tumbled out, scrambled to his feet and fled back the way he had come. Clockwork raised an arm and triggered at the runner's back, but the Corolla absorbed most of the buckshot. The fleeing man grabbed the back of his head where he'd caught a few rounds of buckshot. "Yeow!" he yelped as he ran out of sight.

"Call it in!" Stan shouted, and emptied two rounds from his revolver in the direction of Clockwork.

"How could you miss?" Remo asked.

"What are you doing?" Charlie cried. "You'll hurt him!"

"He just tried to kill somebody!" Stan replied.

Remo grabbed them both and pushed them to the earth just in time. Clockwork emptied both barrels up the hill at them. The buckshot that would have imbedded in their flesh sliced into the trees above them and tore at the leaves.

"Oh, Clockwork," moaned Charlie miserably as bits of green confetti adhered to his teary cheeks.

Remo watched Clockwork roll into the vegetation beyond the road, following Ironhand.

"I think you guys can take it from here."

Stan watched Remo for a moment, observed that he

didn't get a face full of buckshot, then slowly raised his head from the ground. He looked down the hillside, got to his knees slowly, then cautiously stood.

"He's gone. Call it in, Charlie."

"Who would do such a thing, Stan? They took out his heart and made him a monster!"

"There's bad men in this world, Charlie," Stan said gently, patting his partner's thinning comb-over. "I'll call it in myself."

He reached dispatch and reported a shooting and an escaped gunman. He wisely reported it as a "costumed" gunner. Let the Corolla driver make the eyewitness identification on the shooter. Only after he over-and-outed did Stan realized the man who had just saved their faces from being bloodied was gone.

Did he have anything to do with these goings on?

For that matter, what in Hades *was* going on?

24

"Don't touch it!"

Sarah Slate glared at him. "Why?"

Mark Howard had a leaf rake from the toolshed and used it to turn over the blackened metal arm. Sparks shot out of the severed shoulder end and the fingers twitched. Sarah was startled again and she jumped against Mark.

"How'd you know? I could have been electrocuted."

Mark was trying to keep his mind on the situation, but there was this young lady clinging to his arm. "I doubt there's enough of a charge in there to kill you, but it might have knocked you off your feet."

Sarah got over her fright, at least enough to put some space between them. "Grandfather Archibald didn't put batteries in Ironhand's arm," she insisted.

"I think there've been some updates to the Archibald Slate design," Mark said. They bent over the arm, a stark, ugly thing in the patio light, and Sarah frowned.

"Look at these bolts," she said.

Mark looked at the five steel bolts that had been holding the arm to the socket. The bolts gleamed, shiny and new.

"The bolts held," she added.

"Yes?"

"Mark, that means the steel had to rip in order for this arm to come off."

Mark had nothing to say about that.

"Well?"

"Well?" he asked lamely.

"Don't play dumb with me, please. Your friend Remo tore through steel plates in order to get this arm off."

"Probably old steel. You know, corroded."

"I am not stupid, Mark."

"No."

"What I saw happen here was quite out of the ordinary," she added.

"Yes."

"I'm not talking about Ironhand. I don't know where he came from, but modern technology can explain what Ironhand did today. Nothing I know of can explain what your friend Remo did."

"No?" Mark was furiously trying to conjure an answer. Sarah waited a moment, then looked away, sighing dismissively. Mark Howard felt crestfallen, but now was not the time to worry about it. "I need a container," he said urgently. "Wooden or plastic, something nonconductive to carry the arm. Two of them, in fact. The other one is around somewhere."

"What's the hurry?"

Her answer came around the corner in a flashing of lights. The squad car was gone in seconds, somehow failing to notice the broken fence.

"They'll be back soon," Mark said.

Sarah nodded and went inside. Mark watched the arm twitch a few more times.

Then his ankle was crushed.

He sucked in his breath and forced himself to take steps. He was a fool! He should have expected...

He collapsed, his upper body landing on the patio bricks, but his CIA training kicked in and he took the fall with a judo roll. He ended up on his back, staring at the second arm of Ironhand, which was clenched like a vise on his ankle with intense pressure. The pain was incredible, but he couldn't afford to surrender to it.

Sarah emerged from the back door and shouted his name.

"Sledgehammer!" Mark gasped.

She flung down the plastic box and ran to the shed. Mark Howard wanted to scream as the pain reached his endurance threshold...

Sarah Slate didn't have a sledgehammer, but in her hands was a wood-chopping ax that looked just as powerful. The heavy steel head had to weigh ten pounds, and she brought the back end down on the steel elbow joint. Sparks flashed out of the shoulder socket.

Mark Howard felt the fingers tighten and experienced the nauseating sensation of his ankle bone being crushed.

"Don't stop!" he shouted.

"It'll break your leg," she protested.

"Do it! Fast!" Mark Howard pointed, and Sarah Slate glanced into the yard. The second hand was crawling over the lawn, coming at them.

"Oh, God," she uttered, then she set about her business with a fierce expression, bashing hard on the first arm. Two times, three times, ignoring Mark Howard's agony.

The hand released but it looked undamaged as it clawed toward the woman like a fast-moving spider.

"Sarah!" Mark gasped, and made a lunge but failed to grab the thing in his bare hands.

Sarah Slate cocked her head, raised her ax and brought down the blade between the fingers, splitting the steel hand like firewood.

The fingers continued to function, pushing the hand backward. Sarah swung the blade up and around in a wide circle, hit the arm at the wrist, sending it tumbling into the grass.

The second burned hand was damaged, but with three functional fingers it scampered onto the patio and dragged noisily along the bricks. While the second hand hurried up in close pursuit.

Mark Howard forced away the pain of his ankle and looked for a weapon, reaching for the small stack of bricks next to the back step. They were old cobblestones, the corners worn smooth, but they just might work. He witnessed Sarah bash the blackened arm away with her ax, but the other arm slithered around her feet and came fast at Mark Howard as if it had acquired a taste for his blood. This time, it went for the gut.

If it got a good grip on his abdomen and applied crushing force, it could do a hell of a lot more than just break a bone. It could cause massive internal damage—irreparable internal damage.

"Hands off!" Mark said angrily, and brought down his cobblestone brick, flattening the hand just a foot away from his body. The fingers curled up under it again and clawed forward. Mark Howard began bashing the fingers hard and fast, unleashing his anger, cursing with every breath, and his fury seemed unending.

Finally a small, slim, flesh-and-bone hand gripped his arm midstrike.

"I think that's enough," Sarah said.

Mark looked at her, the vivid scarlet of his rage fading until it was just her beautiful face he saw. Then he looked at the hand in front of him. The fingers were flat, like soda cans smashed on the highway.

"Where's the other one?" he gasped.

"Right here." She gestured at the plastic box. Inside was the slowly moving hand and arm. Its five fingers had been amputated with the ax and tossed in after it.

"Are you hurt?" Mark Howard said.

"Not a scratch," Sarah said with a smile.

Such a flood of relief rushed through him he almost wept, and the tension left his body. He went limp into Sarah Slate's arms.

The young woman took a minute to realize he was unconscious, and it took her a moment to understand what he had said before he passed out. Something like, "Thank God in heaven."

Despite everything that had happened to her on this day, she felt peaceful for a moment. She gently stroked Mark Howard's damp face.

25

Remo Williams pressed the 1 button until he heard it ringing.

"Hi, who's this?" answered an eager man in a controlled Southern twang.

"Give me Smith and give 'im to me now."

"I'm Bill. Won't I do?"

"I want Smitty."

"I think you got the wrong numbers, but that's okay. Come on over and let's party. Bring some babes."

Remo wasn't in the mood for this. Harold W. Smith had installed a computerized system designed to weed out the flurry of calls he was receiving on the specialized call-transfer system used by his enforcement arm in the field. Unfortunately, this required that Remo spend the first minute of every phone call conversing with some stranger. The voice was supposedly computer generated, but Remo had begun wondering if it really was.

"Smitty, get on the line now."

"See, nobody cares about poor old Bill anymore," said the man on the other end. "I'm old news. Even my wife pretends I don't exist."

"Smitty, in two seconds I'm calling the Associated Press."

"Aw, come on—"

The voice was interrupted by Harold Smith. "Remo, what's the problem?"

"We don't have time to go over the list," Remo said. "Mark is wounded."

"What? How seriously?"

Remo calmed himself, but it wasn't easy. His relationship with Smith had been getting sour in recent months. Remo couldn't put a finger on why exactly. "Mark has a hurt ankle. The bone isn't broken but it's definitely been bruised. Lots of soft-tissue damage. Chiun's fixing him up."

"What happened? Give me a report."

"Okay, Smitty, the big man himself showed up here at the Slate house. Ironhand. In the flesh. He had the same sort of death-rays or whatever it was that we ran into in Spain. He fried our circuits." Remo quickly briefed Smith on the series of events that ended with Remo and Chiun returning to the Slate house and finding Mark Howard laid out on a sofa, soaking the upholstery with his lifeblood.

"Chiun's figured out what it is that is doing this to us," Remo said finally. "We've run into something similar before."

"Tell me," Smith said.

"Remember those nutcases in Berkley, California, who had the big proton phazer-firer inside the statue?"

Smith took a few seconds to decipher the explanation. "The old Soviet weapon. It gathered and expelled protons in a particle beam."

"Yeah, whatever. It's the side effect that was unhealthy for Chiun and me. Normals don't feel it, but it screws with the enhanced Sinanju nervous system. That's what was explained to me, anyway. What we're running into now is almost the same thing."

"Remo, we tracked the history of the Soviet technology. It was believed to have been closely guarded. We never saw evidence of a leak of the data. It seems unlikely someone else got access to it."

"Is there anybody else there I could talk to? Somebody with brains maybe? No? I guess I'll have to explain it to you, Smitty. They used to have this old style of government over there called communism. Look it up in the dictionary and it says '*see corruption.*'"

"I know about communism…"

"Then stop asking stupid questions. The commies *always* took the low road and the new Russia hasn't cleaned up the old act, so *of course* somebody tried to sell the plans at one time or another. And maybe this wasn't even from the Russian plans. Maybe somebody developed it on their own."

"That's not likely."

Remo felt as if steam was about to shoot out his ears. "I just got the crap kicked out of me by a pile of scrap metal older than you. How likely is that?"

"All right. Let's explore that possibility. What makes you think this may be independently developed technology, Remo?"

"Try to be a little more condescending, would you? They're not using it as a weapon. If they knew how to turn it into a weapon, they'd use it as a weapon, don't you think? But whoever invented it this time sees it as a power source for the generators inside their animatronics. They're using it as a way of creating rapid fuel-cell charging or some such. In Spain they had all the robots plugged into it, so the bad feeling went away when the charging stopped. Ironhand was not like that. He had this little doohickey inside of him and whenever he needed to rev up his little shock-shooter, he'd start the power charger and send our nerves into underload."

"I see." Remo heard a flutter of keystrokes on the either end of the line, then Smith said, "Remo, I am initiating a search for this type of technology."

Remo was relieved that Smith was at least taking him seriously. "You had better believe it. Whoever is retrofitting the droids has pretty nearly wiped us out accidentally. What do you think is going to happen if they figure out how to use it against us deliberately?"

"Yes. That is a real danger."

Smith quickly arranged for their transportation back to Folcroft. "I want Mark under the care of our doctors, and I want him available to assist me as soon as he is well enough."

"Smitty, we have got to squash this thing. If it got loose, it could be bad news."

"I understand, Remo."

Remo hung up the phone, knowing that Harold W. Smith did not understand at all.

He went upstairs to check on Mark Howard, and on Chiun.

26

At the front of the aircraft Mark Howard was reclined, sipping water and being cared for by Ms. Sarah Slate. Chiun pursed his mouth as he watched them.

"He's feeling no pain," Remo said.

"He's besotted and it clouds his judgment," Chiun said. "The emperor will be angry to find the Slate woman accompanies us."

"He'll get over it."

"The young prince will suffer Smith's disfavor for this rash action," Chiun added.

"Mark had no choice in the matter. I told him I'd lobotomize him if he made a fuss."

"That is a lie."

Remo sighed. "Hey, Junior," he called up to the front of the aircraft, "you better not give me any shit or I'll remove your frontal lobe."

"Huh?"

"Just watch yourself."

Mark shrugged to Sarah.

"There," Remo said to Chiun. "Now it's true."

Chiun faced out the window, his eye on the wing.

"Chiun, how do you feel?"

"Irritated."

"You know what I mean."

Chiun concentrated on the wing.

"Hey, old man, I asked you a question."

The Master of Sinanju Emeritus turned on Remo Williams with fire in his eyes, but Remo Williams didn't let him speak. "Listen to me, Chiun, dammit. I know what that neural disruption stuff did to me and I remember what happened when we were in Berkley. We nearly got our nerves fried."

"I remember," Chiun said testily.

"Do you remember that I had to get Anna Chutesov's help to drag you out of the room?"

Chiun colored, his green eyes flashing like an angry child's eyes. "Do you have a reason for insulting me or is this simply your form of in-flight entertainment?"

"What do you think? You are old, Chiun. It's stupid to dance around it."

"I am in full possession of my faculties!"

"I didn't say you were infirm. You're a Master of Sinanju in your prime. But you are not as strong as I am, and I almost got my brain drained today. The only reason you survived is because you kept your distance."

"Now you label me a coward?" Chiun hissed, but without conviction.

"I am saying you were smart enough not to walking into a fight you could not win," Remo said. "Chiun…"

"Yes?" Chiun demanded, his curiosity evident.

"Chiun," Remo said at last, "whatever this is, it is not a rock."

Chiun's face clouded, then he understood, and he hissed like a snake.

27

The President of the United States of America had a killer headache. It wasn't about to get any better and he knew it. He was watching the clock on the small display on his desk telephone, a small titanium device supplied by the Department of Defense and said to be bug proof and EM-blast proof. The phone clock was synchronized automatically by the U.S. Navy's atomic clock, which was said to be the global standard for time-keeping. The President didn't know why the fighting folks needed a clock that was that precise and he didn't want to ask. He hated having technology explained to him. He wasn't stupid, but he had a hard time listening to techno-rambling or electro-babble or whatever they called that kind of talk.

He was about to get an earful of it and he was not looking forward to it.

The whizzing hundredths of a second closed in on the top of the hour. When the time came he would get a phone call. The call would not be late. The President would be mildly disappointed if the call was late.

At 08:59:57:96 the phone rang and the President

was startled, which was silly—it wasn't as if the caller was sitting there staring at the atomic clock. Was he? The caller was just maniacally punctual. Right?

He grabbed the phone. Not the titanium one, but the bright red one with the dedicated line.

"Good morning, Mr. Smith."

"Mr. President," Smith replied.

"How is everything out your way?"

"Our enforcement arm has arrived on-site with the ill-advised accompaniment of the victim of the attack. She will be contained. The threat to my assistant and my enforcement arm remains…"

"I wasn't asking for a debriefing, Smith," the President growled. "I was saying hello."

There was a wait, then Smith said, "I see. Hello, Mr. President."

The President should have known it was a waste of time to try to engage the head of CURE in small talk. But the President thought of himself as a people person, a down-to-earth man, who liked to get to know human beings on a personal level. The whole official side of being President was just a little too dry, too official. What was the harm in loosening things up a little?

But not with Smith. Never with Smith.

"Okay, then, give me the debriefing."

"Yes, sir," Smith said with respect but without a hint of deprecation. "As you know, the recent technology thefts from our military operations have severely undermined our superiority in military security and offensive automation systems."

"Not yet they haven't," the President corrected him. "Only if the blueprints are distributed."

"Most of the systems will be distributed in the form of CAD files. That's Computer-Aided Design."

"I know what CAD means."

"CAD files can be sent electronically. In all likelihood, the party that has come into possession of those files will have stored encrypted copies in multiple sites around the world. Retrieving them all successfully would be highly unlikely, even if we apprehended the perpetrator and received his cooperation."

"But it could happen," the President said, yanking the desk drawer open and finding it entirely empty. Would it hurt to keep a bottle of Tylenol in the Oval Office?

"Regardless, it would be foolish to have confidence that we had, in fact, retrieved all copies. Servers of all types automatically duplicated their stored data remotely, for replacement in case of catastrophic failure such as fire or flood. Those copies sit on servers that might then make remote copies. At any point in the process, data mining software of various benign and malicious types can channel the data elsewhere for other uses."

"All right, Smith."

"I think it is safe to say that, at the moment that the data escaped our control, we could never again expect to have it fully under our control."

"Yes. Yes. Hold on."

The President stabbed a button on the titanium phone, but he squeezed his eyes shut at that moment. He hit the wrong button. It wasn't his office assistant who answered.

"Yes, Mr. President?" said an alarmed British man.

"Ah, I'm sorry, Mr. Prime Minister. Hit the wrong button."

There was an exasperated sigh. "Again?"

"I said I was sorry."

"You know my popularity in the polls goes down every time I even talk to you on the phone."

"Isn't this a secure line?"

"Oh, they know. Somehow they know," the Prime Minister said, low and full of suspicion. "Don't you call here anymore."

The President heard a click. He punched the phone again. The correct button this time. After his assistant brought him a couple of Extra Strength Tylenol he got back on the line with Smith.

Smith was still there, which was a mild surprise. He continued. "The Department of Defense has transferred most of their highly sensitive systems to new locations as a precautionary measure. They have not moved the Full-spectrum Environmental Monitoring Robots, however."

"Yes, well, the system is designed for the White House. Moving it would be the same things as shutting it down."

"That's not a bad idea."

"Wrong. It's a defensive system, Smith. It is designed to keep intruders out, even if the intruders are there to take the system itself."

"Not these intruders. Remember, they have assimilated some of the great achievements in stealth technology we developed ourselves. There has not been time to reconfigure the White House defenses to accommodate those technologies. Also, the intruders will likely be deposited into the White House from the air. The Full-spectrum Robots don't cover the airspace over the White House."

"We've got lots of security that does, however."

"You also have a spy in the highest levels of military security."

The President forgot his headache. "Say again?"

"A spy."

"Who?"

"I don't know. But it is the only explanation for the events in recent weeks. The intelligence needed to stage the various threats came from multiple sources. Their only communality came in their being reported to the highest levels of military and intelligence command. Possibly they gleaned some intelligence on CURE through whatever source they have."

"But I'm the only source of intelligence on CURE," the President complained. "Are you saying I may be bugged?"

"No, Mr. President. You have never possessed some of the intelligence the thieves have had on security measures around the research sites. It's someone closer to the research. One of the Joint Chiefs, perhaps."

"What?"

"It might be the secretary of defense."

"Are you *kidding* me?"

"It could even be the secretary of homeland security."

"Smith, you're way out in left field. I know those men. I respect those men, even if I disagree with some of their political views. They are loyal Americans."

"I think one of them is not." Message delivered, Smith returned to the unresolved issue. "Do you intend to order the dismantling of the Full-spectrum Environmental Monitoring system at the White House?"

"No. I see no need. Is there anything else, Smith?"

"Perhaps it would be best, then, if my enforcement arm performed security watch on the White House, at least until I have another course of investigation."

"Sure. Fine. Send them on up. They won't get half-way across the lawn."

Then the President hung up on Smith. For a change. He frowned at the red phone, then put it away. He had become too defensive, but Smith had stepped over the line.

On the other hand, Smith was usually, annoyingly, right.

Maybe it would be better to have Smith's muscle on hand, just to keep an eye on things.

The President grabbed his titanium desk phone.

"Sandra? Get me the man in charge of the U.S. atomic clock. No, I'll hold."

It took surprisingly little time to find him.

"Yes, Mr. President?" answered the secretary of the navy.

"Ronald, your clock's slow."

The head of the U.S. Navy said, "Who told you this, sir?"

"Is it true?"

"Well, yes. I just got the communiqué myself. There was a malfunction in the processor that coordinates the synchronization. But it is just a few seconds from true."

"Fix it."

"We'll have it right in minutes, Mr. President. My understanding is that the master synchronizing clock…"

"Not another word, General. Just fix it."

"But how did you know, Mr. President?"

"Guess I just know some folks with a better clock, General," said the President.

The general chuckled nervously. "With all due respect, sir, there is no better clock. The Navy's hydrogen maser and cesium chronometers are the most precise—"

But he was talking to himself.

28

Jacob Fastbinder III stepped out of the front door carefully, taking the first big step as if his leg was not trustworthy. When he was on solid ground he turned and locked the door behind him. The house was a low concrete structure that was actually half submerged in the desert soil. The concrete walls were three feet thick, the roof almost as thick, designed to keep the structure cool when it had served as a produce distribution plant in the late 1960s. A chiller, which once kept the warehouse refrigerated, was just so much collapsed, corroded wreckage alongside it.

"That's Fastbinder?" asked the attorney.

"That's him," said museum manager Margo.

"That guy looks old. I thought Fastbinder was in his fifties."

Margo shrugged and chewed her gum. The attorney watched the bent man for another few minutes, then asked, "They have an air-conditioner in that place?"

"Don't think so. Know what it would take to keep that place cool? It's big as a mansion!"

The attorney gave her a doubtful look. "I'll bet it smells like a sewer."

Margo lost her friendliness. "You're being unpleasant."

"Well, I am an attorney."

"Yuck." Margo left, no longer feeling obliged to be sociable. Attorneys, after all, weren't people.

The attorney had no use for these back-road weirdos. He, for one, got no kicks from Route 66, and had not enjoyed his drive on it. Even the Town Car he rented in Tucumcari couldn't seem to pump out enough air-conditioning to combat the searing heat of New Mexico. The doddering old Fastbinder wasn't even halfway to the museum yet.

"Holy shit, how long is this gonna take?" he said.

There was a gasp of horror and an eight-year-old girl in braces and pigtails pointed a stiff finger in his direction. "Mommy, did you hear what this man said? He said the *S* word, Mommy!"

A sweat-drenched pantsuit with a rotund, middle-aged woman inside it came at him fast. He thought she might tackle him. "What kind of a man are you, saying words like that in front of a little girl? Where is your decency? Where is your respect for human beings? It's sick and disgusting."

"Mommy, he said a bad word! He said it. I heard him. He said it!" The girl was sobbing and dancing. "I heard it, Mommy!"

"What happened?" Margo said, arriving to investigate the mayhem. She skewed the suited man with a look. "What did you do to this little girl?"

"He said the *S* word!" the girl wailed.

"You did *what*?"

"Right here in the gift shop!" the girl's mother whined. "What kind a man does that?"

"He's no man," Margo sneered. "He's an attorney."

The eight-year-old girl screeched and panicked, thrashing her limbs mindlessly, knocking over a rack of New Mexico State Bird postcards, which in turn toppled a wire stand holding hundreds of New Mexico shot glasses. The girl curled up behind a display of vinyl Indian moccasins wailing, "He's gonna sue me! Please don't let him sue me!"

The next thing he knew, the attorney was being manhandled out the front of the museum and gift shop. He didn't fight it. It was too hot and Margo was too powerful. But he had never been so humiliated in his entire life. He waited in front of his Town Car.

Damn, he hated this son of a bitch Fastbinder. Couldn't the son of a bitch walk any damn faster?

"Goot evening," said Jacob Fastbinder III in his pronounced German accent, putting on a crooked, wrinkled smile. "You are zee attorney, ya?"

"Yes, sir, Mr. Fastbinder. I'm here on business from the board of directors."

"Oh, ya." Fastbinder laughed. "The board is certainly having these days some troubles!"

"Yes," the attorney answered dryly.

"Maybe they will go into bankruptcy soon, ya?" Fastbinder laughed more heartily.

"We're talking to our creditors," the attorney said defensively. "Some are willing to negotiate."

"I know you jab at me. I will never negotiate. But maybe I will buy back zee company, when the price hits rock bottom!" More laughter.

The attorney smoldered as he removed the envelope and handed it to Fastbinder. "I doubt you could afford it, Mr. Fastbinder. Even in bankruptcy, the company has assets worth…"

Fastbinder opened the envelope and displayed the check to the attorney. The attorney swallowed.

"Not worth more than that." Fastbinder chuckled. "And I get one like this every six months."

"No wonder the firm's going bankrupt," the attorney said. "How'd you manage to get a severance like that?"

"I outlawyered the lawyers! It was easy, once I realized that lawyers are filthy pigs who are helpless away from the slop trough. They thought I was insipid when I wanted half the profits from my U.S. controls group patents. They thought the group was a dinosaur that would fold up in no time."

"And now it's the only profitable business unit," the attorney concluded, stunned. "How could those people have been so short-sighted?"

"Not people, lawyers," Fastbinder said gleefully.

Margo appeared, her Keds crunching on the pea gravel parking lot. She whispered to Fastbinder, shooting glares at the lawyer, then raised her chin high as she strode back into the museum and gift shop.

"I hear there has been troubles. You must pay for the damages, please."

The attorney opened his mouth, closed it again, opened it again. "You have got to be kidding me."

"I am not." Fastbinder stopped smiling. "My manager says we suffered a loss of forty-two post cards of zee cartoon mosquitoes and thirteen shot glass. The post cards are seventy-nine cents each or three for two dollars, so that comes to fourteen dollars. The shot glasses are $3.25 each with no quantity discount. So the total owed is $56.25."

"You have to be out of your mind."

Fastbinder shrugged.

"First of all, I didn't break the cheap tourist crap. The idiot kid broke it."

"My Margo says it was you who caused it."

"Your Margo is an obese idiot. Secondly, you probably buy that junk for pennies."

Fastbinder shrugged. "True. The postcards cost me eight cents each in boxes of a thousand. The shot glasses are thirty-nine cents each wholesale in two-hundred-unit lots. However, if you will read zee disclaimers posted in zee store it says, 'You Break It, You Bought It.' It does not say, you 'Break It, You Will Be Charged Zee Wholesale Price For It.'"

The attorney was stunned. "You know what, Fastbinder, I wouldn't pay you fifty-six dollars and twenty-five cents if it would save my life. I've had enough of you desert freaks."

"Yes. I see. Good day." Fastbinder strolled to his gift shop and the multimillion-dollar check fluttered out of his hands.

"Hey! Your check!" The attorney raced to grab it, then ran huffing after Fastbinder. "I need a receipt for this!"

Fastbinder stopped on the wooden front porch of the Museum of Mechanical Marvels and Gift Shop. "No, thank you."

"You gotta take it!"

"I'll take it after you pay what is owed."

"It's worth millions!"

Fastbinder made a haughty shrug.

"I told you I am not paying for the postcards!" the attorney sputtered.

"Come back when you have changed your mind."

The attorney knew he couldn't go back to the law

firm without a signed receipt for the check. He'd be out of the firm. So he swallowed his pride—his last tiny morsel of pride, as it turned out—and went inside to pay the $56.25.

"You should also say 'I'm sorry' to Margo," Fastbinder suggested.

The attorney apologized to Margo the museum manager, and then Fastbinder took the check.

By the time he returned to the law firm in New York, the attorney had convinced himself that he should return to prostitution, the career that got him through law school. Being sodomized by old men was unpleasant, sure, but it was less degrading. Plus, he had made some great contacts in business and government during six years of practicing law—he knew senators, CEOs, lobbyists, hundreds of well-to-do potential customers. He'd make a lot more than he ever did while attending Harvard.

A classy man-whore with his boyish good looks would have clientele up the yin-yang, and more self-respect to boot.

SELF-RESPECT was a subject near to the heart of Jacob Fastbinder III. These days he had a lot of it, but he was no stranger to self-loathing. Once, for a while, he'd seen himself as lower than dirt.

It was in Cologne, Germany, at the company headquarters. Fastbinder's first clue that things were not right was when he was told to sit and wait. His father was in a meeting, but would get to him eventually.

In the few years he was with the family company, Fastbinder had never before waited for his father to finish a meeting.

"He requires that you make a study of this document," said his father's assistant as she handed him a leather-bound book. Fastbinder took the book, then glared at the assistant, who shrugged and poked at the bridge of her glasses. "This is what he said." She went back to her desk.

Fastbinder began reading the book, *The History of Fastbinder Machine Werks Through A.D. 1975,* published by the company on its half-century anniversary. Fastbinder had read it before, when he was a teenager, and had done so under duress, and he knew most of this history anyway. His father talked about the company history at the dinner table, incessantly, as if he thought somebody besides him cared.

After an hour, Jacob Fastbinder III was allowed in to see his father, who was not in a meeting at all. "How was your reading?" asked Jacob Fastbinder II.

"Dry as stale bread," his son complained. "The only amusement I received from it was finding important gaps in the history. For example, there was another World War. A second one, after the first one. It was in the forties, I believe, and my understanding is that Germany played a part."

His father was not amused. "You are a smart-mouthed punk."

"I'm exaggerating, of course. There's a whole quarter of a chapter devoted to the Second World War, but not one use of the word 'Nazi'. Quite skillful of the author."

"And necessary. But did you learn anything new, Jacob?"

For an answer, the younger Fastbinder sneered and dropped the book with a thump on the oak-and-glass table in front of his father's overstuffed sofa, then dropped himself in the sofa. "What's this about, Father."

"History."

"I mean, this meeting," the younger Fastbinder said.

"So do I." His father turned, clasped his hands behind his back and began to pace the office somberly. "We are here to discuss history, and your place in it."

"I hope I never become one of the lifeless slugs who fill the pages of that piece of trash."

The elder Fastbinder nodded as he walked. "Nor do I. But that is not the true and complete history of this company, as you observed, Jacob. There is more to the story."

"Yes. Nazis, for example."

"There is more than that. More than even you know. More than I knew until I was a grown man." He stopped and glared from under his lowered brows at his one and only son. "The Fastbinder patriarchy has its secrets."

The younger Fastbinder was interested now, but tried not to show it. "Such as?"

His father resumed pacing. "I have been weighing this decision, whether it is time to tell you about all this. You are not yet ready for this knowledge. You have an immature disposition, a recklessness, a disregard for propriety. But I am forced into this by certain unforeseen events."

"What unforeseen events?" This intrigued the younger man; the defamation of his character by his father was nothing new.

"I will get to that in due course. First I will tell you the true history of Jacob Fastbinder I, if you will hear it. Will you?"

The younger man forgot to be flippant. "Certainly."

The older man nodded, then surprisingly, took a seat

in the matching leather chair, looking fatigued. "My father invented nothing."

The younger man cocked his head. "What do you mean? He has more than a hundred major patents."

"All stolen. He was a good engineer, a skilled and talented technical analyst, but with no creativity. All the achievements he claimed for himself were the works of others."

Before his son could utter the scoffing remarks that were on his lips, the elder Fastbinder held up a hand and continued. "It was in October of 1918. Jacob Fastbinder, my father, was in France as an equipment officer. He was helping to erect another of the fine big German cannons, with which to bombard Paris. As the gun was being erected under my father's supervision, the Germans were attacked by a small scout team of American soldiers, who killed most my father's soldiers and crew and destroyed the gun before it could fire a shot. This is recorded history."

His son nodded. He knew all this.

"But the record is distorted. In truth, the Americans did attack, but Fastbinder was responsible for the death of all those Germans."

The younger man frowned, but stayed silent.

"It was at night, when the gun was not yet reinforced. The barrel was in place, but the steel outer casing had been brought to the field in pieces. It was an experimental way of making these large weapons more portable, you see. The gun could not yet be fired, and it was still vulnerable, and that was the night the mechanical man came to tear it down."

His father waited, silently daring the younger Fastbinder to make a joke. His son said, "Mechanical man?"

"Yes. In the late nineteenth and early twentieth century there were all sorts of electric and steam-powered mechanical robots in the carnivals of Europe and North America, but they were frauds. Mostly they were cheap tin suits with a small dwarf or child inside, moving the arms. One or two truly functional mechanical men had actually been built, but they were failures. They would try to walk but fall onto their face. One of them crushed his own head when he saluted the American flag. But that night, in France, my father saw a mechanical man and knew at once that it was different, a genuine work of mechanical genius."

"How did he know?" Fastbinder III demanded.

"Because it was in the battlefield, side by side with U.S. soldiers. No one would send such a thing on a secret military mission if it didn't function. He watched it for minutes, as it crept with the Americans closer to the gun position. He saw the mechanical man traverse uneven terrain, and crawl on all fours with amazing speed, stand itself upright again, all extraordinary feats for an automaton."

"It was a man in a suit," the younger Fastbinder protested.

"This my father considered, but he saw the thing turn a full circle at the hip, then extend its head on telescopic neck supports, and he deemed it impossible for there to be any human being inside the metal skin. My father sounded the alert as the Americans closed in, and the battle was commenced. The mechanical man killed many Germans. He took the point, the bullets unable to penetrate his metal plating, and walked up to the Germans who would not leave their protective post around the precious cannon. The mechanical man crushed their skulls with his hands.

"My father decided then and there that must possess the mechanical man, which meant he must subdue it without destroying it. He thought of a way to accomplish this. He ordered the cannon to be fired."

"What?" the younger Fastbinder asked, astonished.

"Your grandfather told one of his men to aim the cannon at a small dirigible hovering a mile from the battlefield. Whoever was controlling the mechanical man was in the cockpit of that aircraft. If the controller was knocked out of the sky, then the mechanical man would no longer be a danger and the Germans could gain the upper hand in the battle. The gunner protested, but my father assured him the gun was strong enough to fire a few rounds, even without its structural reinforcement. My father, however, threw himself into a deep gully at the moment his gunner obeyed the order and fired the cannon."

The elder Fastbinder smiled sardonically.

"The gun burst apart," his son stated.

"Yes, of course, but amazingly enough it managed to lob its shell with enough accuracy to punch a hole in the dirigible. Father saw it spiral to the ground when he emerged from the gully. He was surrounded by dead men, American and German. The mechanical man was flat on its back and not moving, but it was still functional! The creature knew it had toppled and was trying to right itself, even without remotely issued commands! But it was damaged, and it could not stand, and my father spent the rest of the night digging a hole for it."

"Why?" the younger Fastbinder asked.

His father held up a hand. "He put in oilcloth to line the grave, then used a strong metal bar to lever the mechanical man down into it. He covered it with oilcloth and only just had it buried again when German reinforcements arrived. My father threw himself to the ground, pretending to be unconscious until he was found and revived and hailed as the only surviving hero of the Americans' savage attack."

His father chuckled. Jacob Fastbinder III frowned. "What happened then?" he demanded.

"The handler of the mechanical man came in search of him. It was one night later, and my father had expected it. He had done enough of a quick study of the mechanical man's batteries to know that a rescue attempt must come very soon, and it did. As he stood watch on the burial site, he saw it move. A hand came up from the soil. The mechanical man was being ordered to disinter itself."

The elder Fastbinder was amused, imitating the gesture with one bent arm clutching at the empty air above his head.

"It was another dirigible he saw in the night sky, only a mile away. My father alerted the German army and they went gunning for the aircraft. The dirigible descended and my father buried again the hand of the mechanical man, then left France. After the war, in secret, with just a few hired Frenchmen whose labor and silence could be bought, he came again to the battlefield and unearthed the mechanical man. They loaded the rusted thing into a hired truck and then my father shot the Frenchmen in the back for their trouble, burying them in the hole.

"The mechanical man had not corroded too badly,

due to the oilcloth Jacob Fastbinder wrapped him in, but repairing it was a long and tedious process. My father learned more about advanced engineering in the next thirty months than in all his years of school and internship and military field work. The mechanical man was more advanced than anything he had ever seen or heard of, and my father saw his future. He began to patent and produce the new technology, and that is how Fastbinder Machine Werks was founded. Do you believe me, Jacob?"

The younger man was stunned, but he nodded. "I suppose I do. You're not much of a practical joker, Father."

"True enough. Soon, my father learned the identity of the mechanical man." With that, his father went to his office desk and took out a small, faded book, putting it on top of the Fastbinder history book.

It was a ratty old paperback novel from America, with a prominent "10¢" displayed in the upper right corner. The ridiculous illustration showed a flamboyant robot standing head and shoulders above cowering German soldiers in the uniforms of World War I.

"'*Ironhand Smites the Kaiser*'?" Fastbinder III read. His father nodded. "'Ironhand joins the heroic American troops in the Great War, fighting for freedom against the vicious, cowardly Germans.'"

Again his father nodded and said, "And now, my son, you must think I am truly mad."

"This is just cheap paperback trash."

"Fiction was a clever disguise for a genuine phenomena. Ironhand was exposed to the world by its creator, even promoted, before it was taken under the control of the U.S. government. The dime novels and a few public appearances by a shoddy imitation Iron-hand convinced the world there had never been a gen-uine article. This secrecy made it easy for Jacob Fastbinder to patent the secrets of Ironhand and, indeed, found the Fastbinder Machine Werks."

The younger man looked his father square in the eyes. "I guess I don't believe you, after all."

"Why would I make it up?"

"I do not know. But this?" The younger man tapped the face of the robot on the paperback. "This is prepos-terous."

"I am glad you are skeptical. It is a strange story. But I can convince you easily enough."

"You have evidence?"

"Of course." The older man also tapped the steel face on the book cover. "I have him."

In SILENCE the father and son left the offices of Fast-binder Machine Werks and drove to the family's old house on several hundred acres of fallow land outside Cologne. The father of the first Jacob had tilled this soil, but now it was leased to other farmers or simply al-lowed to grow wild.

The old house was still maintained just as it had been when Jacob Fastbinder died in the 1950s. Jacob Fastbinder III now understood why it was kept—it was a place to house the family secrets—if what his father said was true.

What would Jacob Fastbinder III do if he discovered his father had become a lunatic?

But his father was about to prove he was not a luna-tic.

Into the cellar they went, and into the workshop adjoining the cellar and hidden behind a fake wall. It was a sprawling shop packed with old, broken electronics and mechanical devices and endless rows of work-benches.

"I never even knew this workshop existed," the son said.

"I am the only one who knew until I showed you," explained his father.

There was dust everywhere, and corrosion and rust, and beneath the veil of time the young man glimpsed promises and mysteries. He imagined great engineering feats, invented and abandoned, waiting to be rediscovered. By him.

One worktable was empty, in a back corner.

"Help me with this." The old man grasped a corner of the tabletop, face clenched as if it was a great exertion to move the tabletop, which was really quite light in weight.

When the wood-plank tabletop hit the floor, the young Jacob looked into a box like a coffin. Ironhand was there.

His father began to talk again as he puttered with devices on the next table, explaining that Jacob Fastbinder was a sort of bumbling mechanical genius, the kind of man who could not have a coherent conversation about screwing a bolt into a nut. He did have a talent for reverse engineering, it turned out, and managed to parlay the innovations inside Ironhand into numerous works of mechanical sophistication.

"Of course, he nearly destroyed himself and the company by choosing to put his developments into the hands of the Nazis. Despite the promises of the man in charge, a German thousand-year reign failed to happen.

The corporation was broken up, which is why Fast-binder Machine Werks is these days just a fraction of what it was—with just three factories making parts for automobiles and other machinery."

"Yes," the young son said in a daze.

"But that is sufficient. We machine very good engine blocks and transmissions," the older man added. "The romance of the business may be lost, but we are profitable for the last twenty years and the Fastbinder family is still wealthy. You're not listening, Jacob."

The old man got no response. He sighed and opened up the belly cavity on the old mechanical man, inserted the battery pack and twirled the wing nuts to secure the leads.

Ironhand sat up at the waist.

"It's true," the young man gasped.

"See this gyroscopic control next to the battery?" his father asked. "Look familiar?"

"Grandfather's first patent?"

"Exactly. And this is a mechanized compass, allowing switch actuation with a featherweight magnetized needle. The family fortunes were made on all these things, and it all originated with these very components."

"Let's see it in action," the younger Fastbinder exclaimed. "Have him stand up and walk around."

"That is not possible."

"Why?"

"This is why," the father said. "This series of tiny relays. They're a work of genius that even Jacob Fastbinder could never fully understand or repair."

"There are hundreds! Like spiderwebs!"

"Thousands. They controlled the mechanical man

through its hundreds of functions, in series, sometimes automatically, based on various inputs."

"It's like BASIC programming."

The elder Fastbinder shrugged. He had little patience with the technology of computers. He saw them as tools of the accounting department, and yet these days there were Apple IIs being requested by every department in the company. He knew they were powerful, but he was an old-timer who couldn't comprehend the programming and the logic behind it. It was too late to start learning it now.

Ironhand sat there, a hunk of old steel, internal mechanisms working softly. Just a machine, without consciousness.

To his son, the elder Fastbinder said, "I am dying."

The young man looked up at him.

"And I have a son unworthy of replacing me."

Fastbinder III opened his mouth to speak. Years later he remembered all the emotions he was trying to come to terms with at that moment.

"Why," he uttered finally, "do you find me unworthy?"

"Jacob, you're an impulsive man. You have not demonstrated you can be a valuable man."

"I have ambition."

"But no will. I have yet to see you make a difference in the Werks."

"I'm director of engineering!"

"And you are adequate in that role."

"What more can I do?"

"Be a leader."

The young Fastbinder saw the whole picture now. His father was ill, forced to reveal this bizarre family secret as a way of kicking his son in the pants, force him to become someone truly deserving—by the old man's standards—of the leadership of the family company.

"How much time do I have?" he asked. "To prove myself?"

"Before I die, you mean? Two years, maybe five. Yes, Jacob, there is plenty of time for you. Do you have what it takes to make use of the time?"

For an answer, Jacob looked at the mechanical man. "Let me work here, in grandfather's workshop. Let me see what I can learn from him."

Jacob could tell that his father thought this was a curious request, and Jacob realized then just how dull a man his father was. Why, he had never had the desire to work in this workshop!

At that moment he understood that he, Jacob Fastbinder III, was made in a different image—not the successful businessman his father was. He was like his grandfather, the first Jacob Fastbinder, the man who claimed Ironhand.

THE SEED OF SHAME that his father planted in his being was only as monumental as his excitement over the discovery of his past. It was just two months later that these opposing forces collided again.

"What is this?" his father demanded hotly. This time, Jacob had not been kept waiting outside his father's office for even a minute.

"A patent application," Jacob said. "I have learned much from Ironhand."

His father's anger was commingled with shock. "From Ironhand? The thing still has secrets to tell?"

"Perhaps if you had spent a few hours poking around

in grandfather's workshop you would have discovered this yourself," Jacob said. "Have you ever earned a single patent for this company, Father?"

"No, and neither shall you," Fastbinder stated flatly. "You'll risk everything! Don't you understand? Somebody in America already invented this—this nested relay switching matrix."

"Ninety years ago," Fastbinder reminded him.

"That does not matter if there is someone in America who is still wondering what became of Ironhand. It is a miracle we were never shut down, but at least now those patents are far in our past, too. We cannot afford to dredge up this secret again."

Jacob noticed his old man was pale. How long would it take him to die? Hopefully not five years. The young man said, "Ironhand walks."

"What?"

"What grandfather could not understand, I do understand. I have mapped his programming system, repaired the corroded relays, and now he walks. Soon I'll have his frequencies and command codes mapped out and I'll be able to operate him perfectly, just as his makers did."

His father looked stark. "No. No more work there. It is reckless and I should never have allowed it."

"Father, this is my way. It was your father's way. I can be a success, but not like you, not by being a financial executive. I must be an engineer."

"Then do it elsewhere."

In silence, the young Jacob stood and reached for the paper.

"This stays with me." The elder Fastbinder slapped his hand on the patent application.

So this was what it was reduced to, finally, the old power struggle. Jacob Fastbinder III was not going to allow himself to lose at that, not again, not even one more battle.

"But the knowledge goes with me," the young man said. He extracted a small flat thing from his briefcase. His father looked confused. "It is a floppy disk. All my notes from Ironhand are stored on one five-inch piece of plastic."

"Give that to me!"

"Of course, Father," Jacob said, flipping the thing onto his father's oak desk. "It is only a copy."

"Give me all of them."

"Not possible. I made a dozen copies. Some are hidden around the country, some are in safe-deposit boxes in the U.K. and Switzerland."

Now the old man understood. "You would blackmail your own father?"

The younger man sneered. "What were you trying to do to me, Father?"

"Make you into a useful businessman!"

"Manipulate me. Force me to become hideously mundane, like you."

"Son, please, do not reveal what you have learned."

"I will. To the highest bidder. And let it be known that you refused to make use of my patent. It is substantial. People will want to know why you turned away your own son with his profitable new technology."

"Every word you speak is another knife thrust into my heart," the old man said, full of bitterness.

"Better the heart than the back," his son retorted, exposing his own anger now. "Decide, old man. You have ten seconds."

Jacob Fastbinder stayed with the family business and was promoted to director of technology, eventually even buying out his father's share in the firm. A year later the value of that share had tripled with the introduction of the new nested relay switch product line, giving unprecedented computerlike control to component makers, without investing in bulky, expensive computers. It had applications in luxury cars, armored vehicles, aircraft, cruise ships, you name it.

Jacob Fastbinder III was a great success, but not the success his father had envisioned. It didn't matter. His father's time was over, even if it did take the old man a long four years, three months and six days to finally die.

THE ADVENT OF CHEAP computerized controls made the famous nested relay switch system obsolete not long after the elder Fastbinder died and Jacob Fastbinder III became executive director of the company. Without a hugely profitable invention to shine his star, he was judged solely on his management skills, which were less impressive. Before long he was ousted from the director's chair.

Only the family link to the company, and the need to save corporate face, motivated the board of directors to give Jacob Fastbinder III control of a new start-up firm in the United States. A grand new opportunity, the press releases promised, but Fastbinder knew he was being set up. A large-scale failure in the United States, and the board would have the public justification it needed to eject the last descendant of the company founder.

All went as planned. Fastbinder American Controls Corp. generated big losses. Fastbinder was ousted, but the board agreed to allow him to receive, as severance, a share on sales from his personal patents, which were licensed to the U.S. division. This was an easy concession for the board to make, as there were, in fact, no profits at all coming from the U.S. division.

Fastbinder III sold his shares in the parent firm and kept only his German homes. Still a wealthy man, Jacob went into seclusion on his desert estate in New Mexico, near Tucumcari, and held a press conference that appeared entirely superfluous and self-aggrandizing before the fact. None of the big media outlets sent reporters to listen to a bitter ex-CEO spout vitriol about the company that fired him.

The only tidbit of interest came when Fastbinder explained he "…removed himself from the company in an effort to escape the long history of associations between his company and its sympathy for the Nazi cause during the war."

In truth, there was no longer any public perception of a link between Fastbinder Machine Werks and the Nazis—until the press conference rekindled it. Fastbinder's bad PR sent Fastbinder Machine Werks into financial stutters. His timing helped—the world was finally getting around to taking legal action against firms known to have helped the Nazi cause.

He received calls from various legal organizations asking if the family ever possessed artworks and treasures looted by the Nazis. "Oh, the family never owned such valuables. The corporation, however…I seem to recall a few interesting paintings and boxes of jewels in a basement vault."

Fastbinder allowed his U.S. and German properties to be searched, and they came up clean except for a lot of antique machine parts of no value.

Fastbinder Machine Werks came up clean, as well.

"Tell those nincompoops to look in zee basement vault!" Fastbinder said to the head of the UN agency charged with the investigation.

"Well, the thing is, Mr. Fastbinder, we can't find the basement vault, and nobody on the board seems to know where one is."

"They told you this?" Fastbinder asked incredulously. Had he forgotten to tell the board about his father's secret vault in the headquarters subbasement? Oh, *shiest,* now the company was going to look like it was trying to cover up. Too bad for the company.

"I know it exists. Zee executive director of zee board of directors described it to me personally," Fastbinder said. "He never saw fit to allow me to view it myself, however." Fastbinder told the UN exactly where in the basement they might search for fresh wall repairs.

The vault was found. More Than Three Stolen Paintings Found In Fastbinder Werks Vault! thundered the headlines in the London newspaper. Fastbinder had a copy overnighted to New Mexico. The German papers were too uptight to do the story justice. Fastbinder Vault Reveals Only Four Paintings. Hmm, Fastbinder thought, maybe he should have left more of the family art.

A week later, the London media exclaimed, Each Of The Three-Dozen Fastbinder Masterpieces Identified As Art Looted From Jews By Nazis! Even Fastbinder had to smirk when he read it. The "masterpieces" in question had, in actuality, been the least valuable works of art in the entire lot—which Fastbinder had liquidated for more than thirty million euro after his father finally kicked the bucket.

In the end, Fastbinder Machine Werks settled with the former owners of the paintings. The sum was nine times their value—Fastbinder knew this since he had the paintings expertly appraised before deciding to sacrifice them to the cause.

The sacrifice was worthwhile, he decided, when the financial toll on Fastbinder Machine Werks became apparent. The company leaned in the direction of bankruptcy. Amazingly, the U.S. division was suddenly profitable as Jacob Fastbinder III's patents began selling hugely. It was the only thing keeping the firm alive and yet every dollar was a slap in the face. The company sent squadrons of lawyers to New Mexico to plead with Fastbinder to temporarily rescind his rights to half the patent profits. The U.S. division was now propping up the rest of the firm but was not quite enough to keep it from looming bankruptcy. Even the executive director of the board of directors appeared one afternoon on his doorstep. Fastbinder laughed in his face and shut the door, letting the man stand out there in the ninety-five-degree heat. The executive director lost his cool and started pounding on the door.

"We will make you director again!"

Fastbinder opened his front door on a security chain, laughing. "Did you get that, Mr. Hippolwythe?" he called.

The executive director was shocked to see a man come from around the corner, holding a miniature cassette tape recorder. He also had a camera and took a photo of the sweating, pitiful mess of a man.

"This man is a reporter for my favorite newspaper in zee United Kingdom," Fastbinder explained to the executive director.

The story was perfect fodder for the U.K. tabloids. The paper the next morning had a narrow front-page photo, so tall it went from the top of the page to the bottom, showing the sweat-stained, rumpled executive director of Fastbinder Machine Werks with his mouth gaping open. It was an ugly image. The headline next to it screamed, Pathetic Head Of Machine Werks Comes Crawling Back To Fastbinder Heir Begging Him To Resume Control Of Crumbling Company!

Oh, if only the executive director would have blown his brains out or jumped off a building. Instead he put on a fresh shirt and suit, tidied his hotel room in Albuquerque, and took 112 assorted prescription tablets. He was still sitting there, hand neatly on his lap, when the maid came in to clean up. She gave the tabloid a quote, but "He left the room so spotless, I didn't even need to sanitize!" was not quite inflammatory enough for their tastes.

Oh, well, the rest of it made fine reading. Fastbinder had the articles laminated and hung in his bathroom.

29

The gods rewarded Jacob Fastbinder III for his skillful deeds. They presented him with the gift of a son.

"Weren't you an intern last summer at zee headquarters in Tucumcari?" Fastbinder asked the teenager who showed up on his doorstep.

"Yep. Wanted to check you out. You're an impressive dude, Pops."

"I seriously doubt I am your sire," Fastbinder said, and began to close the door in the boy's face.

"Remember when you were scouting New Mexico for the new U.S. division? Like about sixteen years ago?" the kid blurted. "Remember the blond real-estate agent with the huge hooters? That's my mom. I turned fifteen last Thursday. You do the math."

Fastbinder did the math. Yes, that was about right.

"Hey—" the kid grinned "—I know it's gotta be a real humdinger of a development. You probably wanna do a DNA test."

"Yes." Fastbinder was quite thoughtful. "That would be best."

"What would you like? Blood? Urine? Sem—?"

"This will be sufficient." Fastbinder snatched out a small handful of the boy's shaggy blond hair.

"Jeez Louise, Pops!" The kid grabbed his head. "That smarts!"

THE KID SHOWED UP again three days later. "Heard you rushed it through the system," the kid announced. "I'm legit, huh, Pops?"

Fastbinder was still feeling thoughtful. "Yes, zee tests confirm you are my progeny. How do you know I rushed it through zee system?"

"Pops, your e-mail is *totally* unsecure. I've been eavesdropping on you for months! Nice to meet you, Dad, by the way." Fastbinder abruptly found himself in a wiry, unbreakable bear hug.

After that, Fastbinder played nice, inviting the kid inside.

"So, then, how is your mother?" He struggled to recall her name. He could not even remember her face, although the image of her lace-clad bosom was forever burned into his memory.

"Carla. She's fine."

"Er, and your name?"

"Jack. Jack Fast. Like it?"

"I am not certain."

"My mom's last name is Ashland, but she made my last name Fast. After you."

"All right, Jack Fast, let us be frank with each other. What is it you want from me?"

Jack Fast looked disappointed. "Aw, Pops, I don't want nothing from you, I mean, not like money or anything. I just wanted to get to know my old man. After all, you impress the heck out of me."

Fastbinder became even more suspicious.

"Besides, if I was after cash or something, well, I wouldn't go yanking your chain with all this family re-union stuff. I'd just head straight into extortion."

Fastbinder glared.

"You know, the Culbreadth Control." The kid laughed. "Whatsamatter, Pops, I throw you for a loop?"

Fastbinder *was* thrown for a loop. Maybe several loops. "How do you know about it?"

"Listen, Pops, you've done some really swift stuff, but you know diddly about Internet security. You know that there's all these electronic trails out there linking you to Culbreadth? It's gonna get your ass into a seri-ous sling if anybody ever starts looking. See, this guy Culbreadth comes to you with the control, right? That's twenty-one months ago. You see the potential and make an offer, but Culbreadth wants way too much. So you hit-and-run him."

"It was not me who ran down Mr. Culbreadth," Fast-binder retorted defensively.

"Whatever. The good news is, he's met his maker, and you've still got his hard-copy files, so all you have to do is make sure the files in his computers are erased. Right? Which you did, fine, and you overwrote them really good and the hard drive was all shot and every-thing. But here's what you forgot, Pops—there's an electronic record of you getting into his system over the Net."

"Where is this record!"

"Where ain't it, Pops? Your ISP. His ISP. Every damn place between here and Albuquerque, and over the Internet that can be like a hundred places."

With that, the kid showed Fastbinder how to hack

into the records of his Internet service provider. To his astonishment, there was a complete record of every keystroke his computer made while he was tied into the remote PC belonging to Mr. Culbreadth. "Here's where you overwrote all his CAD files. Here's where you overwrote all his e-mail. Here's where you visited Tits of the Week. Don't worry, though. I'm Jack the Hacker. I make it go away."

With that, the teenager opened up a high-level Telnet connection into the servers and began tapping out commands that Fastbinder didn't know. He watched the lines of his activity records evaporate. "Watch the record of the CAD file go away," the kid said. They disappeared. "Now watch the e-mail files erase command." They vanished.

Fastbinder looked at the kid, who was looking cagey all of a sudden. "What about zee last one. You know, zee Tits of zee Week?"

"Oh, I'll erase it, Pops," the kid said seriously. "But that one is gonna cost ya."

Fastbinder stared at the boy in disbelief.

The kid exploded into hyena howls of hysteria. "I'm kidding, you dope!"

"I see."

"Wow, Pops, you have got one humungous stick up your butt!"

"I suppose I do."

"You need somebody like me around to help with butt-stick removal."

"And to assist in butt-sling avoidance," Fastbinder added. "By zee way, I like zee haircut."

The grinning kid felt his new crew cut. "Had to do something. I had a big empty patch. Can I move in with you? 'Cause Carla is heading for Vegas."

THE KID MOVED IN and Fastbinder went through culture shock, but the rewards far outweighed the annoyances. Jack Fast was as independent as they came. Fastbinder found himself with a son he didn't have to be responsible for.

Fastbinder also discovered his kid was brilliant—like no other Fastbinder before him. "All of us were nothing but reverse engineers. You're the first creative genius we've ever had," he told Jack a few months later.

"Aw, jeez, Pops," Jack said. "I just like fiddling with stuff is all." He closed the small aluminum door on the power unit. "It's just a proton beam chisel, really. Not even an accurate one."

"This could be the greatest leap in portable power technology in decades," his father insisted. "No one knew that proton beams could be used for this. They are too busy using zee technology to carve computer chips out of old porcelain teacups."

"Lets see if it works before you get all gushy," the kid protested. But the proton beam generator worked very well. That was the thing about Jack—whatever he set his mind to create, he created. He told Fastbinder how, when he was eight, he had formed a boys club that played unbelievably sophisticated jokes on the townsfolk. The other boys couldn't hold an interest in the club and girls at the same time, so it all fell apart when puberty hit the group. Jack had been more or less a highly sociable loner since seventh grade.

With access to Fastbinder's desert workshop, Jack went into creative overdrive, churning out amazing—and sometimes amazingly useless—technological creations. Like his father, he loved old mechanical junk.

Fastbinder had brought all of the marvels from the old family home in Cologne, and for years he had been accumulating more antique apparatus through a global network of buyers. His collection was vast.

When Fastbinder saw the potential in the boy, he started coming up with funding. He even bought the boy a proton beam chisel, an obsolete experimental model that had to be shipped from Singapore. The shipping cost was more than the device, which the National University of Singapore Research Center for Nuclear Microscopy considered to be scrap.

The research center had enabled a whole new realm of microscopic chiseling to be performed with its research, but Jack Fast made it into something else entirely. His miniaturized devices, based on the technology from Singapore, created a microscopic burst of high-speed subatomic particles channeled into a tiny electric generator, converting it into large quantities of available electricity for extended periods.

"Will you patent it?" his father asked.

"Nah," Jack said. "I'm keeping it a secret."

"For what purpose?" his father asked.

"Pops, think about it. Ironhand will run for months with this baby inside him. Think what he could do. He could walk all the way to White Sands without needing a battery change. All the way and back."

30

Remo sat in the chair as Chiun stood near Smith's desk.

"Ignore him, Emperor. His brain has jellied," Chiun proclaimed

"My brain is fine," Remo protested.

"It is sad indeed when a teacher discovers his pupil has learned nothing despite a lifetime of education. He was a simpleton when I found him and a simpleton he remains."

"Go eat a cow," Remo responded.

"See the disrespect? Witness the lack of understanding?"

"I'm inclined to agree with Master Chiun this time, Remo. You've demonstrated poor judgment recently."

"And you can go to hell. You have no clue what's been happening, Smitty. This is a weapon we might not be able to overcome. It's not a rock or an arrow or a bullet or a bomb. We're not slithering around it or dodging it or outrunning it."

"Every weapon is a hurled rock," Chiun responded without emotion. "Once I had thought my pupil listened to my teachings. Now I know he was hearing the words but not understanding their meaning."

"Every weapon is not a rock," Remo said. "This time the weapon is something different. For once, being a Master of Sinanju is a disability."

"Fah!" Chiun swiped the words out of the air.

There was a knock, then Eileen Mikulka, Smith's long-time secretary, opened the door and rolled Mark Howard into the room in his wheelchair, clucking all the while.

"Thank you, thank you so much, Mrs. Mikulka," Howard kept saying, until she was satisfied that he was comfortably situated, had a full cup of water and was not in need of medicine, Kleenex or other items or services. She finally closed the door behind her.

"Sorry I'm late," Mark said. "What did I miss?"

Chiun glared disapprovingly at Mark's bandaged ankle. Remo watched the Long Island surf roll in. Harold Smith was in a rare state of indecisiveness.

Mark got a whiff of the ill will in the room and said, "The doc gave me the okay to get back to work. Where should I start, Dr. Smith?"

"We're still trying to get a full profile put together on Archibald Slate and the original Ironhand, as well as trace the history of the antique robot samples you brought back from Spain," Dr. Smith said. "Our top priority, however, is to find out everything we can about the system used to charge the robot power supplies. Unfortunately we have a lot of possibilities. The technology was either stolen from the Soviets or developed independently. If stolen from the Soviets, it might have occurred any time in the last fifteen years. If developed independently—well, it could have been anywhere."

"Like the Pentagon," Remo said.

"We'd know if it came from the U.S. military," Mark answered.

"You didn't know about Ironhand."

"That's different. He was classified and forgotten seventy years ago. The proton discharge device has to be a lot newer than that."

Remo sighed. "What did you get from Sarah?"

Mark Howard looked startled. "What do you mean?"

"I mean, about Ironhand. What happened to him? Where has he been all this time?"

"I haven't learned anything like that."

"Bringing her to Rye was a bad decision," Dr. Smith remarked, addressing Mark. "Allowing her to come to Folcroft was also foolish."

"That's my doing," Remo announced before Mark could open his mouth. "Being here doesn't mean she'll learn anything about CURE. She's the best link we have to the old Ironhand."

"I do not see her as a reliable intelligence source."

"Got news for ya—she's the only intelligence we got."

"Remo," Chiun remonstrated, "you shall not insult the emperor to whom you owe your contractual allegiance."

Remo looked up at Chiun. "If it's true it's not an insult. Where are the Ironhand arms?" Remo asked finally.

"Under analysis."

"Any idea where Ironhand ran off to last night?"

Dr. Smith shook his head. "No trace of him. We're also tracking the robot that was his accomplice. This Clockwork. We have not determined if it is the original machine used in the television program, or if there was more than one built. Until we learn more, our best course of action will be for you and Master Chiun to police the possible upcoming attacks."

Remo waited.

"The Department of Defense is in a unique state of high alert. Vital military research projects all over the country are being relocated, but the emphasis is on secrecy. The President insists on it. If the American people come to think the highest levels of their military are worrying about burglars—public faith in the government would suffer."

"And the President's popularity would go into the toilet," Remo added. "Up for reelection, isn't he?"

Smith didn't acknowledge the comment. "There is one research project that has not been relocated. It is FEM, the Full-spectrum Environmental Monitoring."

"Kind of girly name," Remo noted.

"It protects the White House. It is made up of thirty miniaturized mobile units, patrolling the grounds in shifts of fifteen and relaying data to command computers and into the subterranean command centers. They have sound, motion, thermal, vibration and atmospheric sensors. They're Gee-DAM controlled, of course, but also have a high degree of information processing and the ability for independent decision-making. If they detect intruders with guns, they can call for ground troops. If they detect biological or chemical agents, they can call for HAZMAT. One of the units can perform any and all these functions."

"How come we've never seen them?" Remo asked. "We've been to the White House."

"It has been up and running just a few weeks," Smith explained. "The units still call in a number of false alarms, but the programming is being tuned daily. It could emerge as the most capable defensive system for any sort of a secure site."

"If the White House shares it," Remo clarified.

Dr. Smith slid an eight-by-ten photograph onto the desk, appearing slightly sheepish. "The current FEM unit configuration."

Remo examined the photo.

"A robotic rodent?" Chiun sniffed.

"It's a cyber-squirrel," Remo observed.

"Its a FEMbot," Smith explained.

"Say again?"

"Full-spectrum Environmental Monitoring robot. FEMbot."

"I see."

"To the casual observer, the only way to distinguish it from a genuine White House squirrel is the markings. All the FEMbots have the same forehead markings."

Remo noticed that the mark was a series of white streaks in the brown squirrel fur, and the streaks formed a lopsided *W*. "Somebody at the DOD is brown-nosing big-time."

Smith scowled. "I agree it's foolish. I pointed out to the President that one of these units might be photographed by a White House reporter or visitor and surely attract attention. The President believes the units will keep themselves so well camouflaged there will be little opportunity for such a thing to happen." His words trailed off, full of doubt, and he added, "The President does not believe the White House is threatened. He also does not believe that the two of you will be able to penetrate this new security perimeter."

Remo and Chiun both stiffened.

"I think he is wrong on both counts, of course."

Remo nodded. "You want we should keep an eye on the place?"

"For tonight, yes," Smith said.

"Fine. We'll go stake out the White House."

REMO PUSHED MARK out of the office.

"Really, Remo, I can do it myself."

"This is a cool set of wheels, Junior," Remo said. "Wanna go down and try it out in one of the first-floor corridors? I bet I can get this baby up to eighty."

"No, thank you!"

"I'll take that." Mrs. Mikulka was out of her chair the moment they left Dr. Smith's office and she muscled Remo out from behind the wheelchair with unassailable determination. Chiun chuckled.

When Mark Howard's office door swung open, it almost grazed the front of the massive desk that dominated the room like a hippo in a hot tub. The floor space was narrow. Mark usually had to shuffle sideways to get behind the desk to work.

Experimentally, Mrs. Mikulka wheeled Mark inside. The foot rests wedged against the front of the desk while the rear wheels were still sticking out the door.

"This will never do," she decided.

"No, no, it'll work. It will just take a little jimmying." Mark began wiggling the wheelchair back and forth, inching it around.

Mrs. Mikulka huffed. "This will not work, Mark."

"Sure, Mrs. M. Just another minute or so and I'll be inside."

"Then what? You'll never get behind your desk."

"I'll work on the front."

"There's no room for your legs to get under. You'll add a bad back to your medical problems."

"I'm sure it will be—"

"Not another word from you, Mark Howard. I'm calling maintenance." Mrs. Mikulka strode away. After a few more tiny movements, Mark realized he was completed wedged in. His front wheels tight against the desk, his back wheels jammed at an angle in the door frame.

That was when he realized he needed to go to the men's room.

Remo was pretending to hold a cigar in one hand and a telephone in another. "Hello, room service? Send up some more room."

"That was the worst Groucho Marx of all time," Mark said.

"Seriously, who did you not sleep with to rate this closet? Aren't there empty offices on both sides of you?"

"They're no bigger than this one."

"You just take out a few walls and you'd be in good shape."

"That doesn't exactly help me right now."

"What do you mean? I'll have it done before you're back from the little boy's room."

"No. Please, no, Remo. And stop invading my privacy. I don't need to know that you know when I need to—you know."

"What privacy? You're shifting around like an eight-year-old in mass. Can I at least get you unstuck?"

Mark sighed. "That would be helpful."

MRS. MIKULKA RETURNED to find Mark Howard still in his wheelchair, but the wheelchair was now four feet off the ground. It turned and emerged backward from the office. Remo gave her a smile and placed it on the

ground again, giving Mark a crash-landing for the benefit of the elderly secretary.

"Unstuck. You could stand to loose a few, Mark. I
think I pulled my back."

"Maybe we have some wheelchairs at Folcroft that
are more narrow," Mark said.

"Mark, you are not going to try to cram yourself inside of that office," Mrs. Mikulka declared. "Not until
you are ambulatory again. Come with me, please."

Remo almost had hold of the wheelchair handles,
then found himself facing a mask of maternal determination that sent him into retreat. Mrs. Mikulka wheeled
Mark Howard right back to Mr. Smith's office.

"Dr. Smith has more room than he needs," she announced, and when they entered the director's office
she explained the difficulties down the hall. "You'll be
more than happy to have Mark as a roommate temporarily, won't you?"

"Nod, Smitty," Remo called from outside the door
after an uncertain moment.

Smith nodded. "Yes. Of course. That's an ideal so-
lution. You'll need a desk."

Mrs. Mikulka stepped aside as an upended desk
rolled into the office, followed by a Folcroft maintenance worker who manned the dolly. "Afternoon, Mrs.
M. Where'd you like this?"

Remo couldn't tear his eyes away as Mrs. Mikulka su-
pervised the arrangement of the new office layout, careful to allow plenty of room for Mark's wheelchair. Phones
arrived and were installed by another maintenance
worker. Dr. Smith seemed resigned to the chaos, but in reality it was handled with great efficiency. When the door
closed twenty minutes later, Mark was firmly ensconced.

"Just like old times." Mark grinned sheepishly. "I'm sorry to have this thrust on you, Dr. Smith. Don't think you were given much choice."

"It's perfectly acceptable, Mark, but I have to admit, I've rarely witnessed Mrs. Mikulka in such a take-charge mode."

"I'd say this pack has a new alpha male," Remo remarked.

"Are you finished?" Chiun asked, slipping through the door. "I have been waiting in the rental car."

"I thought you told me you were going to the cafeteria for a burger and fries," Remo protested. Chiun's look would have curdled yak milk. "Well, my supervision here is done."

Remo felt oddly ebullient as they departed, despite his current less-than-affectionate relations with Dr. Smith. In the outer office he made a big thumbs-up. "Good work, Mrs. M."

Mrs. Mikulka crinkled her wrinkles. "Why, thank you, Romeo."

Mrs. Mikulka watched them go, mulling over the odd pair that had just left. She'd watched them come and go for so many years they had become a part of the scenery.

But she had never been too clear on who they were. Relatives of Dr. Smith, she had been told more than once. She didn't know if that was true, and she didn't really care. But two things she had picked up over the years. They ate a lot of rice and they hadn't aged much. Why, she herself looked older now than the Asian gentlemen, and he had seemed ancient to her at one time.

What was their strange attachment to Folcroft Sanitarium? And what about Dr. Smith's late nights, and the two men coming at all hours? What was actually going behind those always-closed doors, anyway?

As always, when these thoughts began getting dark and suspicious, a pleasant puff of distraction floated into her mind as if from nowhere to whisk them away. Which was fine, really. Mrs. Mikulka wasn't sure what was crouching in those dark corridors of suspicion and she would just as soon not know.

31

Playing security guard was always boring work. Didn't matter if it was an office building in Dayton, Ohio, or the White House. You basically just kind of stood there waiting for something to happen.

The security around the White House was always good enough by most standards, but never very good by Remo's.

"This false president has little respect for us," Chiun noted as they slipped along the outside of the White House grounds, skirting the cameras and sensors that watched the place.

"He doesn't know anything about us," Remo answered.

"You should not talk, Traitor of Sinanju!"

"Come on, Chiun, I'm not a traitor."

"You have disposed of fifty centuries of learning and tradition."

"I haven't disposed of anything. You're overreacting."

"Overreacting? How dare you!"

"I dunno, how?"

"I never overreact!" Chiun snapped explosively.

"Sorry, I must have been thinking of somebody else."

They slipped past the concealed military patrol and stepped up to and over the fence, which, at something like fifteen feet high, didn't appear easy to step over.

"Keep an eye out—this is FEMbot turf," Remo said.

"You are worried about these mechanical vermin?"

"No."

"Do they not constitute some new and unassailable threat?"

"No."

"Why not? They are computerized! They have radio waves and mobile telephones built right in! Surely they will neutralize and nullify the Masters of Sinanju and all their skills."

Remo stopped in the evening shadow of one of Washington, D.C.'s famous cherry trees. "Little Father, I know why you're pissed off."

"I am angry for many reasons. Almost anything you say has a good chance of being correct."

"Look, Chiun, I know the *real* reason."

"I doubt it."

"You think I'm sullying the Sinanju reputation and hurting future business."

Chiun stared at him.

"I'm right, aren't I? It doesn't matter that we've had our batteries drained and our butts kicked. All you care about is that I admitted as much to Mark and Smitty. You think they'll somehow communicate this information to the kings and queens and despots that hire assassins like us."

Chiun looked away and fluttered his hand in the

night. "If only you had come to realize this before you spoke to Smith."

"I did."

"Liar."

"First of all, Smitty's not going to gossip about it on the heads-of-state grapevine."

"He will."

"Second, we've had our ass kicked once or twice before. The Sinanju reputation hasn't suffered."

"How would you know?"

"I know we're getting paid an obscene amount of gold for doing this job, and it's more than we were paid under the last contract," Remo said. "Our fee keeps going up, so our value must be increasing."

"Our value to other emperors is what matters," Chiun lectured. "We do not know when Smith's gold will run out, and we must take into account our value on the market."

Remo nodded distractedly. "Let's talk about it later, okay? We're about to face down our first FEMbot."

Chiun said nothing, putting his hands in his sleeves. Remo was more wary, but it was tough to be worried about a contraption that announced its presence the way the FEMbot did, with a rhythm of low-grade whirring sounds from internal drive motors and the clicking of relays and the popping of minuscule air-pressure actuators.

The sound was below the level of most human hearing, but to Remo it was as loud as the beeper on a garbage truck in reverse. It didn't look real, either.

"Is it my imagination, or is that squirrel goose-stepping?" he asked Chiun. "Maybe it is a Nazi android squirrel FEMbot."

The FEMbot was aiming at their tree. Remo lowered his skin temperature to fool its thermal sensors and he stood more still than most people would have found possible. He and Chiun conversed in a low, steady drone of sound that would loose itself in the ambient noise of the evening. Whatever the FEMbot used to look for intruders, it wasn't working. The fake squirrel never gave them a second look.

"That thing probably cost the taxpayers ten million," Remo said as the squirrel laboriously dug its claws into the tree and scissored through the branches.

"All that good money for a device that falls apart at the slightest touch," Chiun said, batting the FEMbot on the top of the head. The FEMbot was instantly transformed into so much scrap metal in a bad nylon fur coat, which slammed into the earth so hard it imbedded itself.

"I'll take this side, you take that side," Remo said. "Try not to do that anymore, okay? There's probably a keeper on the premises who'll come looking for his malfunctioning Nazi android squirrel FEMbot."

"Then the robot rodents should keep their distance from Chiun, Master of Sinanju Emeritus."

"Yeah. I'll spread the word."

THAT WAS WHEN the boring part of the job set in. Remo kept moving, kept an eye out and found himself ridiculously at his ease when it came to stepping around cameras and sensors, making himself unseen to the Secret Service patrols, and making himself generally nonexistent as far as the FEMbots were concerned. He circled the entire building every half hour, invariably finding Chiun tailing one of the executive defense squirrels. Chiun would toss cherry twigs onto the lawn around the robot, making it turn sharply, then turn again, until he had it spinning in circles. This was apparently not good for the drive systems that moved the stiff little legs. The squirrel would eventually jerk and come to a halt, internal servos whining, and there would be a burning smell.

"I asked you to leave them alone," Remo said in a whisper that didn't distract the canine sentinel that was almost within arm's reach. A hundred feet away, Chiun smiled and waved, showing no sign he heard Remo's admonition.

"Oh, great," Remo told the Rottweiler. "Now the old goat's going deaf on top of everything else."

The Rottweiler was oblivious to both intruders and continued his Because-He-Can activity. Chiun, however, sneered. "On top of what else, Remo Williams?"

"I knew you could hear me. I asked you not to touch the FEMbots."

"I did not touch it," Chiun sniffed. "And if I had?" He nudged the robot with his foot. The robot vanished, but not so fast Remo missed seeing it go.

He also witnessed Chiun's quick slice-and-snatch, but didn't comment on that, either. Just sighed and resumed his patrol.

When the FEMbot reached an altitude of twenty-seven feet, it entered the EDS MUAV LAWZ, and that, naturally, sent the military into a tizzy.

THE DOOR BURST OPEN. "Mr. President!"

The First Lady was instantly awake and sitting up in bed, eyes wild. "What's happening?"

"Haven't I told you folks to knock first?" the President asked.

"Security emergency! Get up, please. You, too, ma'am."

"What kind of security emergency?" the President demanded, putting down the legal pad on which he had been journaling.

The Secret Service agent tried not to look, but his eyes were drawn irresistibly to the notepad for a fraction of a second—just long enough to read the words "Octet of Evil" doodled in big, block comic-book letters. There were many explanation points after it. He looked away quick. "There's been a breakdown in the FEM system. Please come with me."

"Whoa, partner." The President put his hands up. "A breakdown is not an alarm."

"There's been an anomalous event," the second Secret Service agent explained.

Dammit! the first agent thought. He hated it when the Chief Executives started getting cocky. And they all did, right around the third year. But he also hated rookie Secret Service agents. Didn't he know—you never, ever give the President too much information.

"Describe anonymous in this pretext," the President added.

"Context, dear," the First Lady said, still frightened.

"We think we've got a micro-unguided air vehicle in the vicinity of the White House," the agent informed him.

"This follows an aberrant malfunction in the fielded FEM units," the rookie added detrimentally.

"Stay here with the First Lady." The President swung his legs out of bed and dragged on his long flannel robe, scuffed and patterned to look like suede.

"We're here to escort you below."

"You will stay here with my wife. I'll be back in a minute."

"Mr. President—!"

"Agent," the President interrupted, "there's a certain senator whose husband used to be Chief Executive, and this senator is requesting an increased Secret Service guard be assigned to her. Interested in a transfer?"

The agent began to tremble visibly. "No, thank you, sir. I'd prefer death by fire ants, Mr. President."

"Then stay with my misses, Agent, she's quite nice by comparison."

The President made a quick jog to the Oval Office, brushed off the aides and agents who tried to get his attention and slammed the door behind him. A fine powder of plaster crumbled down from the ceiling. The President snatched a phone out of his desk.

"Yes, Mr. President?" answered the director of CURE.

"Your boys on the property?"

"I would assume so, sir."

"You told them what I said, didn't you? That they couldn't beat my robo-rats, and they took it as a challenge?"

"Er, that is possible, sir. I'm monitoring the alerts on the Executive Defense System Micro Air Unmanned Vehicle Low Altitude Watch Zone. The signal that caused the alarm was from a small object that was, in fact, traveling away from the White House."

"Yeah? So?"

"Its mass makes it, possibly, a FEMbot."

"But you're not a hundred percent sure? What if it isn't your boys?"

"Do I appear as a boy to you?"

The President shouted and leaped to his feet. It was the old man, who was standing before the desk as if he had been waiting there patiently for minutes. But the President knew he would have noticed an unexpected senior citizen when he first entered the Oval Office. Especially one with severe sunburn.

"Is that Master Chiun? May I speak to him?" Smith asked.

"He may not," Chiun answered.

The President hung up. "Why you been havocing up my artificial wildlife?"

"Because they are a hindrance to the safeguarding of this symbolic domicile and the figurehead who dwells within."

"Yeah, well, you busted some of them up. They're eleven million each."

Somehow, there was now on the President's desk a pile of brown hairy things with wires coming out the end. Squirrel tails! The President sputtered as he counted them. "That's 122 million U.S. tax dollars down the drain! How'd you like it if I took that out of your salary? I get the impression you're paid handsomely for your occasional contributions...."

That was as far as he got. The old Korean's eyes were cold, deadly cold. "Surely you would not break your contract with Sinanju. No leader ever breaks a contract with Sinanju. Especially if this is his most effective alternative."

The old man nodded at the desktop full of faux squirrel tails. When the President looked up again he found himself alone.

The old Korean had a point. Clearly the FEMbots were not the last line of presidential security that their Pentagon sponsor had proclaimed them to be.

32

Harold Winston Smith had waded into ethical quagmires more times than he could imagine, and his own indomitable self-control and analytical abilities gave him a unique advantage in determining what was ethical in the face of conflicting moral judgments.

Smith was not emotionless, as some accused him of being. He was not without imagination, as several former CIA psychiatrists had concluded from extensive testing. But these emotions were extravagances of human cognition, and with a little self-control they could be submerged in the psyche, making it easier to weigh the opposing sides and make the most ethical choice.

Smith was also uniquely disinclined to regrets and remorse. Once he made a decision he knew was the correct one, he did not allow himself to second-guess or wallow in doubt. That was a waste of time and energy, and served no purpose.

So when Dr. Smith decided it was time to violate the privacy of the President of the United States, he did so with a clear conscience and absolute lack of self-interest.

He was not inclined to believe that the President was a traitor, but someone close to the President probably was, based on recent events. The intelligence needed to stage the break-ins in Arizona and New Mexico, in Virginia and Illinois and Oregon, had all come from various government agencies. This intelligence didn't coalesce in any manner below the executive level—either the President or someone close to him was feeding the data to the thieves, or the thieves had scrounged the information themselves from a variety of secure federal agencies. The latter source seemed less likely to Smith.

So, what top-level officials might be corrupt? The President. The cabinet. One or two advisers. They were supposed to represent the greatest American patriots, but Smith knew from experience they sometimes turned rotten.

CURE had extracted a few bad apples from the governmental barrel in its history. In fact, quite recently CURE proved that a powerful U.S. senator from California was found to be selling U.S. war plans—hundreds of documented military options for almost any crisis, in almost any conceivable theater, all sold to one of the worst former tyrants in the Middle East.

Smith was therefore quite surprised when he heard the President make his very first phone call to the traitor himself.

"Senator Whiteslaw, this is the President."

"Good evening, Mr. President. What can I do for you?"

"I need your expertise, Herb, one more time."

"Always happy to help."

Smith had only just programmed the wiretap and had

hardly expected to have this fall into his lap within three minutes.

"The FEM system is a washout. It failed a major test," the President said.

"I wasn't aware a test was scheduled," said Senator Whiteslaw questioningly.

"It was an impromptu sort of thing, but it was real-world enough to prove the FEM system is really flawed."

"They are still being optimized. Their capabilities are getting better every day. Who tested them?"

"Experts. Herb, the FEMs never even knew these guys were on the grounds. And now I've got a bunch of fake squirrel tails sitting on my desk."

"Mr. President, you allowed them to destroy the units?"

"No. They just did."

"But, Mr. President, that's got to be a violation of a bunch of federal laws, and it's not exactly professional behavior—you should have these men detained!"

"Whiteslaw, shut up."

Silence. Smith wondered what further surprises were coming.

"How can I help you, Mr. President?" Senator Herbert Whiteslaw said finally.

"I need to know if I have a spy in my cabinet."

"What!"

"You heard me. We've got a technology advantage on the rest of the world. It cost us billions and it took years to get here. It's being erased more every darn day. I don't want to be the President who allows the U.S.A. to go from superpower to just plain global power. Anybody can be a global power. For God's sake,

Unpopular Science

France is a global power!" The President took a deep breath. "I need to put a stop to this."

"You want me to go back undercover, Mr. President?"

"You tell me, Herb. Will it do any good?"

"I can't promise anything, but I do still have my connections in the Middle East. They're the kind of people who might know who is selling the plans. Who knows where the trail might lead?"

"Good. Do it."

"Mr. President, you are asking me to risk my reputation, my future in politics."

"You'll be sanctioned by me."

"Sanctioned?"

"I'll back you up, Herb, a hundred-and-ten-percent. You get busted, I'll go public. You'll come out looking like a hero."

"All right, Mr. President. I'll get started."

The call ended. Mark Howard yanked open the door and pushed his way inside, finding the CURE director looking thoughtful.

"Dr. Smith?"

"Mark, listen to this."

Smith replayed the just-ended conversation. Mark Howard recognized the voice of Senator Herbert Whiteslaw at once and became visibly alarmed. By the end of the call he looked like a man who didn't know what to think.

"What's your take?"

Mark shook his head. "I honestly can't tell you," he said. "I thought Whiteslaw was in WITSEC."

"The records say he is being held in the witness protection program while his case is sorted out," Smith said, leaning over his screen. "The highest-security files have him documented as a potential top-level traitor. He was told he is under danger of assassination and was put in the witness protection system for his own safety, but the Homeland Security is monitoring him for evidence of betrayal."

"The evidence CURE had," Mark Howard said. "And altered."

"It served its purpose," Smith said. "Still, I wouldn't have given my approval for using it if I thought the President would free the man."

"So why *did* the President free Whiteslaw, and create this fiction in the records of the federal intelligence departments?" Mark asked.

Smith stared into space, weighing the possibilities. Some of those possibilities were quite troubling, and he jumped when the red phone rang.

Smith and Mark Howard stared at one another as Smith picked up the receiver and punched on the speaker. "Yes, Mr. President?"

"So, Smith, what's your verdict?"

Mark's eyes grew wider.

"My verdict on what, Mr. President?"

"I'd rather not play games, Smith. I bet you tapped my line. Maybe you have had my line tapped from the very start, but I'm guessing you heard the call I just made."

"Yes, Mr. President. Mr. Howard and I were just discussing it."

"You have some questions to ask and they're pretty important ones. If I give you the wrong answers, then you'll have to make some mighty big decisions."

Dr. Smith felt the rumble in his chest as the mighty

weight of all this settled into his chest like a quarry full of massive boulders. "Yes, I understand perfectly."

Mark Howard did not. Not quite.

"You had better ask those questions, Smith, so we can move on. One way or another. I'll call you back in five minutes."

33

Secret Service Special Agent Martina Vespana had long ago decided that all politicians were nuts and desperately in need of protection by sane human beings such as herself.

She was as competent and cool as they came, and despite her lack of skill in the political glad-handing department, she was noticed for her dedication. Despite not knowing enough of the right people, despite not having kissed enough of the proper backsides and despite the fact that she was equipped with the wrong sort of natural plumbing, she managed to get a high-ranking White House assignment. Based on her job performance, of all things!

She considered other career choices during the bleak days of the previous administration. Her fanny and her pride could take only so much presidential man-handling. She was sure she was going to lose her cool if she had to put up with those busy executive hands and those furtively whispered invitations to "see Little Rock."

She was almost pushed too far. Another few gropes

would have been the last straw. Just one more thumb-jab in the...

Then came salvation. An intern. A cigar. A lot of media scrutiny and a few lies. Bad news for the nation but good news for Agent Vespana. Slick Willie's manners improved overnight.

She had nothing to fear from his successor in that department, and in fact the current Man seemed level-headed, less of a lunatic than the others.

But you have to be a lunatic to be President, right? And every once in a while some of the lunacy came out unexpectedly. Like in the middle of a full-scale White House Alert, Level Red-Beta. Red-Beta meant the President went deep underground and stayed there until somebody told him it was okay to come out.

She was quite surprised, then, to see him emerge onto a balcony just over her head.

"I need to see you boys right away," the President said, as if he was talking to somebody right there with him. But he was alone. Nobody around except Vespana.

"Mr. President, get to deep cover," she insisted.

"Evening, Agent. Good to see you on the job."

"What is your security situation, Mr. President?" she demanded.

"I'm just fine. I am just fine, Agent."

Vespana felt better. The operative phrase today was *fine*. If the President said he was *good* it would have told her he was, in fact, in extreme danger, probably under threat of immediate physical harm.

"Then why are you—?"

The President went back inside the White House.

Vespana grabbed for her radio and demanded to know what the hell was going on.

34

"I guess I'm a little slow on the uptake, Dr. Smith," Mark Howard said. "The President knew we were tapping him. What questions does he want you to ask him?"

Smith's eyes were heavy with dread. He had not expected this and wasn't prepared for it. Even a man such as himself could not emotionlessly contemplate throwing the nation and the world into political chaos.

"He wants me to ask him if he is a traitor," Smith explained, his words dull. "If he is a traitor, he knows that I will order his assassination."

Mark sucked in his breath, then shook his head tightly. "But he wouldn't have staged this if he was a traitor, right?"

"If he thought it through ahead of time," Smith answered. "Maybe he realized too late that we may have tapped him. He's trying to bluff us."

Mark shook his head. "But we would know by now!" he insisted. "The President couldn't hide his culpability in... I don't even know what you think he might be guilty of!"

"I do not assume he is guilty of anything," Smith replied carefully. "But now we are faced with the possibility. We must rule it out immediately. I hope that is what he intends to do."

The red phone rang.

Smith picked it up. "Mr. President."

"SMITH," said the President of the United States of America sitting in the Oval Office. "I've got a herd of consternated Secret Service agents who will start pounding the doors down in a minute, so we have to get this going."

"Are my people present?" Smith asked.

"They haven't showed up," the President said.

"We're here," the draperies corrected him.

The President almost shouted. "Come out of there, would you, please?"

Remo Williams stepped into view, smiled shortly, his teeth exceptionally white against his blood red, pebbled complexion. "Evening."

"Is the other one with you?"

Remo nodded in the President's direction. The President glanced over his shoulder and found the ancient face of the Korean assassin just five inches from his own.

"Wah!" exclaimed the President, at his most unpresidential.

The Korean didn't speak or twitch or even move his glass-hard green eyes.

"That's impolite," the President accused.

"You summoned us," Chiun answered.

"Yes. We have got to clear the air around here. Things are running a little amok."

Chiun shrugged. "It is democracy. It is perpetually

in a muck. Popular mandate is the least efficient form of government."

"My government is not—" The President raised a hand to put a stop to himself. "You two. Bear witness."

The President knew about these men. He was pretty sure that they could see it if he lied. He was now under trial, and if he was guilty, the punishment would be death. They were his jury and, if needed, his executioners. Smith was going to serve as judge.

But the President couldn't have asked for a more fair trial, and he knew it, which was why he asked for it.

Smith asked, "Mr. President, why did you authorize the release of known traitor Senator Herbert Whiteslaw?"

"What?" Remo asked. "He's free? As in un-incarcerated?"

The President nodded, not at all surprised that the man could hear the words from the telephone.

"I told you to let me solve that problem, Smitty."

"Allow the President to answer the question."

The President did. "I was the one who sent him under cover originally. His trips to the Middle East were authorized by me. His assignment was to sell sensitive U.S. military secrets. The secrets were forgeries. It was part of a strategy of deception that would have helped us during the war in Iraq."

"Buzz! Wrong answer."

"Remo, please," Smith said.

"The stuff he sold was legitimate."

The President nodded stiffly. "We found out, through other channels, that the real plans had somehow made it into the hands of the enemy. We—I—did not believe Whiteslaw was a double agent."

"Even when we told you so?" Remo asked incredulously.

"Remo, please stay out of this," Smith insisted.

"No," the President said.

"So you brought him back into the inner circle? Does that seem really, you know, *smart?*"

"Remo…"

"When the current crisis erupted, I needed my experts," the President responded. "That means Whiteslaw. He's ex-Silicon Valley. He's got his fingers in every high-tech program the Senate knows about. Even if I have major disagreements with him in terms of political views, he was an invaluable adviser."

"Except he sold out the whole freaking country," Remo growled.

"Mr. President, why did you not heed our report on Whiteslaw's activities?" Smith asked.

"Because you didn't tell me anything I did not already know. Nothing I hadn't authorized him to do—from what I could see."

Remo glared. Smith said nothing. Chiun was just standing there, too close. The President continued, "I started seeing the pieces falling into place after my discussion with you today, Smith. I went through the list, and every time I thought about Whiteslaw, something felt wrong. It may be that he's dirty."

"*May be?*" Remo asked.

"That's correct. I don't believe he is. I won't believe it until I've got proof. If he is innocent, his undercover contacts just might lead us closer to whoever is really behind all this. If not, well—innocent or guilty, he'll serve a purpose. Whatever he does next will make for some interesting watching."

Remo Williams looked thoughtful, but Chiun sighed in disappointment.

"Come on." The President grinned. "Tell Smith if I'm sincere or not."

"The President is not lying, Smitty," Remo announced. "He's not plotting with Whiteslaw."

"Now, if you're satisfied, as well, Smith, let's talk strategy," the President said, sitting up straighter.

"Aren't you supposed to be in the basement?" Remo asked, suddenly alert. "There are a bunch of Secret Service outside the doors who're plotting to break the door down and some of them have even started perspiring."

"False alarm." The President glared at Chiun. "I'll stand them down." But before the President lifted the second phone, Remo held a hand over it. Remo and Chiun were staring into the ceiling, as if listening to the rats in the White House attic. Then they looked at one another, frowning.

"What?"

"The alarm is no longer false," Chiun stated, then twirled and slipped toward the window. The President jumped to his feet and by then he was alone.

The eldest and only son of Jacob Fastbinder III stabilized the air pressure, then keyed open the door to Fastbinder's new jet.

"You're on your own from here, dudes!"

The first metal cylinder, which was tapered at both ends like a hand-stretched glass Christmas ornament, rolled obediently out of the custom-widened side door of the passenger compartment. The second cylinder got stuck on something.

"Hey, come on, you big tub of lard, get going!" Jack Fast yanked the stick left and right. He heard the cylinder collide with something inside the aircraft. "Oh, great! Did you bend another seat support? I'm gonna strip your gears. I'm losing my patience with you and it's already down to eight degrees in here. Take this!" He turned the aircraft on its side.

The cylinder, much wider and shorter than the first cylinder, bonged against another seat but tumbled out of the jet and started the journey to earth. The journey would take a long, long time as free falls go.

"Pops," Jack radioed.

"Yes, Jack, are they on their way?"

"Yeah, Pops, but I think that fat tick-tocker bent the seats, just like in the tests. We need a better jet. I'm getting tired of replacing passenger seats in this little prissy thing. We need something with real bomb doors. Maybe the Canadians—"

"We're not going to buy a bomber, Jack!"

"Aw, jeez, Pops!"

Jack signed off and scowled into the stratosphere. "Fine. I'll build my own darn airplane."

THE CYLINDERS TUMBLED just seconds before righting themselves, and then they were ultra-aerodynamic, slipping through the thickening atmosphere in virtual silence. They were black, without signal lights, so they remained unseen. The coating of paint on the exterior allowed military scanning waves to slip over them as easily as the airstream. The ground control that was constantly monitoring the skies over Washington, D.C., never even knew the oversize Christmas ornaments were above them.

The Fastbinder jet never entered restricted airspace, simply followed its flight plan up the coast. The cylinders would plummet straight into the ocean until they brought out their guidance wings, which were scarcely more than ridges distending from the metal. They created just enough of an alteration in the course to steer the falling cylinders inland, still unnoticed. The ridges guided the cylinders directly over the White House, then pulled inside to allow the free fall to continue.

The tremendous speed of the cylinders might have punctured all the way into the underground bunker levels, but bombing the President wasn't the intention.

The intent was to make a soft landing on the White House lawn and snatch up the most high-tech rodents in existence. FEMbots had an estimated black market value of thirty-five million dollars each.

The cylinders contained no living tissue that might be crushed by the sudden deceleration of the most severe High-Altitude/Low-Opening jump in history.

The first cylinder burst and loosed a compacted wad of dense fiber the size of a bed pillow, which unfurled into thousands of black streamers—a cloud bigger than the entire White House itself. The streamers were torn away in a millisecond by the intense force of the wind, but not before slowing the cylinder markedly and not before pulling out a second wad of compact fiber. Another billowing cloud of paperlike streamers. And a third. Finally the cylinder had been sufficiently slowed to deploy a trio of extreme heavy-lift parachutes, which opened in series and brought the cylinder to a crunching, 11-G deceleration. If there had been a man inside the cylinder, he would have become human remains in that instant.

The three huge parachutes carried the cylinder for only three more seconds before the ground loomed up beneath it and the cylinder's tapered end penetrated the lawn soil. The landing looked smooth, but again it would have turned human occupants to jelly.

The three parachutes transformed simultaneously into flames that consumed them and vanished in a moment, allowing the second cylinder to land without tangling.

WHEN YOU WATCHED airspace over the White House, you used protocol. You never, ever deviated from the proper vocabulary of the operation.

But Sergeant Julian Cleary couldn't help himself. There had been one alert tonight already, still unexplained, and the watch crew was tense. Cleary was nervous. So what if he used a few nonsanctioned exclamations?

"Mother of crap!" He got a hold of himself and reported, "We've got an eminent catastrophic strike. It just showed up, at two hundred feet!"

His commander appeared. "Too slow to be a bomb."

"To fast to be anything but—shit!"

On his screen, the warning lights blinked and the audible alerts screamed and the tiny indicator showed the twin objects coming to a stop on the White House grounds within seconds of each other.

Sergeant Cleary and his commander rolled their eyes up to the ceiling. They were the on-site watch team, so whatever the objects were, they had just come down right above them.

They frantically began making alert calls, which were redundant since the event had been witnessed by three other watch teams stretching from Washington, D.C. all the way to NORAD in Colorado. The military response was already launching.

Which left Julian Cleary with nothing to do except watch and listen. Any second now, he was sure to feel the tremors of the explosion that would erase the White House from existence.

What the hell were they waiting for?

36

Remo watched the first display as if it were the Fourth of July—great clouds of paper appeared and disintegrated instantly. He also saw the effect it had on the falling objects. They slowed greatly. Then came three parachutes, which slowed the devices more but still dropped them to the earth hard. The tapered lower ends were lengthy enough to, penetrate the earth before deforming into an accordion of crumpled metal, further cushioning the impact.

Remo was moving fast, hoping Chiun had the same idea he did since there wasn't exactly time to discuss it. That idea was to move in fast and take out these amazing mechanical mothers before they got a chance to user their proton-ray thingamajigs.

Chiun was right beside him as he drifted across the grounds at inhuman speed, like a pursuing wraith, and used the flat of one foot to knock the cylinder off its pedestal before it was even fully settled. The impact was greater than Remo had counted on. Whatever the cylinder was made of, it was tough stuff.

Instead of wrenching off the base, the base bent and

the cylinder slammed into the ground broadside. An eight-foot panel ejected from the cylinder on small explosive puffs and revealed the contents.

"Whaddaya know, Ironhand lives again," Remo said, snatching the metal door panel out of the air. The metal had a strange lightness to it, as well as incredible heat from the friction of the descent. He began vibrating his fingers, not allowing them to contact the metal long enough to absorb the great heat.

Ironhand threw its arms into the air as Remo brought the metal panel down. It was a fast move, but not fast enough. Remo turned the panel and slipped it past the robot arms, cutting deep into the chest cavity. Remo didn't know why, but he felt this was where he needed to create damage to prevent the debilitating proton discharge.

Ironhand scissored its legs and launched itself to its feet with the corner of the panel imbedded deep in its chest. It stepped out of the cylinder with a skip of its feet.

"You look like Tobor the Great playing hopscotch," Remo said, slipping up alongside the mass of metal. Ironhand struck at Remo fast. Very, very fast.

"New arms, I see. Very shiny." Remo held one and twisted it at the shoulder socket. And he kept twisting.

"Learned a thing or two about dealing with your type," Remo said, easily stepping under the blow Ironhand sent at him with its free arm. "First of all, you guys broadcast your moves worse than professional wrestlers. Also, you may be shiny but you're not too bright."

At that moment, Remo steered Ironhand's free arm into its face and wiggled the hand so fast it made gray smoke.

When he let go, Ironhand's fingers were ultrasonically welded to its face. The robot began rotating its torso rapidly in both directions, trying to free it.

"I gotta hand it to ya," Remo said, yanking off the other arm and slamming it into the chest of the robot. "Get it? Well, do you?"

The chest panel dropped off. Remo reached in and yanked out a chunk of quarter-inch-thick steel plating, then several other pieces until he had the guts of the robot exposed.

What's a proton emitter supposed to even look like? Because there were lots of different gizmos mounted inside the mechanical man and Remo couldn't begin guessing what any of them were for. But he knew he had to find out quick. Ironhand was like a landed fish, flopping around trying to get its hand freed, which forced Remo to weave and bob as he began yanking out parts.

There was a flash of electricity as something shorted out and Ironhand came to an abrupt halt. Remo could feel the surge of electricity coursing through the man machine, then draining away abruptly. Ironhand was out of power.

Something started up, something whirred, and Remo was abruptly cast into a pit of lifeless blindness. Ironhand was recharging itself, and Remo Williams's senses were cast into a void.

He thrust out his arms as he collapsed onto his knees and felt his hands come in contact with something that burned and froze and began sucking out his own existence, like a chain from Hell tugging on his soul. Had his fingers closed on the thing itself, the proton emitter? Did he feel Ironhand moving to strike him down? Was he even still alive?

Remo didn't know the answer to any of these questions, but he exerted his will, or he attempted to, or he thought he did, and as blackness fought to claim him, he imagined he was wrenching the heart out of the machine man.

37

Jack Fast wasn't a happy boy. "Those meatballs gutted the Big I, Pops!"

"Get out of there, Jack," Fastbinder ordered, his voice distorted by the digital satellite feed.

The laptop sitting on the copilot's seat beep shrilly and Jack jumped. "I got a fix on Ballboy, Pops! He's sending!"

"Jack, don't do anything risky."

"What in tarnation is happening? You seeing this, Pops? This is all freaked out." Jack could hear his voice rise as he grew more agitated every second. "He's not on the White House grounds anymore. He's moving away. His gyros are totally out of whack."

"They apprehended him," Fastbinder said. "They will get him away fast as possible, just in case he is wired to blow zee House up."

"I'm not buying it, Pops. If it was the Service they'd have stuck him in a sealed vehicle so he couldn't get communications out. Ballboy is still sending full-strength, it's just all messed up. The GPS is fluctuating like—like— Hey, Pops, Ballboy is rolling down the street!"

"That is unlikely, Jack."

"Yeah, look at the fluctuations in the GPS feed. It'll model out to pi, I guarantee it. It must be those weirdo friends of Senator Whiteslaw who nabbed him. It isn't the Service at all…"

Fastbinder read volumes in the thoughtful tone in his son's voice. "Jack, please do nothing that is foolish."

"I gotta know, Pops. These jerks have caused us nothing but trouble since the beginning. They killed Ironhand, Pops! He's an heirloom. He's what we're all about."

"He's a machine only, Jack. He can be reconstructed."

"You're not getting it, Pops. It's not about Ironhand—it's about this pair of reprobates who keep ruining everything we do. We gotta stop 'em. We gotta."

Jack Fast steered the aircraft into a bank so sharp he felt the blood travel into his legs. Time to return to the scene of the crime.

Fastbinder was still talking on the radio, trying to convince the teenager to keep his distance. "We will get them sooner or later. You risk getting caught or shot down."

"They'll never catch me, Pops. Not if I dive."

There was a moment in which Fastbinder said nothing. "Do not dive—I beg this of you."

"Sorry, Pops," Jack said, "I'm diving already."

38

The Air Force general opened the door fast and hard, breaking the nose of the lieutenant who collapsed to the floor, the coffeepot he'd been rushing to refill shattering against his head.

"Your lucky day, Lieutenant," the general barked. "If there had been coffee in that pot you'd be looking at years of skin grafts."

"Yeth thir, General," said the lieutenant, holding his spurting proboscis in one hand and his gashed scalp in the other.

"Have this cleaned up," the general snapped at his assistant.

The assistant, a captain and decorated fighter pilot, snatched at his lapel and spoke into the clip-on mike. "Cleanup in Command Control."

General Elvgren "Sick Puppy" Rover was already shoving his way through the crowd around one of the banks of flight controllers. "Show me."

"Right here, sir," said a button-pusher.

General Rover looked at a dot on the screen. It was different from the other dots because it had a red circle blinking around it.

"What of it?"

"It came out of nowhere, Sir. One second it wasn't there, the next second it was just there. Now it's going Mach 4, Sir."

Rover shouted, "It's a missile, you idiots! Shoot it out of the sky!"

"When it first showed on the screen it was going Mach point five, General, Sir."

"What the hell is this geek going on about? Captain! Where the hell—?"

"Here, Sir!" His assistant had just now elbowed his way through the pack of onlookers. He withered under the disapproving glare of the general, then quickly straightened. General Elvgren "Mad Dog" Rover disdained any sign of weakness. "He's saying the aircraft is an aircraft, Sir. One-half mach is too slow for a missile, Sir."

"You screwed up the ID, son, that's all," the general accused the flight controller. "You got some dinky plane and this missile mixed up together."

The flight controller tried to decide how best to defend himself against the accusations of General Elvgren "Ruff! Ruff!" Rover. He decided on the straightforward truth. "It is not my identification, Sir. NORAD's had a lock on it since it entered the ECUSSA."

"Excuse you what?" Rover demanded.

"East Coast United States Secure Airspace," Rover's pet captain explained.

"What happened to Secure East Coast Air Watch?"

The crowd tittered. The air traffic controllers looked at their screens to hide their amusement, and even a visiting Pentagon official scratched his ear to hide his mirth. A janitor rolled his eyes as he pushed his mop bucket into the hall in a big hurry.

"What's wrong with you people?" Elvgren "The Bitch" Rover exploded.

"The SECAW designation was retired more than a month ago."

"What? Why?"

"To allow the new designation to be used—District of Columbia And Surrounding Environs Coastal Airspace Watch Perimeter. DOCASECAWP. It failed to roll off the tongue, Sir. The designation was therefore changed to ECUSSA."

"Why in blazes didn't they just change it back to SECAW, then?" demanded General Elvgren "Fido" Rover.

There was silence. The flight controllers looked at one another questioningly, and the officers mulled it over or pretended they knew the answer. Rover's captain said simply, "Nobody thought of that, Sir."

"That's why they call me 'Smart Puppy' Rover, Captain."

"Yes, Sir."

The Pentagon official, who had once worked in acronym development, was feverishly writing notes on his palm with a ballpoint.

"What about the BOIID?" interjected the controller, who added quickly, "The Belligerent of Indeterminate Identification."

"Shoot dat BOIID. Didn't I say that first thing when I walked in here? What's everybody still talking about it for? Captain, I want court martials for every man in the room. You, too."

"A moment of your time, Sir," the captain said.

The exasperated Air Force general accompanied his assistant into a private corner. "We can't shoot it down,

Sir. That's why I asked you to be consulted in this matter, Sir. The aircraft is behaving like an EVIDA—it's an Extreme Velocity Intrusion Delivery Aircraft."

"Never heard of it."

"In development by the Navy. Top security. But the grapevine says the prototype was stolen recently. No other aircraft we know of could go from a slow stealth airspeed to Mach 5. EVIDA is designed for it, Sir."

General Elvgren "Sly Dog" Rover nodded thoughtfully. "The Navy's, you say?"

"Yes, Sir."

"Shoot it down."

The captain turned to the loiterers in Command Control. "General's orders. Shoot down dat BOIID."

"General's orders. Shoot down dat BOIID," echoed the Pentagon official, who appeared to have some authority here.

"General's orders. Shoot down dat BOIID," radioed the controller whose task it was to relay such orders.

General Elvgren "Bow-Wow" Rover asked quietly, "You sure I'm not supposed to know anything about this Evita?"

"EVIDA, Sir. No, Sir. Even I am not supposed to know."

"Good. Let's get out of here before they start singing."

The room continued echoing with calls of "Shoot down dat BOIID," and did, indeed, come dangerously close to becoming a chorus.

"EVENING, Little Father."

"Hello, Remo. Rested?"

Remo got to his feet, evaluating the grinding of

bones in his chest. "Small fracture," he said offhandedly. "Nothing too serious."

"I know this, of course," Chiun said.

The smell told Remo he was no longer on the grounds of the White House. He found they were standing in an alley.

"What did you bring that for?" he asked.

"This contrivance?" Chiun asked. "I deemed it could be of value to us. We shall present it to the Emperor for evaluation by his laboratory hirelings."

"It's Clockwork. It's the robot we saw helping Ironhand in Providence," Remo said. "The one from the TV show. He had a key in his back for winding him up."

The robot's body was a copper ball more than two yards in diameter. Out of the gasketed opening at the top protruded a scrawny copper tube of a neck, topped with a copper sphere of a head the size of a basketball. He had ears that were pounded out of tin and riveted in place. A mouth was etched into the metal surface and almost hidden under the layer of scratched stealth paint that coated it head to toe.

"He is not a windup toy," Chiun said. "He was once powered by a device such as this." Chiun held up a small egg-shaped lump of steel with dangling wires.

"You took that out of Clockwork?"

"You removed this from Ironhand."

"I did?" Remo gazed at the thing. "I remember trying. I wasn't sure if I'd managed to actually do it."

Chiun showed concern for the first time. "The mechanical man kicked you in the chest, and I thought you were senseless, and yet you did not release your grip on what you were grasping. You pulled this out of Ironhand and he ceased to function. It was a foolhardy thing to touch it, Remo."

Remo relived it in his memory, the blackness that came upon his senses and seemed to erase his consciousness. "Little Father, it was not like dying. I've died. Death I know." He fixed the old Korean master with haunted eyes. "This was worse."

Chiun nodded, but couldn't understand what Remo had endured. Perhaps, Chiun thought, Remo was correct about this device. Perhaps it was a weapon that was more than just a rock.

Now Remo scrambled to his feet and backed away. "Little Father, get away from it!" The source of his concern was the big round ball of a mechanical man, which stood quite still.

JACK FAST SAW the fighter planes come to intercept him. "Hi, guys." He grinned and waved.

The fighter jets spit out white bursts of fire, and Jack nudged his joystick just enough to dip the EVIDA. She dodged the burst and was past them in an eye blink.

"'Bye, guys," Fast said as they were left behind.

He had one hand on the stick and another on the laptop on the seat next to him, keying in every command he could think of to optimize his reception.

"Come on, Ballboy, what's the problem?"

He snapped off a quick repeating command to Clockwork, ordering it to send an emergency black-box data dump. If that fat moldy old robot reject could send even a couple seconds of data stream, it would be enough to tell Jack what was going on in the past few minutes. The glow of Washington, D.C., rushed up under the aircraft at exhilarating speed, but Jack hardly noticed. He had an eye out for another intercept.

An orange light appeared on the controls. The wing temperature was climbing into the danger zone.

"Navy piece of junk!" Jack exclaimed, leaning out the window and staring at the tiny stubs of the fully re-tracted wings. "Why didn't those morons use tita-nium?" He throttled down to Mach 2.2 until the temperature climb stopped. He could stay in the cau-tion zone if he was careful….

The proximity alarm screamed and a pair of closing fighter jets came at the EVIDA from out of nowhere.

"Fine, jerks, let's see how this grabs ya." Jack did-dled the joystick and spiraled toward the city just as a burst of fire scorched the air over him.

"HE'S GOING DOWN in D.C.," the pilot radioed. "Com-mand, you've got a real mess about to happen."

"He's trying to pull up," added the pilot of the sec-ond fighter.

"He'll never be able to—"

"He's leveled it! Look! What the hell is that thing he's flying, anyway?"

"Officially," the second Air Force pilot answered, "I have no idea."

"THIS ONE IS NOT functional, Remo," Chiun insisted. "It was damaged when it flew over the fence and rolled down the street to this alley."

"You tossed it over the fence?" Remo asked.

"Then steered it into this filthy dark place with my feet. Perhaps I should take up soccer."

Remo pictured it, the little Asian man carrying his

inert body into the streets of D.C., nudging along this bizarre metal ball with tubular arms and tube-mounted treads for feet.

"I hear activity inside this thing."

Chiun shrugged. "Dead machines are like dead humans. A car will continue to make pulses of electricity for days after it crashes."

"This is more than that." Remo could hear the rising concern in his voice. "There's a gyroscope in there."

"I hear it," Chiun said.

"It's stabilizing."

"Of course."

"The gyroscope is still under power. Let's get the hell away from it, Chiun."

"Remo, I understand if you are fearful, but this machine is broken. We may safely transport it to the Emperor. Even I can see the need to understand its workings."

What Remo was hearing was like a rising scream, although he knew it was tiny. A minuscule gyroscope inside the robot, like the gyroscope in an aircraft autopilot, was stabilizing after the wild fluctuations of Chiun's soccer-ball routine. Any moment now it would reach its baseline and then...what?

"We go now."

Chiun put his hands into his sleeves and wrinkled his brow, prepared to take a stance, but then the haunted, hollowed, stricken eyes of Remo blazed into him. Rarely had Chiun been the target of that look.

"*Now*, Chiun."

But even as he said the words, both of them felt and heard the subtle steadying of the gyroscope inside the foolish-looking machine. Remo made a sound in his

chest that hurt his broken bones and he willed his body
to move fast, move hard, just *move*. He had done it before when the blackness came down on him and he
would do it again, but it was a nightmare that came back
to devour him. The round ball head twisted and then
blackness came.

Chiun felt the blackness, just as he had felt it in the
grounds of the White House, and he felt Remo's hands
wrench him by the wrist, carrying him off his feet,
sending him above the ground to the end of the alley
where the blackness slipped away with the distance.
Chiun gathered his senses about him and met the slime-
coated alley floor easily, turned and skimmed the earth
back the way he had come. If the thing avoided recharging itself, he would have time to best it.

The danger was over temporarily, but the damage
was done.

Remo lay where he had fallen, his eyes open. He
wasn't stirring. He was more than still. He was rigid,
as if long dead.

Chiun felt real terror. What a fool of an old man was
he! His pupil had done this great deed once tonight, and
Chiun had exposed him to the madness again! How
much of this could one be expected to endure?

"Remo, hear me and return!" Chiun cried as he
struck the flailing arms and thrashing head of the mo-
ronic copper man. "Remo, the blackness is no place for
a Master of Sinanju. It is *beyond* the Void!"

JACK'S FINGERS were tense on the joystick as he rock-
eted just 1,100 feet above Washington, D.C.

"Here's Jack. Talk to me, Ballboy."

The computer beeped as if in answer.

"Cool!" Jack Fast exclaimed, and steered on an intercept course.

CHIUN FELT the pressure waves echoing along the street as if some gigantic bullet was approaching, but it wasn't coming down. Simultaneously he felt the burst of static electricity that flew out of the metal creature disintegrating under his hands.

"Is this a friend of yours?" Chiun asked, snatching the head off of Clockwork. The eye lenses rolled crazily in their sockets. "Then rejoin him!"

He angrily shot-putted the heavy metallic head into the skies over Washington, D.C., as the approach of the low-flying aircraft became an assault of pressure waves. Chiun's senses were imperfect at this moment, and the aircraft was coming with extraordinary speed; momentarily, the old Master questioned the accuracy—

The head and the aircraft came together with Chiun-like precision.

THE INTERIOR of the aircraft became a sound chamber filled with screaming alert signals.

"HOLY TOLEDO!" Jack Fast exclaimed, not hearing anything. His attention was riveted on the needle-sharp nose of the EVIDA aircraft. A deformed metallic thing was impaled there, shaped like a flattened basketball. Amazingly, the brass bowler hat had survived almost perfectly intact.

"Clockwork!"

One rolling eye dangled in the slipstream, then was

jerked out by the force of the air. It was then that Jack noticed the EVIDA was vibrating uncontrollably.

Clockwork's skewered head was screwing up his aerodynamics big-time.

CHIUN FELT the rumbling of the city, then the shock wave of the passing aircraft thundered this filthy corner of Washington, D.C., like an earthquake, cracking the crust on the street filth so that the stench blossomed anew.

Chiun was beyond noticing. He didn't care that he had bested the enemy. It no longer mattered that the thing of copper was reduced to bits and pieces of metallic waste that might as well have gone through a junkyard shredder.

He took the wide-eyed creature from the filthy pavement and carried it into the streets of the hideous city. His ancient, bony fingers could feel the beating of a powerful human heart inside this body—but what else remained? Did *anything* else remain?

"Fight it, Remo," he whispered. "Claw out of the blackness. Do not let the blackness imprison you beyond the Void, where there is nothing."

Chiun took a taxi to the airport, then boarded the aircraft hired for him by Emperor Smith, although he was not truly aware of doing these things. At one point Chiun heard the flight attendant tell him a car would be waiting for him at the other end. Smith's machinations coming into play.

Chiun was speaking all the while, quietly, whispering, and sometimes weeping. "Old fool!" he would say occasionally, but usually his words were for Remo.

What frightened Chiun the most was the feeling in his own breast, the dreadful emptiness.

There was a connection between a Master and his Pupil, and when a Master died or a Pupil died, the other knew and felt such an emptiness. It was perhaps one of the myths of Sinanju, based on a wish more than the true nature of the art.

Chiun hoped this was just myth, just a Sinanju old wives' tale, because at this moment that place was empty, as if Remo Williams had ceased to be.

"Remo," whispered the old man.

His words went unheard.

39

"Dad, you there? Come on, Pops, talk to me!"

"Jack, I had given you up for dead!"

Jack almost breathed a sigh of relief as he muscled the EVIDA under Mach and felt the click of the wings locking into their fully extended position—but the plane kept shaking.

"Loser IIT dropouts!" Fast exploded. "Why can't the Navy hire some real engineers to design their gear?"

"Jack, say again?" Fastbinder radioed.

"Can't talk now. I'll call ya back, Pops." Jack reduced speed even more and felt the aircraft wobble uncertainly in the direction he steered it. He was out over the Atlantic when his air speed reduced to three hundred miles per hour.

The EVIDA project leaders boasted a stall speed of 125 miles per hour.

"So why is the darn thing stalling?" Fast exclaimed. He pumped more juice into the engines and pushed the EVIDA into a tentative stability that wouldn't last long. Fast thumbed on the autopilot and grabbed the laptop.

He groped under the passenger seats, which were installed by the brilliant engineers at the Navy who intended for the EVIDA to be hidden in plain sight by pretending to be an officers' transport plane. Fast yanked out a cushion with a label that said that, in case of a water landing, the cushion could be used as a flotation device.

The EVIDA choked on her fuel as Fast blew off the cockpit entrance. "Good riddance," he told the 1.6-billion-dollar hunk of junk as he stepped out.

He deployed his stealth chute and drifted away as a pair of fighter planes screeched a few thousand feet overhead. The fighters watched the EVIDA ditch in the Atlantic, but they never saw the young man who ejected.

Fast wasn't a happy camper. A heck of a lot of work had gone down the drain tonight. His only consolation was that, maybe, if he was lucky, the data dump received from Clockwork, now stored in his laptop, might give him a clue about who it was who had beat him.

Because tossing a robot head onto the nose of a screaming jet took special skill. Fast would need ingenuity and strategy to overcome such skill.

His flight goggles' nosepiece extended to cover his mouth and nose. His empty cushion covering was a backpack that was filled halfway with steel air cylinders. There was a waterproof pack alongside them that accommodated the computer. Fast zipped it closed as he drifted down to the surface of the Atlantic.

Just before he submerged, Jack took a last look at the lights of the shore.

It was gonna be a heck of a long walk.

GENERAL ELVGREN "Bad Dog" Rover was reading the paper and pretended not to notice his assistant was on the phone. The captain hung up.

"Sir, the BOIID went into the Atlantic."

The general's wolfish grimace came and went, detecting something unsaid. "We shot it down?"

"It was shot down," the captain said. "By someone. Over D.C."

"Gang crossfire?"

"Unknown, Sir."

"If it was over D.C., then it was gang crossfire."

"Well, the street gangs in D.C. are some of the best-equipped in the world," the captain said uncertainly. "Still, this aircraft was designed to take antiaircraft rounds—"

"Not so far as we know, officially," Rover said, rattling his newspaper. "Gang crossfire. You writing the press release?"

"Yes, Sir."

"Gang crossfire."

"Yes, Sir."

40

First came the Emperor.

"We should move him to a hospital bed."

"That will do him no good. You have done every foolish test your charlatan doctors could think of."

"It would be better than laying him out on the floor."

"Be gone, Emperor," said Chiun.

Next came the prince.

"We know how the proton device functions, anyway. The labs are working on it."

This mattered not at all to Chiun.

"We may be able to repulse it. You know, turn it off. It would require some sort of counteractive device."

The prince left, eventually.

Next came the woman.

"I am capable of caring for him," Chiun snapped.

"It cannot hurt for another to care, as well," said Sarah Slate, taking the hard, limp hand in her own as she lowered into an identical cross-legged position. She looked Remo and said nothing. She left hours later, but she came back the next day, and the next.

Chiun took rice, he took water, but he seemed to fade.

And all around, the world seemed to fade with him.

41

Sarah Slate came into the room again, to find nothing changed. For days it had been like this.

"I have held my tongue."

There was no response.

"I thought I knew you," she said to the frail, gaunt little figure in the kimono.

Chiun emerged from his meditation. "You do know me. Leave me be."

"My family," she said sternly, "traveled the world for generations. We had incredible adventures. We knew many peoples. I thought I recognized the kind of man you were from reading the histories of my family. I thought I knew you, but I was wrong."

"Then we can end this pointless discussion. Depart now."

She was angry; Chiun didn't know why and didn't care why. He just wanted her to go away. Now she was scribbling on the walls with a reed brush dipped in ink, which she must have brought with her.

"Look, old man!"

Chiun raised his head.

"I thought this was you. I was wrong."

She threw down the bottle and the reed, splattering the floor with black ink, and stalked out of the room full of hot indignation.

Leaving behind her a sad old man, and the empty shell of another man, and on the wall, scrawled larger than life, the simple lines of a trapezoid pierced by a single slash mark.

It was the symbol of the House of Sinanju.

IT WAS A POLTERGEIST, or a demon, certainly not a human that came into small suite of rooms in a convalescent wing of Folcroft Sanitarium. The doors literally came off the hinges and rattled to the floor, but by then Sarah Slate was near to death.

"Chiun, stop!" Mark Howard cried as he hoisted himself out of bed as fast as he could move.

"Who are you?" demanded the Master of Sinanju Emeritus, one finger pressed against her throat. "Tell me this before you die."

Sarah Slate opened her mouth, fighting for breath, her body flattened against the wall as if buried under tons of rubble. "Who are you, really, old man? Tell me before I die."

"I am Sinanju, as you know! But what fool knowingly insults a Master?"

"What kind of a Master insults another Master?"

"I will not engage in word play with one such as you."

"Chiun, you're killing her!" Howard said, dragging at Chiun's bony arm.

"I intend to."

"For God's sake, why?"

"Because I have exposed him," Sarah croaked as her face colored. "He has not the strength to save his pupil."

"There is no way to save him or I would have done so."

"I can save him," Sarah said, her last words coming out in a ragged, empty breath.

Her neck was abruptly released. Chiun's eyes were green fire that burned her. "I do not believe you."

"You have nothing to lose," she gasped.

"In this you are correct."

"What is going on?" Mark Howard demanded.

Sarah tried to smile as she forced herself to walk. "A Slate goes to resurrect a Master of Sinanju. Again."

42

"What potion will you pour in his gullet?" Chiun asked bitterly.

He hated her, this woman who dared tantalize him with hope when he knew there was none—and yet she believed in herself. Certainly this woman's ancestors were acquainted with the greatness of Sinanju. But to dare claim to have saved the life of a Master was outrageous.

Sarah Slate sat on her legs in a child's pose, rested her hands on her knees and, with a wave of her hand, indicated Chiun should take his seat across the limp body of the Reigning Master of Sinanju.

"Tell me about this man," she said.

"No," Mark said, standing off to the side.

"What would you learn?" Chiun asked. "Already you know he is Master of Sinanju."

"That is not the all of him," Sarah Slate replied. "He has a past and a future. He has known love and loss. In this he is like all human beings."

"You don't know what you're asking, Sarah," Mark Howard said. "There is knowledge you cannot have."

"For what purpose would you know these things?" Chiun demanded.

"He is lost. He is beyond the Void. Masters have ventured there before."

"Never by choice," Chiun said. "Never to come back."

"Yes. Some came back," Sarah said. "At least one did. A master who called himself Go."

"I know of Master Go," Chiun said. "Go did not travel beyond the Void. Our histories are carefully kept."

"As are ours," Slate replied. "Master Go was in search of gold when he met Andrew Slayte, an ancestor of mine. My ancestor also sought the gold. In Spain they met a mesmerist who tricked Go and drained him of all his thoughts."

Chiun stared. "This is a fairy tale."

"It is in the history of my family."

"That does not make it true."

"Andrew Slayte was more than a partner to this Master Go—he was a friend."

"Phah!" Chiun waved the air away as if it smelled bad.

"Andrew knelt by the side of Go and used his voice to entice Go out of the emptiness beyond the Void. He reminded Go of all the wonders of Sinanju. He reminded Go of a girl Go loved, back in the village. Even, he reminded Go of the vipers' nest outside the village where Go loved to play when he was a boy, teasing the snakes for entertainment. Go heard Andrew Slayte's voice and recovered."

"This is too simple a cure," Chiun protested.

"But it is all that is needed," Sarah said gently. "Master Chiun, you do not bear the responsibility of bringing him back to our world. All you must do is light a tiny flame of remembrance in him. Any memory at all, if it is potent enough to reach him, will be light enough to see by, and then he will see all of it, everything that was wiped away."

Chiun was silent as stone. Sarah said, "Tell me of this man, Master Chiun. Tell me about something or someone he loves. What gives him great joy?"

Chiun looked over Sarah, at the black slashes of her symbol of the House of Sinanju.

Chiun spoke in the voice that was so gentle and beautiful that Mark Howard swore it came from someone else. "There is a beautiful girl," said Chiun. "She is Freya. With hair like gold. It is his daughter, who loves him, and he loves her."

Sarah Slate smiled, as if she, too, knew joy at this recollection. Sarah leaned close to the prostrate Master and spoke in a gentle, soothing voice. "Remo, do you see Freya? She's with you. You love her with all your heart, and she loves you. She has hair of gold. She is beautiful. She is the most beautiful girl in the world."

Mark Howard was silent, but the words were reaching him, too. Yes. The most beautiful woman in the world. He didn't know if he was thinking about Sarah Slate or Freya, daughter of Remo Williams, and for a moment it didn't matter.

43

He was in horror and misery and it was the horror of blackness unending, where there was no vision or sound, no smell or touch, nothing. Eternal awareness of eternal emptiness.

The horror melted into the mundane, and with profound relief it was forgotten. Emptiness, after all, was easy to forget, once there was anything to erase it.

In an instant his identity surged back into his thoughts. He knew who he was again. He knew his past again. His name was Remo.

Where was he?

He was in the desert, near the rez, and he was watching the most beautiful girl in the world. Her name was Freya, his daughter, and she loved the rabbits, and she loved Remo.

"'Bye, Daddy," she said as he left, but it wasn't a sad leaving because she said "'Bye, Daddy." So naturally did she let those words come from her lips that he knew it was true. Remo was Freya's dad and there was nothing better than that.

He was drifting like a peaceful ghost through the village. "Remember when I introduced you to the Sun On Jo?" asked Remo's father, Sunny Joe Roam.

Remo pictured Sunny Joe's introduction of him to the Sun On Jo people. They had accused him of being a half-white. What else had Sunny Joe said? Brought to us by a vision. That would be Remo's vision of the desiccated remains of Ko Jong Oh.

Then Sunny Joe Roam called Remo the next Sunny Joe.

Another tidbit that had been floating around unused in his head for years. Yes. Remo was the next symbolic leader of the Sun On Jo tribe. But the Sun On Jo were a pacifist people. They had hidden their great talents for generations—it was part and parcel with their origins. Ko Jong Oh had instilled in them secrecy lest they bring down the wrath of Sinanju, who could allow no other village of assassins to compete with them.

But how could Remo, the embodiment of Sinanju, the dynasty of great assassins, become the leader of these people with their philosophy of nonviolence?

Did he want to? If not now, would he want to someday? Would the Sun On Jo want him?

It would be a peaceful, quiet life on the rez. Didn't he deserve some peace and quiet?

As he drifted through the village of Sun On Jo like a weightless cloud, Remo passed through people and a horse and a fence, but then he crashed into something that he couldn't pass through. It was Mark Howard's stupid rental car, still propped up against somebody's house, and it fell over with the loudest, most annoying racket possible.

SOMETHING CRASHED. Something banged.

"Dammit all to hell!" He grabbed his throbbing head and staggered to his feet, then landed upright against the cabinets of the small kitchenette.

"Please. For the love of god. I am *begging* you. Stop banging the damn pots."

"Ah, you have awakened finally. I thought you might sleep the day away."

"Shove it, Chiun," Remo said. "My head's killing me. What time is it?"

"What time is it? You have been addled by too much sleep. Go purchase yourself a Swatch if you cannot know the time inside." Chiun touched Remo's forehead. Waves of pain radiated from the spot into Remo's skull and he sat down hard, back against the wall. He looked around and found himself in the three-room suite that he and Chiun shared at Folcroft.

"Feel like I've been out for days. What happened?"

Chiun didn't answer the question, guiding Remo back to his mat and fussing over him. There was a concern in his eyes that Remo didn't miss.

"Did I really get whacked, or what?"

"I suppose so, my son."

"Are you okay, Little Father?"

Chiun stopped fussing and descended into a cross-legged position, a look on his face that Remo, who knew him so well, could not read well.

"I must ask your forgiveness, my son. I led you into great danger."

Remo scowled. "Come on, Chiun, what are you talking about?"

"In the alley, after we left the clapboard palace of the pretender to the American throne."

"Yes? It was you who saved me, remember, Chiun? Ironhand turned my lights out."

"But there was the other. The ball-shaped copper man."

"Yeah? He fired up the sense-sucking death rays again, didn't he? I told you he would."

"Yes, you did." Chiun lowered his eyes.

"So I got knocked out again. So call me Scarlet O'Hara for having fainting spells. What's the gloomy look all about?"

"You were wounded more grievously than you may think."

"I don't want to think. It hurts when I think."

"It has been four days."

"Ouch." Remo touched his head. "No wonder I feel crappy. What happened? I mean, what would knock a guy senseless for four days?"

"That is what the young prince is trying to find out. He now has the mechanical heart that you tore from the breast of the first monster. He is having it studied."

"What about Clockwork? What happened to him. Did he hurt you?"

"Of course not," Chiun said, regaining some composure. "After you laid down to rest, I dismantled him. His trainer came along to retrieve him and I knocked his plane into the sea."

"Cool. Case closed then, eh?"

"According to the Emperor, the case remains open. As you have not yet stood up with confidence, I shall handle the preparation of the evening meal. It shall be haddock and jasmine tea."

"I'd like some Advil in mine," Remo said. "It's evening?"

WHEN THEY ENTERED the office it was past midnight. Mark Howard watched Remo from his own temporary desk. Smith gave Remo a careful appraisal. "Feeling better?"

"Better than when I was unconscious? No. Got any Excedrin?"

"Do not give him any," Chiun warned.

"Joking," Remo said. "See, I have my sense of humor back so I must be feeling better."

Smith said nothing. Chiun was silent.

"'Course, if humor matters, then you geezers are both minutes from the grave. Smitty, if you're gonna chew me a new one for taking unscheduled coma time, then let's get it over with."

Smith tightened his mouth. "Remo, we have much to discuss, but it can wait. We know who's behind all of this."

Mark Howard pushed a color eight-by-ten photograph at them. "Jacob Fastbinder III."

"He's ugly, but what makes him guilty?"

"He's got a very interesting history," Howard said. "It goes back to World War One."

"Oh, cripes." Remo grabbed his head. "Do I really have to hear it? Especially now? Little Father, can't you give me a mercy nerve pinch to make the throbbing stop?"

"I've tried. As I said, Remo, the hurt was deep...."

"Okay, let's go get him." Remo stood up. "Where we going?"

Mark gave him a brochure.

Fastbinder's Museum Of Mechanical Marvels
On Historic Route 66
In Scenic New Mexico!

"Oh, brother," Remo said, and left the office without walking into the doorjamb, although it was a near miss.

Smith looked worriedly at Chiun. "Should he be in the field, Master Chiun?"

"The time for concern is done. He will recover, Emperor, and perform his duties without fail. He is muddled now, still in the clutches of his extended slothfulness. I predict it will have passed before we arrive in the land of the Recently Annexed Mexico."

Smith nodded. "Master Chiun, I'd have to say you don't sound too certain of your own words."

Chiun snapped out of his own lingering distraction, and his self-anger simmered like a pot of gruel that had been bubbling on the fire for too many hours.

"The Master of Sinanju is never uncertain, Emperor, as you well know."

Then he followed Remo out the door. Quickly.

44

The phone bleated eight times, stopped, then started up again. Finally the sleeping man groped for it and pulled off the receiver. He sat up, manipulated his face vigorously and looked around. The hotel room didn't help him out. Every hotel room in the Middle East looked alike. He glanced at his wrist, found it empty and finally located his watch on the bedside table. The tiny window told him it was Thursday.

"If it's Thursday, this must be Cairo." Oh, yes, now he remembered arriving in Cairo from Qatar and getting drunk, alone, in his room at the Hilton.

So who would be calling him in his room in the Cairo Hilton?

"Hello?" he said finally into the phone.

"It is Fastbinder."

"Mr. Fastbinder, have you heard from your son?"

"I have."

"Oh, thank God," breathed Senator Herbert Whiteslaw of California.

"You are so fond of Jack?" Fastbinder asked.

"I was worried something horrible had happened to the boy."

"Something horrible did happen. He was two days hiking across the floor of the ocean to get back to zee dry land. He is exhausted. He will fly back home day after tomorrow."

"I can imagine."

"What is it that you have set us up against precisely, Mr. Whiteslaw?"

"If I knew that, I wouldn't have come to you for help, Fastbinder."

There was a pregnant pause. "If zees men ever learn the identification of you or me, then we are as good as dead. They seem to be gifted with some outstanding abilities."

"You're telling me. I've seen them in action, remember?" Whiteslaw flipped on the light and began hunting for his bottle. He almost groaned in disappointment when he found it on the counter, empty. There were disgusting tongue smears inside the neck of the bottle.

"Jack thinks he has a way to neutralize zees two," Fastbinder said.

"What? Really? How?"

"This he could not explain to me clearly, so I am certain the explanation would be entirely lost upon you. Sufficient to say these two have a Achilles' heel, unique to them, and Jack believes he knows how to use it."

"Well, that's great! We still have a green light on the plan then, do we?"

"It will be delayed," Fastbinder reported.

"No, no, no. Fastbinder, there's no time for delay. My strategy is based on a timeline that I can't control."

"Senator Whiteslaw, we must be empowered to defend ourselves against these men in case they come for us. We will delay. Until Jack can build this defensive system. Until such time, we cannot risk further exposure."

Senator Whiteslaw groaned. "So I'm sitting here pretending to be an undercover agent in the Middle East while your goofy high-school kid finds time to invent new weapons technology? I'm not encouraged, Fastbinder."

"It will take little time. A few weeks, perhaps."

"Weeks, huh? He doesn't need to go to college first?"

Fastbinder's accent thickened. It always did when he was agitated. "Herr White-zlaw, you underestimate Jack. He is the greatest mind in four generations of Fastbinders. He is an engineering genius. The world has never seen the like of him."

"Yeah, but he's got a girlfriend, so it balances out."

"You need not depend on Jack. Go elsewhere for assistance."

"You need me, Fastbinder," Whiteslaw barked. "As much as I need you."

Fastbinder chuckled.

"What's so funny?" the senator asked.

"You, and your confusion, I find humorous. The truth is I do not need you, Senator."

"Only I know where the military research is."

"But I do not need that! For me, stealing these secrets and selling them is more or less a hobby. I am semiretired, you know? You, on the other hand, are a driven man, and there is only me and Jack who are capable of helping you to meet your objective. Or maybe not. Maybe you have other irons in the fire, ja? Allow them to assist you—it is of little consequence to me."

"You know that's not how it is. You're the only chance I have."

"That is as I thought. Don't worry, Senator, I think Jack will rise to the occasion and we'll have plenty of time before the elections."

"Until then I'm just supposed to keep playing double agent for the President?"

"And keep praying that these assassins do not locate either of us while we remain helpless."

Senator Herbert Whiteslaw hung up the phone and sat on the edge of the mattress. That Fastbinder was a morbid turd. Was there any real reason to think they could be tracked down?

Who knew with these wacky assassins, the old Asian and the smart-mouthed skinny guy? Who knew what sort of resources were behind them? Maybe they were eavesdropping on him at this very minute.

He peeked out the window shades nervously. Fourteenth floor and no sign of assassins.

Still, if they did show up, Whiteslaw wanted to be ready for them. And that meant liquor. Lots of it.

45

"Howdy." Margo, manager of Fastbinder's Museum of Mechanical Marvels, greeted every customer who came through the door with a great big "Howdy." It wasn't an act, like the old farts who stood inside the Wal-Mart. Margo was the genuine article, friendly as all get-out.

"How-dee," answered the little man in the robe that added a turquoise glow on his paper-thin flesh. The man was older than Margo's grandma but standing upright, after all. He cocked his head, listening to the gift shop sound system and smiling.

"It's the latest Molly Pardon. You a Molly admiree?"

"He only likes her for her cleavage," said a much younger man who entered behind the Asian gentleman.

"Ms. Pardon is not as talented as Ms. Wylander—" the elderly man said conversationally, but he never finished.

"Oh, don't. I just can't take it today." The younger man, who looked constipated or worse, turned on Margo and never even noticed he didn't get a "Howdy." "Looking for Fastbinder. Is he around?"

"No. You another lawyer?"

"Do I look like a lawyer?" The man spread his hands slightly and looked down at himself. He was in a crisp, pale yellow T-shirt and casual slacks. The shoes were nice but too much with the outfit.

"Well, maybe you look like a lawyer about to clean his garage," Margo suggested.

The flesh on the forehead of the old Asian man wrinkled up, his mouth opened in delight and his green eyes positively danced.

"Heh, heh! A lawyer about to clean his garage. Heh, heh!"

The young man breathed out, and the words "oh, God," were in all that exhaled air. The young man tromped off into the corner and glared into the security camera—the real one, hidden in a plastic fish, not the fake one over the cash register.

"A lawyer about to clean his garage," the senior citizen repeated appreciatively.

"Do you have Tylenol?" the young man called.

"Sold out," Margo said.

"Laudanum? Heroin? Cyanide?" The young man was holding his head as if it really hurt.

"My son is joking," the old Asian explained. "This is what he thinks is funny. After all these years he does not notice that he laughs alone. Is Mr. Fastbinder available?"

"Sorry, sweety. Gone to town," Margo said. She was used to lying for Mr. F. So many nasty reporters came here to pester him that it wasn't really like lying.

Both the men stopped, as if frozen in their tracks, then the young man said, "You're right, Little Father. We flushed him."

"What is that noise this time?" Chiun asked. "It is a vehicle, I think."

"Hey, if tries to fly off, I'm not running after him," the young one declared.

"I certainly shall not," the old man said as they whisked out the door, so fast that Margo didn't actually see them go. She began looking under the display counters.

REMO RAN and the hot air was like a torch flame that singed his skin, but burned off some of the crust, too. It felt good to move like torrid wind in the Southwestern American desert. The headache receded.

He nodded to Chiun as they came upon the low, ugly building. Chiun gave him a last, concerned glance, then they separated. Remo circled right, Chiun left, looking for the source of the rumble. It didn't sound like an aircraft, really, or a truck. Maybe it was a bulldozer. Would Fastbinder try to escape in a bulldozer?

Anything short of a rocket, and Remo had him, and the heavy rumble of diesel engines sounded nothing like a rocket. When he rendezvoused with Chiun on the far end of the building, the old man shook his head.

"I saw no signs of any vehicles."

"Me, either, but he's got something big inside there." Remo said, eyeing the sand-worn brick warehouse. "He has to come out eventually, right?"

They circled to the delivery entrance, but the garage door remained shut. The rumble of machinery became intense, then there was a cracking and grinding like a controlled avalanche.

The saw nothing, but their feet could read the complaints of the very earth upon which they stood.

"Little Father, I don't think Fastbinder even knows we're here," Remo said. "He's too busy excavating a new root cellar."

"This is not any type of mechanized shovel I know of," Chiun said, frowning.

"Let's check it out."

Chiun's gnarled fingers locked on Remo's abnormally thick wrists. "No. I shall go."

"Chiun, I'm fine. The headache's fading."

"Remo, I have learned a hard lesson from this Fastbinder. Have you learned nothing?"

"I learned they're tough mothers with some really bad doodads. But take a whiff, Chiun, they've got none of the proton sense-erasers in action."

Chiun didn't release Remo. "Your words tell me you have indeed failed to learn the lesson. Did I not tell you before when we were at the home of the buffoon in Barcelona, to embrace your fear speck, to make use of it? Still you parade about, arrogant and speckless. Once again I tell you, Remo, that we do not know what surprises these Fastbinders have in store for us. Let our actions come from wisdom, and allow me to enter first."

"Whoa, you had me there until the me-first part."

"You are not recovered fully. If this weapon strikes us again, you will succumb more easily."

"Wrong. You're already more sensitive to that thing, Chiun. You have been since the first time we ran into it. Don't give me that I'm-so-insulted pout, either."

They stood in the hot sands, feeling the earth vibrate. "The funny thing is, if he's digging a root cellar, he's digging it really freaking fast. He must be down forty feet already," Remo observed. "I'm going in. Coming?"

FASTBINDER WATCHED the video feed from the security system, aghast at what he saw.

The bolt knobs on the blast-proof entrance doors turned and fell off. A tempered-steel chain, welded of half-inch links, kept the door from opening, but not for long. A hand came through the narrow opening and tapped the chain. Tapped it again in a different spot. Tapped it a third time, and the link crumbled.

The door swung open and there they were, the assassins. Fastbinder laughed bitterly—not an hour ago he was telling Whiteslaw to watch his back, and the assassins were already on their way to Fastbinder.

He fed more diesel into the engines and felt them increase their massive torque. He fretted over the controls, keeping the needles just under the red line.

"TOBOR THE GREAT at one o'clock," Remo warned, but Chiun was upon the guard droid in a flash, disemboweling him with a slash of fingernails strong enough to whittle girders. The robot was a top-heavy rolling contraption with a fishbowl enclosing his whirling head components, and he spun out of control. Chiun snapped at the thing with one foot and the robot flew across the room, slammed into worktables, knocked over a hunk of metalworking machinery and tipped over, vanishing into oblivion.

More of them came, and Remo threw himself into the battle with one overriding goal—work fast, before any of them felt the need to recharge their systems. He slashed at them furiously, crushing their mechanical body parts, ripping out their motorized entrails. A chrome-plated sauna box with clothes-dryer exhaust hoses for arms was lifted and brought crashing down upon a rolling, wooden camel with spiraling eyes. The camel burst open and showered jagged strands of metal just as it was crushed. Remo stepped around the only two projectiles that escaped the explosion. The chrome robot moaned, swiveled its head and tried to raise one arm, snapping its pincers weakly. Remo kicked its skull clean off and it went limp.

There was an android clown that laughed nightmarishly as it tromped toward Remo on gear-driven spider legs. The helium-dispensing valve in its mouth was once used for inflating balloons at the circus. Now it dispensed hydrogen at Remo Williams, a clicking igniter bolted under its chin turning it into a flamethrower.

Remo was behind the clown before the flames got to where he had been. He bashed the clown in the head and his fist just kept plowing through the fiberglass body until the thing was demolished. The spider legs weren't part of the clown's original equipment. They kept right on walking. Remo smashed the motor and the gear box, then grabbed the biggest aluminum pieces and clapped them together with enough force to shatter them.

There was a sudden stillness. Remo almost didn't trust that they had prevailed without a single incidence of proton unpleasantness. He felt the very air for further above-ground disturbances and found nothing.

"We dismantled them real good. We should be in *Junkyard Wars*."

"I doubt that a contest named *Junkyard Wars* befits a Master of Sinanju."

They cautiously crossed the old warehouse until they came to the great pit, the source of the continuing grinding vibration. The pit was surrounded with fresh, earthy sand. A heavy-duty ramp stood next to it, streaked with fresh grease, as if it had recently launched something directly into the earth.

Remo shook his head, amazed. Chiun was simply perplexed.

The fresh-dug tunnel was now more than sixty feet deep, and they could make out huge black metal gears that were channeling loose soil under a pair of rotating battering rams, which thrust away from each other on hydraulic thrusters and crushed the loose earth into the walls and ceiling of the tunnel.

"What is it?" the old man asked.

"Willy Wonka's Mechanical Mole, from the look of it," Remo said.

"Speak no nonsense. Simply explain."

"It's a mechanical mole, Chiun. For riding into the earth. You know, Journey to the Earth's Middle, Mahars, mushrooms big as mountains, Pat Boone as action-adventure hero."

"Why do I ask you anything, ever?" Chiun demanded. "Are you trying to say Fastbinder is aboard that device? That he is attempting to escape us in this way?"

"Exactly," Remo said. "Kind of cool, huh? I never knew anybody ever actually tried to build one of those contraptions. Looks unsafe."

"Unsafe is an understatement."

Remo said, "We have to stop him right away. What if he's headed for a cave system? They can go for miles."

"You must pursue him immediately," Chiun agreed.

"Okay. Here I go."

Before Chiun could change his mind, Remo stepped into the open mouth of the pit and dropped, touched down lightly on the steep incline of the tunnel, stepped again and came to a stop just inches from the rotating pounders at the rear of the mechanical mole. Imbedded in the wall nearby was the fishbowl-headed robot who had been tossed in minutes before. Now he had the appearance of a Dodge Dart just emerged from the junkyard flattener.

Remo watched the half-moon-shaped hammers extend violently, in opposite directions, compressing the crumbling earth into a solid tunnel wall. It still didn't look all that stable, and he had no intention of sticking around to see how long the tunnel would stay intact. He hit an extended hydraulic shaft with a thrust of his palm, then hit the other one. The shafts bent.

The hydraulics struggled to retract the shafts, and the result was a metal-on-metal death scream. Remo jogged out of the hole and joined Chiun on the ledge to watch the mechanical mole die.

"But what purpose did the hammer heads serve?" Chiun asked.

"Used to compact the soil excavated by the drills on the front of the mole," Remo said. "This thing excavates and reinforces its own tunnel, so it doesn't collapse. But the thing only has one big engine and it drives the drill and the pounder and everything in unison. So if one part freezes up, it all freezes up."

A plume of smoke drifted to the surface, smelling of superheated metal.

"How do you know all this?" Chiun demanded.

"Read it in a book. When I was a kid. At the orphanage. You know, some science-adventure novel from years and years ago."

In the stillness that followed the death of the mechanical mole they heard bolts turning and, through the haze, saw a small hatch swing open from the rear of the mechanical mole.

"I zurrender," Jacob Fastbinder said through a fit of coughing, his accent more pronounced in his fear and lack of oxygen.

"We know," Remo said.

"Zere is a rope up zere somewhere."

"So what?"

Fastbinder stopped hacking and stared up at the entrance to the tunnel, mouth open to make breathing possible, but it was so dark and smoky he couldn't see a thing.

Remo, standing on the lip of the hole, crushed his expensive Italian shoes into the earth and sent down a shower of sand.

Fastbinder spit it out. "You vouldn't!"

"Vee vould," Remo replied. "Vouldn't vee?"

"Vee most assuredly vould," Chiun agreed with a sniff.

Fastbinder dived through the hatch in the mole and was still tightening the hatch bolts when Remo and Chiun stomped their feet in exactly the right spots. They stomped several more times, just to be sure, and by then they had stopped breathing because the air was thick with billowing dust. The tunnel was collapsing, again and again from the bottom up, until the place where it had been was only a sinkhole in the floor of the old warehouse.

THEY BREATHED AGAIN when they were outside, strolling leisurely to the Fastbinder's Museum of Mechanical Marvels.

"Howdy!" Remo said.

"Hello." Margo didn't seem to care for him much.

"Two, please. One regular person, one senior citizen.

how Margo your AARP card, Little Father. Is this the
nly Fastbinder museum, by the way?"

"Of course."

"So we get to see all his collection, right? I mean,
·verything that's not kept up at the house?"

"Yes. Why do you ask?"

"Just checking. You guys recycle? You know, tin
cans, scrap metal, stuff like that?"

"No. Why?"

"Just checking."

Margo handed them their tickets. Remo and Chiun
entered the museum, where Herr Fastbinder's collection of mechanical oddities and novelties waited in
over-air-conditioned splendor. These were oddities and
antiques from around the world, procured at great ex-
pense by Fastbinder's network of dealers. There were
gleaming robots that seemed to have little or no useful
function. There were all kinds of smaller devices in motion, clanking, humming, beeping and generally
accomplishing nothing.

Remo examined a rocking chair linked with a lever
to a butter churn. The sign explained: "Automatic butter churners were said to have been used in Appalachian
homes as far back as 1892. This is a genuine working
model that was used as a prop on the 'Yee Haw!' TV
program. Go ahead—give it a try!

"Think any of this could possibly be, you know,
dangerous?" Remo asked.

"No."

"Better safe than sorry, though."

"I agree," Chiun said.

It took the Masters of Sinanju less than a minute to
reduce it all to scraps and rubble.

Epilogue

After his long trip home, Jack Fast was shocked by what he found there. There was crime scene tape around the museum. The interior of the museum proper was in shambles—although the gift shop looked untouched. There was crime scene tape across the entrance to the Fastbinder house, as well, and inside were ruins.

The depression in the floor, and the one major piece of unaccounted-for equipment, told Jack Fast exactly what had happened to his father. The assassins came and Fastbinder tried to escape using the most dangerous possible method.

"Aw, Pops, ya dope. I *told* you it was a death trap."

Jack's girlfriend appeared around eleven that night and ran into his arms. Nancy was overjoyed to find him alive.

"The police came and couldn't find any clue about what happened, Jack, and they couldn't find you or your dad. Where were you? You could have called!"

Eventually she overcame her anger. They slept in the cool, peaceful ruins inside the old warehouse. Jack Fast was one tired kid.

But he woke up when he heard the clink of metal on metal, and sat bolt upright. He couldn't hear the sound anymore.

When he laid back down, he heard it. Faint, coming from beneath.

Jack Fast grinned, his mind already working at lightning speed, planning his next amazing feat of engineering.

"I'm coming for you, Pops!"

James Axler
Outlanders®

MASK OF THE SPHINX

Harnessing the secrets of selective mutation, the psionic abilities of its nobility and benevolent rule of a fair queen, the city-kingdom of Aten remains insular, but safe. Now, Aten faces a desperate fight for survival—a battle that will lure Kane and his companions into the conflict, where a deadly alliance with the Imperator to hunt out the dark forces of treason could put the Cerberus warriors one step closer to their goal of saving humanity...or damn them, and their dreams, to the desert dust.

Available August 2004 at your favorite retail outlet.

Or order your copy now by sending your name, address, zip or postal code, along with a check or money order (please do not send cash) for $6.50 for each book ordered ($7.99 in Canada), plus 75¢ postage and handling ($1.00 in Canada), payable to Gold Eagle Books, to:

In the U.S.	In Canada
Gold Eagle Books	Gold Eagle Books
3010 Walden Avenue	P.O. Box 636
P.O. Box 9077	Fort Erie, Ontario
Buffalo, NY 14269-9077	L2A 5X3

Please specify book title with your order.
Canadian residents add applicable federal and provincial taxes.

GOLD
EAGLE®

GOUT30

TAKE 'EM FREE

2 action-packed novels plus a mystery bonus

NO RISK

NO OBLIGATION TO BUY

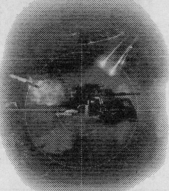